WOLF: BOOK 2

"Answers."

By: A.G. Milhorn

Edited: Dozer Yukon

CONTENTS

CHAPTER 1

Outside the truck window, the sky had finally grown dark and they had left the city behind a while ago, its lights now nothing more than a light blur on the distant ocean of black, where the curve of the earth was barely just visible. The scenery had faded from towers of concrete and steel, to smaller older buildings and finally had given way to rolling hills and thick forests. Highways had given way to boulevards and finally, an exit later, had become an older two-lane road surrounded on both sides by wild ancient sentinels, trees that had seen the Revolutionary War and god knew what else.

Overhead, the moon had risen high into the sky and the stars took the place on the stage, twinkling vibrantly. A tiny red and green dot moved slowly across the ebony velvet sky, a plane, moving silently to some far-off place. Brian felt the thrum of the well-tuned engine as the Ford wound its way ever closer to the Keesogs, a range of mountains that tapered down from the Appalachian trails. Its name came from the Mahican tribes, but Brian couldn't remember what it meant now. His brain was numb and for the first time in what felt like hours, he felt his hand going numb.

Blinking, he remembered where he was.

He was still in the truck with Max, on the road, his chin resting on his hand, his arm sitting on the window sill, staring into his reflection, no longer even noticing the glow of his eyes. Upon sitting up to shake feeling back into his hand, he realized his back and ass was stiff. Stretching as best as he could, he heard his bones crack in his shoulders, the black and grey plush leather seats creaking as he did.

Jesus.

Looking at the clock on the black and grey accented dashboard, he saw the digital clock on the radio gleaming with its white LCD numbers. The radio played, its volume barely above a silent whisper.

7:10 PM.

That shocked him. *How long had they been on the road now?*

"Hey..." he asked his voice quiet and tired, lost just as much as he was. Thinking right now was like struggling to breath water.

"How long have we been on the road, Max? Where does Draco live?" Brian finished, rubbing feeling back into the arm he had been leaning on. He noticed that his nose had left a nose print on the glass of the passenger window and he cleaned it away with the tail of his shirt.

Max sat behind the wheel, his hands on the thick black steering wheel, the instrument panel light casting a faint azure glow onto his soft gray fur. He hadn't spoken the entire trip, leaving Brian in the peace of his own thoughts. *Peace. If only*, Brian thought darkly.

Max looked over at him briefly, his eyes glowing yellow in the dark of the cab.

"A while; Draco lives pretty far out from the city and he likes his privacy. It's an old house out in the middle of nowhere practically. You get cell service and DSL. That's about it and that's only half the time it seems." He told Brian, slowing and then gently accelerating through a curve, a grove of trees reaching over the road, making a natural tunnel.

"Damn. A few hours then. At least two and a half. My ass is numb." Brian frowned, wiggling his hips to get blood flow back into his nether regions. He caught Max nodding a bit in agreement.

"Know what you mean. I'm not a fan of long road trips. Haven't been out this way in a long time. I thought you feel asleep, so I tried to keep quiet."

Brian shook his head. "Nah, was just...thinking. I think. I kind of zoned out for most of it, seems like."

"Yeah you were pretty out there," Max agreed, trying to be personable. As they came out of the curve, the headlights of the truck picked out a long dark stretch of road, straight and with clear fields on either side, the high grass swaying in the night breeze, the moonlight transforming the rolling amber waves into an ocean of silver gray.

After a few minutes of silence, Max tried to talk to Brian and Brian noticed it was awkward, not because Max didn't want to but because, Brian could sense, that Max simply wasn't used to interacting with people much.

"So... uh...did you get a hold of your friend...what's her name...?"

Brian told him. "Ellie and yeah, I did."

"How'd that go?" Max asked, and Brian saw Max's expression tell him what Brian already suspected, which was that shifter hearing was very acute. He must have heard the conversation even in the living room, yet he still had tried to give Brian his space. That counted for points.

Brian shrugged as best as he could, and sat back in his seat with a sigh, partly of being road tired and just tired of all the emotional roller coasters he'd been on the last few days.

"She seemed to blame me. I tried to tell her what I could, but it wouldn't come out right. I don't know why I didn't just tell her. We've been friends since I moved here...she's a shifter too. I don't know why I couldn't, man. I just...locked up."

"Blame you?" Max asked, taking a quick glance at Brian before he turned his attention back to the road. "For what?"

"I guess for not being there for her. We were all close. Hung out a lot." Brian replied, crossing his arms and nestling back into the leather seat, stretching his now longer legs. He felt his toe joints pop and that felt wonderful.

"You could try telling her the truth. Maybe she'd understand. I mean, you can't exactly hide it forever. It's not a crime or anything to be what we are..."

When Brian didn't reply, Max finished. "It's just a bit harder from time to time."

"Yeah. I'm learning that I guess."

For a moment, an expression crossed Max's muzzle and Brian couldn't figure out what it was. It seemed like disbelief or maybe doubt. As quick as it had come, it melted away into the shadows.

"I take it that's who you went to see at the cemetery then...your friend." Max softly stated, and Brian could sense that he meant no harm, so he merely nodded in reply.

"What about work? Are you going to tell them?" Max asked as he slowed to a halt at a lonely stop sign at a four way stop. Taking a left turn, the truck bounced onto a more rural road, this more pitted, rougher, cracked with age. The trees had slowly begun to creep back up in thickness along the roadside and soon the moon was blotted out behind them, the mountains now closer than ever.

"I don't know. It's a pretty inclusive place but I guess right now...I just need to get used to it before I start asking anyone else to take me as I am, if that makes sense." Brian replied, his ears twitching a bit.

"I understand. I can't help you learn about shifting or anything, that'll have to be Raven, but if you...you know...have questions in general...you can ask me. I'll tell you up front, I suck at dealing with people. I'm not used to it. I'll probably be blunt, and you'll think I'm an asshole."

That made Brian smile a bit. The self-depreciation in Max's voice was...charming? Yes. It was charming.

"That's okay. I'd rather deal with people who are blunt than bullshitting."

"A-fucking-men." Max agreed heartily, and they drove for a while more, the road gradually becoming more and more curvy and Brian could tell they were on an incline, slowly ascending the mountains. With a slight pressure in his head, Brian felt his ears pop.

Deciding to take advantage of the moment, Brian plunged in, eager to move forward a bit, to get some distance between his own mind and at the same time, satisfy some of his own curiosity.

"Okay, first question."

He saw Max grin a bit. "Shoot."

"Silver. Is it true?"

Max chuckled a little without actually laughing. Brian had never heard him laugh. That tiny brief sound was the closest he had ever heard Max come to a laugh. It wasn't cruel but rather just amused.

"Well, it hurts like anything else when it stabs you but if you mean do we have a special weakness to it, no. We don't. It's just another metal."

"What about full moons?"

Max took one hand off the wheel and jerked a thumb up towards the windshield. Brian looked and saw the waning moon, a hanging bloated disc of pale silver in the sky, its surface pocked by craters and unmarred by clouds or the smog of the city as the shadow of the earth slowly encroached on its edge.

"Oh. Well, I guess since I'm not slobbering fiend, that answers that."

Putting his hand back on the wheel, Max told him. "No, the moon has nothing to do with it. From what Raven's told me, its hormonally driven. Higher emotions can trigger a change. Sometimes, people get talented enough to where they can shift just a part of their bodies. Just takes time, I guess, but the change back and forth is usually at will. I wouldn't know obviously."

"The biting part I know already I guess. It was way more complicated that I thought..." Brian added under his breath. Max caught it and nodded.

"Yeah. I've heard it's messy for those who don't have whatever it is that you did. I don't even know why—"

Brian interrupted him. "Why you bit me?" The question wasn't angry or accusatory now.

Now, it was just genuine curiosity.

Max seemed far away in his answer, his voice low and reflective.

"I guess I just...just didn't want to lose anyone else. I spend a lot of time on the streets almost every night...I try to make a difference....to...make up for losing my family. I don't ever get to see what happens of the people...their faces blur after a while. I never know their names. But you...for some reason, man, you were different."

"Huh." Brian replied, not sure how to respond that nugget of truth.

Brian felt the truck slow and then it turned, leaving the main road behind, the wheels suddenly crunching on gravel.

"This is the road that goes to the house. Private road. Not marked. Goes for about half a mile into the woods."

"We gotta be up a decent amount. I felt my ears pop a while back." Brian said, now more alert than before, looking out the windows, seeing nothing now but dark trees as they enveloped the road itself and a moment later, their arching branches and thick leaves cut off any view of the sky and they were surrounded by a tunnel of greenish black.

"A fair bit, I guess." Max responded.

Ahead the gravel road with its tree roof canopy went on and after what felt like forever, the headlights of the truck splashed onto a gateway. It was black, wrought iron, set into an old, thick set of gate posts that themselves made up part of a six-foot-high brick and stone fence. The brick and stone were well weathered, faded with time but the grounds around the fence (a wall really, his mind argued) were well manicured and obviously cared for. The iron gate itself look just as ancient, its black gleam reflecting in the bright halogen lights. Its top was rounded and there in the center of the gate where the two halves met, was a heavy iron circle and the metal was cut into a shield, shaped and formed into a coat of arms.

On the shield was what appeared to be the figure of a howling wolf, noble and beyond it, a crown encased with crossed set of arrows and ivy. Words were carved around the shield, following its curve and Brian squinted to read them as Max pulled up to the call box.

Is Fortitudinem Mutare.

"Any idea what that means?" Brian asked, glancing from the gate to Max.

Max shrugged. "Its Latin. I think it means something like 'strength in change'."

Brian head the beeps as Max keyed in a code and looked over to see the call box itself. It was a very modern piece of technology with a glowing blue flat screen made of thick glass that looked practically unbreakable. It was set into a thick metal frame with a dark rounded lens near the top, a grilled speaker and a tiny hole at the bottom. On the bottom of the screen itself, a live video feed showed the top of the truck they were in, the colors the unique shade of electric green that infrared light tended to give its subjects. Above the feed was a set of buttons outlined in white on the digital pad: A numeric keypad, a call button and a transmit key.

Brian didn't see the code Max entered but a moment later, he leaned back into the truck and rolled up his window as the gate hummed. With a clanking of metal and a turning of gears, electric motors engaged and the shield on the gate split in two as it swung wide to let them pass.

As the gates swung closed behind them in the red fire of the truck's tail lights, Brian turned around to face back through the windshield, raising an eyebrow at Max.

"That was higher tech than I expected."

Max grinned a bit again, this time fondly. It didn't fade so fast this time.

"Draco has a good IT team. Well, a person, not a team, but a damn good one."

The drive up to the house itself was marked by softly lit well-trimmed trees and well mown lawns on either side of the trees, both now dark in the night but by morning light they would be a succulent, verdant green. The gravel crunching under the tires was a familiar sound to Brian and it made him think of the nights when he was younger, and his dad came home. The apartment complex they had lived in had a gravel parking lot and the sound of crunching gravel always meant that his dad was there, safe with his mom and himself.

The driveway turned and opened up as the house itself rose out of the darkness, its windows aglow with soft amber light.

To the farthest left of the house was a large garage which was larger than the homes that some people lived in. The doors were shut so he could not see inside of it. The garage appeared connected to the house but it was the house itself that held Brian's attention.

It was nothing more or less than a castle; at three stories high, the home was titanic in size. It stretched back farther than he could see. At each corner, large towers rose up, each topped with battlements. The home itself was square and flat roofed. Smaller additions to the house that seemed relatively modern abutted out of the left and right sides of the home, next to the garage.

The house itself was constructed of brick and stone, with the foundation stones being rounded and well-worn but far sturdier than any modern material. The brick was dark red, faded and pale in places with age and wear. Ancient willow trees had been planted near the back of the house and they loomed over the home, their long trailing vines and leaves cascading down like green capes. Brian counted and saw that, just from where he could see that there were at least twenty maybe more windows on the front side alone, each one large and made of old glass, glass that was probably hand blown. A chimney rose from either side of the house. The front door, he saw was reached by a low set of marble stairs, creamy gray in color and polished to a shine. There were no handrails. The front door itself was made of ancient wood, dark with time and probably stronger than steel. He saw that the door had a knocker carved out of bronze in the shape of a wolf's head.

The driveway itself curved into a roundabout, leading back down the road they had just pulled in from. Soft garden lights highlighted the house grounds, with each light placed at well thought out intervals, giving the grounds a gentle, warm, welcoming feel. Surrounding the house, thick forests went on for miles and in the distance, the mountains of the Keesogs rose and loomed closer than ever.

As the truck came to stop and Max killed the engine, Brian saw another set of cars had arrived here before them and were parked in the round-about. The one closest to the truck was a curvy and aerodynamic candy apple red Subaru Impreza, its windows tinted darkly, and its trim accented with a deep black. Parked in front of the Subaru was a large SUV, a jet-black Expedition or Tahoe, Brian couldn't tell which. He did hear a noise from beside him that made the fur the on the back of his neck go up.

A low and deadly growl.

"What's he doing here..." Max said, eyeing the black SUV, speaking more to himself than to Brian or anyone else. Without a word to Brian, Max yanked his seat belt clear and a moment later, was out of the truck, the door slamming behind him.

Confused, Brian hurried after him as best as he could, his legs refusing to move as fast as he needed them to in order to keep up with Max's slightly longer stride.

"What's who doing here?" Brian called after him, and getting no response, he shrugged and forced his stiff legs to move faster.

Wordlessly Max charged into the house, throwing the door open, not running and not walking at the same time, his movements purposeful, the muscles in his neck and shoulders standing out, flexing under the fur of his arms. Brian saw him ball his powerful hands into fists and his ears flatten to his skull entirely. The fur on the back of Max's neck was on end as well, giving him a terrifying appearance.

"Max, wait..." Brian tried, stopping briefly to shut the door behind him, wincing at how loud it was in the large entry hall. The house's interior was just as stunning as the exterior. The walls were made of rich hand carved wood, and the floor was white marble polished to a mirror shine. Gentle modern sconces provided soft gentle light and a sweeping staircase rose before them, leading up and into the house's upper floors. A large hanging chandelier made of glass and brass chain hung down the stairwell, casting golden light, effusing the whole foyer and entrance hall with a gentility and grace that belied the home's obvious years.

His booted feet slapping roughly against the hard-stone floors, Max turned to the left and a moment later, he and Brian came to a set of closed oak doors. Max didn't even stop. He threw them open violently, the wood banging off the walls, and in a mirror on the far wall, Brian caught a glimpse of Max's face. It was the same face Max had worn when he attacked those gang members: his eyes blazing yellow with hate, his hackles raised, fists clenched, and fangs bared.

His chest heaving, Max took one look at the figure seated in the chair closest to the door and snarled a simple deadly question.

"What the hell are you doing here you son of a bitch?"

Seeing past him Brian saw the target of his angry inquiry sitting calmly in a chair.

In the instant he saw the figure, Brian's brain screamed to flee, or fight. Warning bells screamed silently in his head wailing *DANGER DANGER DANGER*. He felt the flesh and fur on his balls creep and his fur stood on end slightly.

The person sitting in the plush armchair in front of them was a shifter and whether he was a full generation like Max, Brian couldn't tell, but he was in his wolf form and he was one of the largest people Brian had ever seen. The werewolf was enormously broad, making him into a walking tank. His hands were as big as Brian's head and when he stood, Brian knew that he would be at least seven feet high and at least four hundred pounds of steel-bound muscle. Well-groomed and wearing dark pants and a black sweater with patches on the shoulders (what the British called a "wooly" his mind told him absently), the werewolf sat calmly, his dark shoed feet planted firmly under his massive and powerful legs.

His face was savagely aquiline, with a noble and thick set muzzle tipped in a black nose. His body seemed to strain the confines of the sweater and pants and Brian very well thought he could probably crush a car like a tin can. Now, he sat with his thick arms resting neutrally on the arms of the chair, his fingers tipped in sharp black but short claws. His ears stood at attention and his eyes looked up at Max with a languid ease, as if Max were merely an annoyance that he was tolerating and would crush at his leisure as soon as it was convenient for him. One of his jet-black eyebrows move slightly up.

The one thing that stood out most to Brian was the color of the werewolf's eyes.

Like his fur, both of his irises were a deep maroon-red and when the light hit them, they twinkled slightly, turning the color of fresh blood.

The image was made more solid in Brian's imagination: he pictured the werewolf wearing a coat of blood, no, rising out of it, born of it, naked, the thick fluid dripping from his fur, his fangs and powerful body as he ascended to loom in obsidian darkness and red light, as mortal death come to reap anyone who got in his way.

Brian shuddered as a chill crept down his spine.

The huge shifter said nothing to Max but instead turned his canine features back towards a rich and cultured voice that came from the chair opposite him. Brian turned his gaze there and saw a somewhat shorter werewolf that was about six foot seven, but unlike the blood colored, furred monstrosity that loomed in the chair before them, this werewolf was a deep gray with gentle kind eyes the color of an ocean's wave at sunset. He was well groomed and dressed in a tailored suit that fit him well, the dark fabric contrasting nicely with his naturally coloring. His ears were straight and calm, at attention but not at alert. He had long straight hair and like the rest of him, it was gray and had been pulled back into a neatly combed pony tail.

"Max, please. Not now. I asked him to come because I needed Rakinos and his expertise to help us understand. Trust me, I have as many reservations as you do, given our past." the gray wolf said, indicating with a slight nod past Max himself at Brian himself. "Rakinos, this is our mutual new friend."

Rakinos, the blood colored monster, simply gave Max a cold smile and spoke. His voice sent chills down Brian's spine. It was a deep measured baritone. He spoke calmly, his words enunciated carefully and clearly.

"I did come quite a ways up here. There aren't many experts in the fields of lycanthropic genetics and as much as Draco and myself differ on...many subjects...your problem caught my attention, in spite of our past. Unless you would prefer I refer you all to Madison Genetics, of course."

Max stepped forward and Brian saw him go to raise his balled fist back.

"Max. Stop it. Now."

Raven.

Brian finally saw her peek out from behind the chair that wasn't facing him. She looked tired and drawn, strained.

Her voice caused Max to pause and he began to move anyway and then he stopped. His blazing yellow eyes caught a glimpse of Brian in the background in the mirror and something stopped him. He slowly lowered his fist and growled low in his throat.

"You're lucky." He snarled at Rakinos before moving away from the bigger shifter, taking up a standing stance next to Draco, his arms crossed, his large

13

biceps flexed, his forearms tense as he crossed his arms. He looked as if he wanted to kill the bigger shifter and Brian though if he was ever turned loose, he would certainly try.

"Look, I don't want to cause any more trouble. There's been enough of that...I just need answers." Brian spoke up, unaware of where he found the courage to even open his mouth as he stepped forward a bit, easing more towards Raven and putting a few healthy feet of space between himself and Rakinos.

The guy creeped him out and he didn't know why.

Draco's face grew warm and he smiled gently. His accent...Brian couldn't place it. Scottish, maybe? It was very light, lilting and rolled off his tongue like a warm breeze.

"Brian is it? Raven's told me all about you. She came up here just as I came in from Washington, and you are not going to cause trouble. We'll help you any way we can. Please, have a seat and I'll introduce myself and..." Draco took a long and meaningful look at Rakinos, choosing his words carefully. "...And my associate. We'll see if we can find some answers for you. In the meantime, try to relax. You're safe here. I tend to have a knack for sorting out lost causes and getting them back on their feet. Something of a favorite past time." Draco looked at Max proudly, and Brian saw the look of a proud father to a favored son.

Brian carefully made his way across the room, giving Rakinos a wide berth and took a seat next to Draco, with Max on his left. Looking up at Max, Brian gave him the tiniest surreptitious nod that he would be fine.

Max didn't return the gesture, but his eyes acknowledged that he had seen it and his irises slowly faded from the burning yellow to his gentler blues, but he never took those eyes from Rakinos, who in turn, gave Max every moment of that glare right back, without so much as flinching and instead, showed only the politest of interests.

Now, surrounded by friendly faces and faces that provided another yet as of now unknown quality, surrounded by walls of ancient books and paintings, with artifacts under glass, in this library, Brian turned his attention to Draco who in turn faced the young new werewolf.

"Now, start the beginning. I want to hear everything from your point of view." Draco said warmly.

#####

In the two hours it took Brian to tell him, Raven had taken two more blood samples from him; Brian wouldn't let Rakinos touch him. They had headed off deeper into the manor and Max had gone with them, keeping himself between Raven and Rakinos like a guard dog. Brian hadn't seen Max's ears lift once since they had arrived and the tension in the room had been unbearable. Privately, he was glad the three of them had left. It made talking to Draco easier. Draco himself was one of those people who you instantly trusted, Brian found. Talking to him was like breathing. At first, he had been hesitant but as he continued, Brian found that the details he knew and the details he was told flowed easily into a conversation that even now continued. Draco did not interrupt him and instead waited for moments, natural pauses, where he could ask a question here or there. They were few and far between, sprinkled like seasonings.

Draco seemed to be totally at ease with Brian as well, as if he had known him for years. His manner was open and calm, and he was a careful listener. As they talked, Brian had found himself moving around the room, finding sitting making him anxious. Movement, it seemed helped. *The room itself is bigger than my apartment*, he noted, wryly. Every wall in it was loaded with books; the books were all colors, sizes and ages. Some were so new as to be glossy. Others, so ancient, he thought that if he touched them they would fall apart. He recognized many of the names: Blake, Tolstoy, and of course, Shakespeare. There were also names he didn't recognize like Grimmwolf, Bleddynnson and Rowe. One he did recognize because it stuck out among the rest as it was a series of medical and science books labeled with Madison Genetics logo on them.

In between the shelves were display cases, some covered in sealed glass. Items varied from case to case. Some were books so old that putting them on a shelf was dangerous. One he noticed was entirely in Latin and had images in it of dog-headed men carrying baskets and there, on the wall, he also noticed a familiar face.

St. Christopher.

Only this St. Christopher was different from most depictions of him. In most depictions, he was seen in white robes, a darker robe draped around his shoulders, his dark hair and beard framing his tanned face, a scepter in one hand and a cherub on his shoulder. This depiction, Brian noted as he passed it caused him to pause in his story and take a closer look.

This Byzantine depiction of St. Christopher was in a much older form and style, more abstract than the later ones Brian had seen on the medals Catholics wore on their necks. This man was tall, powerfully built, and armed with a long staff. He was dressed in black and green armor with a flowing red cape that draped around his shoulders. What was most striking was in this in painting, he wasn't human at all, but rather resembled nothing less than a full generation werewolf or a shifter in their wolf form. A thick strong neck led up from his fur covered shoulders to his canine features and head, his muzzle sharp and his ears tall, his amber eyes glaring out at the viewer. He was covered in reddish-brown fur and his head was tilted towards the sky.

Draco spoke softly to him, in the moment, breaking the sudden quiet.

"Do you know who that is?" he asked, his voice gentle. Brian's right ear perked backwards, jumping towards Draco's voice.

Brian looked back at him, his hands in his jeans pockets, his tail flicking with his own curiosity.

"Yeah," he said, his tone confused but also wanting more. "That's St. Christopher, right? That's what the Greek around the top says."

"You can read Greek?" Draco asked from his chair, his eyebrows moving up in surprise. Brian shook his head.

"Nah, I can't but I can make out enough of the letters. I'm a writer. I like to collect folklore and stories, but this...I don't know this."

"I take it you aren't religious?" Draco asked, standing and crossing the room to stand next to Brian. His broad strong form towered over the younger werewolf, his looming presence softened by the gentility in his noble eyes. He held one arm at the elbow, while the other stroked the fur on his chin like a man will do to his beard when he is thoughtful. It was an unconscious action, Brian thought, reading his body language.

"Nope. No one in my family really was. Except for my uncle Donny but he was a lunatic." Brian told him, moving his eyes back to the painting.

"Have you ever heard of the legend of St. Christopher and how he came to be a part of the church?" Draco asked, looking up at the painting thoughtfully.

With a shake of his head, Brian told Draco that he had in fact not ever thought about that question.

"The oldest written records of St. Christopher come from 9th century French writings but the most common account of him comes from a 13th century work called The Golden Legend."

As Draco talked, Brian felt his eyes move up to meet St. Christopher's and there he was transfixed by the warrior's gaze.

"The earliest stories say that Christopher's name before he was baptized was Reprobus and that he came from Canaan. They also say that he was what is called a cynocephali, a "dog-headed" man. He served his king and his people there as a soldier and was renowned in battle as a deadly warrior; an unstoppable juggernaut, seeking glory and honor in the battles of his time. They say that the warrior sought out the most powerful king of his day and went to serve him."

Brian listened with rapt attention. He had never heard of any of this from anywhere. Draco carried on, his voice soothing on his ears.

"One day, he saw the king shudder in fear of the Devil. Deciding to seek out this Devil and serve him, Reprobus sought out the demon lord, and after many weeks, found a man calling himself just that leading a band of roaming marauders. He ran with them for a time before seeing that the fearless leader was in fact scared of a symbol, the Christian cross, when he refused to stand in front of it."

The corners of Draco's mouth turned upward in a bit of amusement from Brian's raised eyebrow, his gaze moving from the young werewolf to the armored man in the painting above. Draco felt a sense of pleasure from seeing how closely Brian was listening. It pleased him because most young people these days had no patience for anything longer than a thirty second sound bite.

"After learning that the Devil feared this Christ, Reprobus sought out Christ and instead found an old hermit. The hermit instructed him in the ways of Christian ideals and beliefs about Christ and finally, the day came when Reprobus wanted to consecrate himself to his new ruler that even the Devil feared. The hermit told him that fasting, and prayer was one way and Reprobus said he couldn't, so the hermit told him of another way."

Brian frowned. "What other way?"

Draco smiled and went on.

"He told him that nearby was a river that flooded its banks and made crossing it dangerous and that many people had already died in the attempts to reach the other side. Suggesting with his powerful build, Reprobus could carry the people across on his shoulders to safety and that Christ would be pleased with him for doing so."

"So, what, he carried people across the river on his back?" Brian asked, shifting his weight from one foot to the other, his green eyes glinting in the warm glow from the wall sconces.

"Indeed, he did, so they say until one day a child asked to be carried across. Thinking the task would be easy, he picked the child up and let him ride on his shoulders. Half way out into the raging water, the river began to flood and up to his neck in the water, Reprobus held tightly to the child, protecting him until they made it across where Reprobus set him down and told him: 'You have put me in the greatest danger. I do not think the whole world could have been as heavy on my shoulders as you were'. To which the child replied: "You had on your shoulders not only the whole world, but he who made it. I am Christ your king, whom you are serving by this work." The child then faded away, leaving Reprobus stunned and finding a new-found faith."

Draco noticed Brian's eyebrows go up skeptically at the last bit even more and smiled inwardly. *This one*, he thought, *is perhaps wiser than he lets on, perhaps.*

"What happened then?" Brian asked thoughtfully.

"Stories say he wandered the lands, converting people to Christianity, protecting the weak and innocent, getting into quite a few more fights and battles. He came known as one of God's soldiers and was held in high regard by the people of his day. Of course, every heroic story ends only one way," Draco said, a solemn look fading over his majestic features.

"I know enough of the heroic cycle to know where this is going," Brian added gently. Draco nodded sagely.

"Indeed. You're right, of course. There came a battle after Reprobus traveled to the land of Lycea to comfort Christians who were being martyred there, and there he was captured by the king. Demanding he worship his pagan gods, the king tortured Reprobus in every way imaginable, tempted him with women and more but Reprobus refused to convert and when he managed to convert two of the women sent to tempt him, the king ordered him executed."

"I imagine that didn't go well, did it?" Brian asked, looking up at the painting.

Draco shook his head. "It did not."

After a moment, the gray werewolf continued.

"They tried every manner they could think of and he simply would not die. At last, out of desperation, the king ordered him beheaded and so, Reprobus of Canaan met his fate that day in Lycea under the executioner's sword. He was later canonized by the Eastern Orthodoxy and became a patron saint of protection in Catholicism. They said prior to his final battle, and capture, before his death that he was baptized and when he came out of the baptism, he lost his canine features."

Brian looked up at Draco. "You don't believe that, do you?"

"What? The legend?" Draco asked. "Or the fact that he suddenly became human after his baptism?"

"The latter."

"Oh." Draco said, laughing gently. "No. Not at all. I believe our dear Reprobus, later named Christopher, was in fact, a werewolf, like you and me and that he was a shifter and simply changed form to fit in with his new-found faith, probably due to social pressure more than any spiritual calling. He spent his life chasing glory and power and in the end, died a hero to the less fortunate, even if he sacrificed his identity to do it."

"Were there others like him?" Brian asked, stepping back from the painting and towards the center of the room, the thick rug soft under his boots, his mind whirling.

"Oh yes. The Cynocephali were an entire race, at least, according to the ancient Greeks. They were spread all over the world: India, Greece, Egypt. Then they were gone. Most of the world thinks they were just myth or a mistranslation of the word for Canaanite, but my research shows that they most likely just moved underground with time to avoid the persecution of the Christian advances, especially during the Crusades. I think that they were our ancestors, if not our place of origin, though some say our origins go back much farther than 248 BC, and there are many unanswered questions even if it were true. There are other myths and legends, but I can't substantiate them. I can barely substantiate this, and I suffer my fair share of ridicule from other scholars for even looking at it seriously."

As Brian sat in one of the thick arm chairs, Draco did the same.

"This is a lot of information. There's a lot of the history I didn't know. They never talk about it on the news. It's always talking heads going on for hours about their opinions. No one ever talks about history or facts." Brian said, adjust his tail as he sat.

A dark look crossed like a storm cloud over Draco's face.

"Sadly true. Most of us want to live peaceful lives and just exist. Others," Draco said, and Brian saw his gaze fall to the chair were Rakinos had occupied earlier. "Others have their own ideas about what should be done to address our current civil rights crisis. In the last year, four separate bills have been introduced to regulate shifters in some way, and I've spent nearly all my time fighting them, and so far have I have managed to keep them at bay but this last one, this registration bill, has refused to die. Given the current political climate, it is gaining more traction than I might be able to turn aside. People are afraid, right now. People are angry and confused and when they are such, they do regrettable things. Terrible things."

"I've seen the protests, the marches. Hell, Twitter blew up last month remember, with that hashtag...what was it? Furry lives matter?" Brian replied as Draco winced at the name.

"A well-intentioned but misguided attempt. A finality that most people do not seem to understand in this life, is good intentions and movements are nothing without action and resistance, peacefully, to make a point. One cannot simply adopt a cause from an armchair and be offended and angry for others in their place." The older werewolf told him.

"And here you are," Draco said, taking a deep breath and letting it out slowly, looking Brian up and down. "A young man minding his own business, tossed into our world of politics and violence, of chaos and uncertainty and are now expected to navigate it. I imagine you've been asked a thousand times by this point, especially by Raven but, how are you dealing with…all this?" he asked, and with a wave of his hand, indicated everything.

Brian shrugged. "To be honest, Mr. Riley, if someone asks how I am one more time or asks for one more blood sample I might go crazy. Well, crazier than I already am."

Draco smiled at that. The young man was honest and blunt. He reminded Draco of Max a few years ago with the same stubborn spirit.

"I'll take that to mean you are holding strong. I know what it's like to be tossed into chaos and expected to swim. You seem to be doing well, I have to admit."

Brian *hmphed* gently. "Haven't had much of a choice. Things moved so fast if I didn't roll with it I would have been ran over like road kill."

"I wish I had more answers to give you other than stodgy speculative history. The truth is, Mr. MacGregor, that we don't know much more than you do about what we are or where we come from. We know basics and that's all. As for your specific situation," Draco told him and he seemed to consider his next words very carefully. "As for your specific situation, I must admit, in my…considerable years…I've never encountered a case quite like yours. You truly are unique to my knowledge."

"How many years qualify as considerable?" Brian asked, not being rude but as he had proven to Draco so far, driving home right for the point immediately. He smiled a bit when he answered.

"One hundred and fifteen."

He felt a chuckle threaten to rise from his throat when he saw Brian's eyes go wide. The poor boy's jaw nearly dropped open.

"Say that again…" Brian asked shocked.

"One hundred and fifteen as of three weeks ago."

"That's impossible…."

"Mr. MacGregor, you live in a world where people can change their shapes at will, where we can transport molecules across space and time and freeze light in place. I think, with all due respect, you may need to redefine your definition of that word." Draco chided him gently.

Brian did some mental math quickly. Math was never his strong suit, but this was easy, and the result gob smacked him.

"That means you were born in 1903. You were nine years old when the Titanic sank."

"Indeed, I was. I was nearly on that ship, by the way. Fortunately, my mother simply refused to set foot on it. She made my father wait a further two years after Titanic went down before we immigrated from Scotland to New York. My father worked in construction once we arrived and eventually made enough capital that we invested in Manhattan real estate, which as you can imagine turned out to be quite profitable."

"How can you be over a century old? You don't...well.... I don't know much about how shifters age ...but hell...you don't look it or act it or sound it...how?" Brian asked, the revelation dumbfounding him.

Nodding, Draco told him, and this time a chuckle did escape from the big shifter. He looked over at Brian with a grin.

"Something that is unique to us and our biology with our advanced healing factors is our life span. Somewhere in our early forties or so, we seem to stop aging entirely and enter what appears to be a maintenance phase. Assuming we aren't killed violently, we are the world's first macro-cellular complex biologically immortal life-form. Something the news leaves out because most of them aren't aware of it. There are far older werewolves in existence than I am out there and over time, they learned to keep quiet and fade away, living peaceful lives and staying out of the public eye."

Brian felt the world sway.

That simple truth and its implications hit hard.

Immortal.

The word stuck in his mind like a flaring signal light. It didn't seem real. He was going to outlive, in theory, everyone who he knew and loved that wasn't a shifter. Something about the enormity of the idea was too much to conceptualize.

"I don't believe that...I can't..." he stammered to himself more than anything else.

"Your reaction is understandable and you seem like a rational man, so I'd like you to look at these two images if you will. Perhaps doing so will help." Draco replied calmly and reached around to a side table. He picked up two picture frames. He handed them both to Brian who took them gingerly. Looking down at them, Brian saw they were two black and white images. Well, not black and white but rather sepia toned, he corrected himself. The first thought to cross his mind was that these things were ancient.

The first image was a more intimate family portrait. It had been composed carefully and professionally. In it, a woman sat in a long floor length dress with a long-sleeved white top. The neck and wrists of the top were delicate and made with a rich lace. Her hands were gentle and dainty, and her posture was straight and regal. Her eyes pierced the camera and like the necklace that glinted on her chest, her gaze was sharp and refined, wise and not to be trifled with yet she also had a kindness there behind the stiff presentation. Her thick rich dark hair was tied up into a neat bun. Behind her, a tall broad man stood, dressed in a dark suit, one arm by his side, the other resting lovingly on the woman's shoulder and there, in the middle of them, was a child. The child like his mother wore a long-sleeved white shirt, dark stockings and shined black shoes. His shirt was tucked in and a white bow tie lay nestled under his neck.

The photo looked like countless ones he had seen online of the early 20th century family portraits. Nothing was out of place except...

Except that the entire family were werewolves, the father, the mother and the son, each one fully shifted into their wolf forms, ears and muzzles and fur well-groomed and brushed to a shine. The little boy had a round face, his snout larger and his eyes as big as saucers. His tiny ears and big feet and tail made him for the entire world appear like a puppy that had been put into human clothing, yet his human shaped hands wrapped around a wooden hoop caused a shudder to unconsciously run-down Brian's back. The boy's eyes were the same as his mother's: intense and light colored, even in the sepia.

The next image was composed like the first, only it was a family at the docks, a massive black and white steam liner behind them. All around them the dock side bustled with activity and Brian noticed the one thing that stood out in the image. This family was human, entirely so, but the boy's eyes...those eyes, albeit a few years older, were the exact same as in the first image. These images were not altered. They were real, which meant only thing.

Draco was telling the truth.

"You can change forms like Raven....it's true, then. You really are one hundred and fifteen years old...Jesus Christ....this is wild." Brian's amazement turned to confusion as he looked from the picture to Draco.

"How is it possible that you are a werewolf that young, though? Raven said that shifters don't start to be able to shift until they hit their teens?" Brian asked as he handed the photo frames back to Draco who sat them carefully down in the original positions.

"Yes. I can change forms but in the last few years, I've preferred to say in my canine form. It helps me feel more energetic, and it also helps people realize that not all shifters are the criminals we are portrayed as, nor are we monsters, but people just wanting to live without fear. As to the second question, when a child comes from two werewolves instead of a human/werewolf parentage, they gain access to their shifting ability much sooner." Draco said calmly. Draco paused and considered for a moment before continuing.

"The question, Mr. MacGregor," Draco asked, turning to face Brian once he had gotten the frames where he wanted them. "Is whether or not you can shift. Can you?"

Brian swallowed. It was a topic he had thought about, an idea that flitted through his brain in the quiet moments in the car ride up here, on the rooftop that night with Max and in the bathroom as he looked in the mirror.

"I don't know. I wouldn't know how to try."

Nodding, Draco replied. "I see. With as much as has happened to you the last week, it's understandable. I'd like to work with you and help you to see if you can shift, as well as your other senses, and if you can indeed shift, to learn to master it. Raven told me you had managed to get quite a bit of time free from your work."

Having no real argument as to why he wouldn't want to stay, and already set on asking if he could anyway, Brian quickly agreed.

"I'd appreciate that. Learning about what I can do seems like a decent way to get some solid ground under my feet. I was going to ask if I could stay with Max tonight and then come up here tomorrow. I think I need just a bit of time before I jump in. One night at least. Finally get my head straight and all."

"That would be fine as well. That way you can have time to process this. You've been through a living nightmare. I'd imagine some stability would be a welcome change. You are welcome to spend as much time as you need here. There's no one here but myself and a few others. You'll eventually run into Jackson when he isn't eyeball deep in his computers and network. He's my technology guru, so to speak. He's wired this entire house and grounds and he's quite a genius. Bear in mind he can be...awkward at times. He doesn't mean any harm but sometimes his brain works faster than his mouth can properly filter. He's quite dear to me. The other two people you'll see here besides myself are Mr. Roy Daniels, and he's been with my family for as long as I can remember. He keeps the house in order and lastly there is Miss. O'Hara."

Draco's expression warmed considerably and his eyes grew thoughtful. The moment was lost as he seemed to come back to the present.

"I would truly utterly be lost without her. She's my personal assistant and honestly, the closest friend I have. All of them are trusted and you can be assured they mean you no harm. "

Sighing in relief, Brian replied.

"I need some air for a bit. Just one question though. This house...it's huge. Why all this space just for you and a few others?"

Draco looked up at him as Brian stood up and made for the door to the main hall. He stood as well, and he towered over Brian by. His height was going to take some getting used to, especially the strange mix of refined gentility that seemed to be at odds with his fearsome (if he wanted it) appearance. The cloud returned over Draco's sea-ocean eyes and this time, Brian recognized it not as anger but as pain and Draco's tone told him all he needed to know and after Draco told him, Brian didn't press the matter.

"At one time, I had family living me. My brother and sister. They were born much later in my life and much closer to your birth year I'd imagine. My mother and father still resided here as well. My father had helped design and later built this house. He called it Forest Glen and for many years we lived here in peace. Then one summer, things changed. My sister passed away and my brother and I grew estranged. He left, and I haven't spoken to him in some time, even though he works for the nightclub. He owns half of it, I'm sure you've been told."

The thought of his brother seemed to bother Draco, his eyes becoming regret filled.

"He won't speak to me much anymore. We seem to fight and argue more than relate, so I give him his space. Our sister's death hit him hard and maybe I wasn't the brother I should have been but that's in the past."

Sighing, he went on.

"My mother and father moved back to Scotland not long after, and we still talk from time to time, though it's less frequent as the years go on. I stay here because it's where my family is...even if they are long gone. It's where I feel the most content. It's my home and I've filled it, I think in many ways with surrogate family members, Mr. Mullen and miss Jones among them for a time and now, I extend that to you, Mr. MacGregor."

Standing in that door way, looking at the older werewolf, Brian was struck by how lonely Draco looked, and for a moment, Brian could see the years on Draco as plain as the lights in the room, but there was something more about the old werewolf's manner that was revealed in the weight of those years of experience and it resonated in Brian in an unexpected way.

The look on Draco's face, the sound of his voice. It took Brian a moment to process what the feeling he was having was after so long without it.

It was the expression, tone and warm protective manner a father took when talking with his son, when leveling with him in a way that only fathers could, sharing his own experience in hopes of making life for his son better than his own.

In that instant, Brian decided he genuinely liked Draco Riley and, knowing no more needed said, nodded quietly and made his way outside for a breather. As he left, Draco stood in the doorway, leaning on the doorframe of the study as the younger shifter vanished outside, the outer door closing softly behind him.

Draco's expression hardened and drew together darkly, concern etching itself into his features as he considered all that he had heard and all that it implied as the past rose up around him and the halls of the old house seemed to echo with the footsteps of long buried ghosts.

#####

Max stood across the room, his blue gaze fixed on Rakinos like a snake on a rat, refusing to let the hulking werewolf out of his sight for a moment. He leaned against the wall, his jaw set hard and his tail flicking back and forth restlessly, his arms crossed in an X across his chest, fingers making fists unconsciously. He, Raven, and Rakinos were down in the mansion's science lab that once been a drawing room. Raven had helped Draco design and build it, while Jackson laid out the fiber optic systems that powered the super computer core that was the brain of the entire mansion itself. It was well hidden of course, and this room was a stark contrast to the rest of the stately old home. This room was all glass and cold steel, very modern and filled with microscopes, three computer analysis stations, all tied into the super-computer array in the basement tech room.

The computer array, Max knew, was, several refrigerator sized units packed with god only knew how many components and parts that he had never heard of but all in all, this lab made the one at the shelter look paltry.

Many doctors and scientists would kill to have a lab like this; it had been built originally for Draco to help with the analysis of the lycanthropic genome project years ago and had been upgraded continually with Raven's input once she came onto the scene. Draco had been on the team helping the project with Dr. Harvey Madison and though the two no longer spoke due to Madison's proclivity to see profit before people, the manor lab had proven useful for studying the quirks of the results of that project, something that Draco and Raven, more recently, had taken up as a personal hobby in her free time.

Rakinos, much to Max's distaste, had also helped with the original genome project but was kicked out of the project for wanting to take it into directions that were less than ethical, going beyond seeking to understand the lycanthropic genome and straying into the gray waters of genetic enhancement, and as much as he hated him, Max had to admit, the man knew his subject matter. Draco, Madison and Rakinos, as Max had come to understand it over the years, did not work together directly but rather on separate aspects of the project, though from time to time, Draco did meet with Rakinos and talked with him, as they were some of the only shifters on the project. In many ways, Rakinos and Draco's pasts were tied together.

That didn't mean, Max thought, watching Rakinos work a microscope surprisingly deftly with his large hands, that Max didn't want to kill him several times over and take his time doing it. After his termination from the genome project, Rakinos had vanished off the map, and the world had seen little of him since. The fact that he had showed up now, boded ill in Max's opinion.

The reason for his hatred that was as deep as the river that had carved the Grand Canyon, was simple one.

There had been a clash of protestors at a peaceful rally in Baltimore several years ago near the end of the genome project. Draco and his sister had led a peaceful march in the city to bring attention to shifters rights, which at the time, were being threatened by a recent bill drawn up by a Tennessee state senator, Republican Charles Arkly, which was intended to make schools segregated for shifters and non-shifters, citing a clear and present danger to human children from accidental bites from shifter children, should there be a scuffle.

Draco and his sister had led the movement to oppose the bill and they had been met by counter protestors from right wing groups, including the KKK and Odin's Spear. The rally had been peaceful until Rakinos had showed up with a group of his own protestors. Rakinos was of the mind that shifters and full generations alike were superior to what he considered was the failed evolution of humanity and made the point that, in his mind, shifters would eventually supplant non-shifters in an evolutionary shift of dominance, either through natural selection or deliberate engineering.

Rakinos and his crowd angrily pushed back against the KKK and Odin's Spear, while Draco and his sister tried to keep the peace, but the crowds were simply too big. The police could do little more than watch as guns were pulled out and the sharp staccato of shots began to echo.

The protest became mass chaos.

Rakinos' group clashed with the humans, and the fight had been brutal and brief. When it was done, Draco's sister had been killed by a gunshot wound to the head.

Max had been there, helping Draco as much as he could, though he generally tried to stay out of politics though honestly it was more out of a feeling of debt to the man who had taken him in and set his life back on track. One moment, Draco's sister had been standing there, her auburn hair billowing as she shielded a young woman who was panicking with her own body and the next, she was gone with a single powerful crack of gunpowder. In the ensuing chaos, Rakinos and his group made off before the police could question them. Max held Rakinos responsible for the death of his mentor's sister, though no one ever did learn who fired the shot.

Barbara had been kind and gentle, fiercely alive and warm to anyone who approached her. She had been pursuing a degree in architectural design.

The fallout from her death split Draco's family and Max would never forgive Rakinos for inciting that riot. He'd rather eat rusty nails that were on fire. For Draco to reach out to Rakinos after all this time, showed how much of an unusual situation Brian really was. The fact that Rakinos had dared to even respond and had shown his face made Max even more furious and in his fury, Max wondered how Draco had even managed to contact that red furred bastard after all this time. Draco had not clarified.

"Mr. Mullen I can't solve your problem if you keep glaring at me"

Rakinos deep voice snapped Max back to the here and now and it angered him. Just the sound of it annoyed him and he stepped forward, his arms falling to his sides, fists clenched as he stopped before the lab table Rakinos was working on. Rakinos didn't even bother to look up from his work.

"Does my presence bother you?" the large blood colored werewolf asked, his voice putting on a reasonably fake and well-done mask of sincerity that sickened Max.

"Yes." Max told him flatly and coldly. Rakinos looked up from the eye pieces momentarily and glanced up at Max.

"You can imagine my distress." He said dryly and stood up straight as Raven crossed the room from the DNA analyzer that looked like a microwave with a touch screen.

"Will you two knock it off? What did you find from the samples?" she snapped at them, working herself between Max and Rakinos, pushing Max gently back from the table as she began to type furiously at a workstation, the screen flying by in windows, commands and numbers.

Rakinos turned his head only fractionally to look at her as he spoke.

"So far, nothing terribly special. Red blood cell count is normal, leukocytes are properly functioning, and hormone levels have fully stabilized. Your data from earlier suggests there was an imbalance?"

Keeping her eyes on the screen, Raven refused to indulge Rakinos with so much as a look as she addressed him.

"Yes. I've found the marker in Brian's DNA. The shifter gene was on the Y chromosome, so whomever the shifter was, they were on his father's side. I don't think he knows, but if he didn't have that dormant gene, he would be dead right now. It saved his life."

"It seems like perhaps Mr. MacGregor should be grateful to his werewolf ancestor somewhere down the line. Though, judging on this data, Dr. Jones, it wasn't that far back." Rakinos replied thoughtfully.

As he went back to his work, Rakinos seemed to feel Max staring at him.

"Mr. Mullen, I don't do tricks, so can you please make yourself useful or remove yourself? You're a distraction; besides, your samples here are looking as boring and ineffectual as you are and equally broken. Nothing new to see here." Rakinos told Max bluntly, without looking up at him.

Max had given up blood and DNA samples as well. Raven had wanted to see if there was anything different about Max's makeup that had enabled him to activate a dormant gene and so far, they had come up with nothing. All they had found so far was that, as was to be expected, Max's shifter marker was mutated once on the Y chromosome, leading to it being turned off at birth, making him the full generation that he was. Old news.

"Thanks. I'll take boring over fuck face any day." Max snapped back quietly. Max could never forgive Rakinos for Barbara's death. The man was an arrogant, smug asshole, and for that alone, Max hated sharing the same atmosphere. There was just something about him that made Max's skin crawl.

For the next fifteen minutes, the two scientists worked in silence, and Max stood guard, not trusting Rakinos to be alone with Raven, or alone at all within ten miles of anyone he cared for. That bastard was a living waste of oxygen, Max thought and he desperately yearned to resolve that situation as roughly and painfully possible. To add insult to literal injury, Rakinos had dropped by the Wolves Den one night a year or so ago and he and Max had crossed paths. A bar fight ensued and Max lost. Badly.

One day, you red asshole, Max thought darkly. He forced his tail to stop flicking back and forth and took a stance against the glass wall near the door.

Rakinos, in the meantime, was no longer paying either Raven nor Max any mind. He had moved from the microscope to one of the analysis stations that was hooked into the super computer, subtly positioning himself so his work could not be seen. He had lost himself in the scrolling numbers and the three-dimensional model that represented Brian's genetic code on the screen, working on simulations of genetic expression. Certain segments were highlighted in orange, red and green, but one segment was coded in blue and it was that segment that fascinated him and it was a discovery that he had kept to himself.

It was some type of protein, not one of the usual type associated with RNA information transfer but it was present in all the cells that Rakinos had taken from MacGregor's blood sample. The genes in the blue section seemed to control the transfer and encoding of information into the RNA which in turn was transferred to the cells of Brian's body for implementation and execution but it was the profile of this protein that was strange.

The protein had re-shaped MacGregor's DNA into a triple helix shape, something he had never seen in all his time working for the genome projects or in his own personal studies. He moved through the program he was using for the simulations, marveling at its ingenuity.

The program that he was using for this was a custom piece of software normally used by law enforcement to identify suspects. It would take their genetic markers and would generate a sample phenotype; it was essentially capable of creating high tech forensic sketches. This version had been significantly tweaked by the admittedly genius touch of Draco's annoying and painfully awkward technology expert (who had poked his head into the lab several times to check on his computers) into something more. Now, it could be used to simulate the expression of genes in a given form, to see what the outcome would potentially be.

He had tried several simulations to see the action of the protein in isolation on standard human DNA, but so far all of them had failed. Then he ran the most recent

Anthony Milhorn

DNA taken from Brian an hour ago, paired with an isolated amplified version of the strange protein combination in Brian's DNA profile.

Rakinos felt his jaw want to drop but stifled the urge.

The implications were immense. If what he was seeing was correct...

If the results were accurate (he had no reason to think they weren't) it meant a total revolution in the understanding of lycanthropic science and in fact, confirmed many old legends and stories that science had thought it had disproven: the old stories of werewolves biting humans and turning them. All understanding of those old stories, backed up by a few cases in modern medical journals, indicated that humans bitten by shifters without the shifter gene did not survive. Something Rakinos himself knew about from personal experience, he thought, remembering the drug dealer he had put out of his misery.

Until now.

This would change everything, he thought. All his plans he had made about lycanthropic genetic engineering would change forever. This was the final key that he needed and here it was, handed to him on a silver platter. He needed to think bigger. Bolder.

He needed to move quickly.

"Max can you help me a moment?" Raven asked and out of the corner of his eye, Rakinos saw Max move in to help Raven move a heavy set of analysis chemicals from one bench to another. In that moment of time, Rakinos moved swiftly; he took the DNA sample from Brian and shoved it deep into the pocket on his chest. It vanished like it had never existed. For good measure, he took the DNA sample from Max as well. He needed to confirm this revelation about Brian's true nature but not here, somewhere more accommodating to his own personal projects that had been in development hell for years now.

He quickly erased his work from the hard drive and closed the programs down, leaving a bit of code behind that should help cover his tracks.

Standing, he made it out to look like he was consulting a database on another terminal. He wondered just how far Jones was willing to go with her desire to understand her discovery. Could she be an ally or would she be a hindrance? Needing to find out, he caught Raven's attention.

"I believe you were correct and this is a case of a dormant gene being activated." he said calmly. "Have you considered submitting a paper and your research for peer review or applications of your work?"

Raven shook her head as she closed a cabinet door.

"Not yet. I need more time, more studies. More controls. This protein and its

30

ability to take foreign genetic material and incorporate it into new coding that can be expressed is frankly unheard of. It could do wonders for gene therapy if it could be made safe. We have to go slowly. It's just that simple."

Rakinos shook his head. "Naturally but discoveries like this, they come around once in a lifetime." He moved to stand next to her, dwarfing her with his height while his shadow fell over her. Raven didn't flinch.

"True, but they need to be controlled and contained safely so that no one gets hurt in the process. Discovery must be a gentle process, not a blunt instrument being shoved in. We have to follow protocols. There are guidelines and rules in place for such work, especially when it comes to genetics. You know that more than most." Raven told him as she turned to face him, crossing her arms. Her reference to his past on the genome project didn't cause Rakinos to have the slightest reaction but her tone suggested to him that she was, in her own way, tempted by the power of what they had found.

A dark grin formed on Rakinos' face. The light played with his eyes, making tiny red pinwheels twirl in them. His voice was low and carefully measured but held a dark edge to it, a tempting one.

"Discovery, Dr. Jones, real progress, isn't made by being careful. It's made by being bold, decisive. Context is for kings, for better souls with the vision to see it and use it. You and I could do wonders with this; it could leap our understanding of people like us into the next generation. With your knowledge and mine, we could use this protein and its properties to help our people, to make real change, you said so yourself."

Raven stared at him, meeting his eyes and for a moment she said nothing, considering his words before shaking her head.

"I'm sorry. I'm not ready to move forward with this. Not yet. Not now. I want to make sure of what is here and what it can do before attempting to use it for anything, regardless of its potential. We don't even know what that protein is. Its ability to absorb and integrate foreign material into a genetic code is, honestly, staggeringly frightening. It's beyond anything we have now. Playing God, is not something I want to do."

Knowing that she was a lost cause, Rakinos knew that she would not be tempted and so, he stood back.

"God works too slowly for my taste. I prefer to take the initiative from him, if he won't do what must be done, then someone else should take his place."

Raven suddenly turned back to face him, the clipboard she was writing on tossed down hard on the counter in surprise.

"And that person to take his place is you, I suppose?" she asked in disbelief, her eyebrows raised.

"I'm open to the idea." Rakinos replied back, his dark eyebrows coming together.

She realized then that he was serious.

"I think we're done here." She told him flatly but loud enough for Max to hear.

Max looked up from the chemical containers he was moving. He set one down hard on the metal counter, the sound loud in the lab. He sniffed once or twice unconsciously and gave Rakinos a nasty glare after seeing the way Raven moved away from him. He crossed the room immediately and put himself between the two.

Glaring up at the bulkier werewolf, Max's voice was deadly quiet.

"I'll walk you out."

Rakinos said nothing for a second and merely looked at Max as though he were a precocious child that he was tolerating.

"As you wish." the red furred shifter said finally.

Without a word, Rakinos walked quickly out of the lab. Max had to sprint to catch up to the bigger werewolf's longer stride but there was no way in hell that Max was going to let Rakinos out of his sight. The lab door slowly swung shut as the two of them left, leaving Raven thoroughly annoyed and confused and if she was honest, disturbed. She had heard and read of Rakinos' behavior on the genome project and she finally saw it in person. It was frighteningly intense.

As she sighed in frustration, she realized he was right about two things at least, no matter what her opinion of him was. First, Brian being alive and a werewolf despite, to his knowledge, having no werewolf family, was down to genetics. Someone, somewhere in his family tree had lied to him. It was that simple. The second was that this discovery of this unique protein and its properties had implications for shifter genetics studies and could increase the medical knowledge for the rare maladies that affected shifters, as well as kick into high gear research for human diseases, such as HIV and cancers but she had to go slowly, no matter how tempting it might be. One had to walk before one could run.

There was one other matter, one that was more pressing and much more immediate in its need for attention and resolution.

As she crossed the room back to her workstation, her right hand slid into her lab coat and felt the hard coldness of the glass vial of the blue drug she had stolen from the hospital earlier. Raven glanced down the lab at a workstation that was currently one but locked. She had been running a sample of the drug through the analyzer secretly. Now that Max and Rakinos were out of the lab and she was alone, she took the opportunity to unlock the station and review the results.

As she read them, her mind working fast, she felt her heartbeat grow faster and a cold fear began to climb up her throat.

The drug was truly terrifying.

Chemically speaking, it was unique. Nothing else like it was found during the cross-referencing check she had run. Based on its structure and some of the components that made it up, it appeared to have the properties of a hyper-amphetamine, but there were also traces of some kind of hypnotic cocktail as well, something similar to benzodiazepines but much stronger.

There was also the slight radioactive trace that she couldn't even begin to account for, though she had a theory and it was deeply disturbing:

The radiation would make the drug stable in the immune system of a person whose body was hyperactively healing itself by lowering the body's natural defense mechanisms. In other words, it was tailor made for shifters.

In a normal human, it would absolutely kill them and would produce the accelerated effects of an overdose: she now had three bodies in her morgue at work to prove its lethality.

In function, she could theorize that it served one purpose only:

To turn any shifter that took it into an addicted hyper-strong and very compliant weapon. Someone in the city was making a chemical that would literally turn shifters into a walking army of juggernauts.

But why? And how? There were so many questions and no answers.

Raven felt frustrated and deeply worried.

With the revelation of the nature of that drug that was flooding the streets, she now felt a responsibility more than ever to help put a stop to it by finding its source. She had lost enough people to it and it had caused enough trouble.

The lab door opened with a hiss and Raven looked up.

It was Max.

His face was still sour and his body language tense, but it had lessened to a degree and that was what told her that Rakinos was gone.

"Relieved?" she asked, fingering the vial in her pocket as she did, her gut a mess of tangled apprehension and determination as the next part of her plan from earlier finally had an opportunity to be put into action. She was nervous about it but steeled her courage. There was only one person she could ask for help in finding the source, only one person who was on the streets nearly every night and knew the ins and outs of the underworld better than anyone. Someone who could not only help her end the threat of the drug but take care of themselves in the process.

Max grunted a reply as passed her and asked her if she needed help cleaning up.

"Actually," Raven said, pulling out the vial from her pocket and holding it up in her hands, the remaining liquid sloshing blue inside, giving off a small azure glow that reflected in the darkness of Max's pupils. " I do need your help but we need to keep it between you and me. For now."

Max looked up at her, his dark eyebrows meeting in the middle as he frowned. "What do you mean?"

"I don't want Draco to find out what I'm about to ask you for because he would try to stop it but there's no other way."

"Raven," Max asked, shutting the lab door and crossing his arms, studying her. "What are you talking about?"

"I need your help." and taking a deep breath, Raven told him what she had planned.

######

The darkest part of any city isn't the place where the lights are dimmest. It's not the place where shadows swing in a murderous dance of umbra glazed hazes. The darkest place of any city is rather deep inside the broken pieces of humanity, existing between the spaces, between the shards, existing eternally as the glue that sticks everything together.

Nestled in the heart of the oldest section of Dawson City, among the derelict buildings and forgotten apartments, behind the old fish factory and the old coal power plant sat a building that even the city zoning commission had forgotten about. It wasn't a forgetting born out of time's incessant march, but rather by a steady flow of cash into the right hands, at the right times, with the right words whispered and the right pressure points applied surgically like a scalpel to people's appetites.

The building's original purpose was long lost to most but it sat, draped in the shadow of the surrounding waterfront buildings. Curiously, it was the only one to have power it seemed. Modern quartz lights were spaced at even intervals, making the pools of shadow where one may hide between the piercing beams thin or nonexistent. A fifteen-foot-high fence surrounded it and it was only by passing through a secured checkpoint made of a daunting gate and a set of armed guards could one gain entrance. The other entrance was in the rear of the building, near the docks. The Dawson River flowed there, wide and cold, winding its way through The

Narrows neighborhood, passing by Skid Row and finally emptying into the Atlantic Ocean.

Armed guards patrolled the outside perimeter, each in black uniforms, each carrying a heavy assault rifle and none of them walked with dogs. This was because each one of them were werewolves, shape shifters, shifted into their wolf forms, their eyes gleaming yellow in the dark like floating cigarette embers. Headsets beeped at every check in on the hour even though the windows of the building were dark.

The building's upper floors were every bit the abandoned ruin that the owners of the building wanted it to look like but below ground, was a different story. Below ground was where the real activity took place. The building's owner had blessed it with a gigantic maze of corridors, rooms and sections, all four stories below ground, very nearly touching the water table itself. No one remembered who he was today, but the owner had actually been a paranoid warmonger, profiting nicely from the bombs there were dropped in Japan, having invested heavily in atomic energy research.

The owner was dropped by his heart that went off in his chest, a deadly bomb as any. His name had been David Greer, but no one remembered that either, and no one ever knew how paranoid he had been of being incinerated by the very bombs he had helped build to wipe out others. The entire sub complex beneath this old administration building was his bomb shelter, just in case.

Nowadays, Greer had a different shelter, albeit much smaller, made of concrete up in Pleasant Rest Cemetery under an ornate tomb, inscribed with words that reminded those who would stop to read it that he was dedicated to peace. His legacy, the old network of tunnels and rooms underground, remained intact and it had been repurposed by minds with purposes not all together dissimilar, though far grander and darker.

It was here, nestled in the darkest heart of the city that plans were being made to lay the city itself low, plans that would change the face of Dawson City and shift the balance of power in it forever. The key to the execution of those plans was now finally within reach.

Deep in the heart of the underground bunker, a tall human man in a white lab coat stood before a bank of computers, watching the readouts, his lined face and hard clean-shaven jaw line set in stone. His slate gray eyes and salt and pepper hair matched his glasses, small square lenses that spoke volumes about the importance of efficiency to him. Around him, the lab he was currently in was bustling with activity, humans and shifters alike, side by side, each absorbed in their own tasks. Machines beeped steadily and movements at the door to the lab made him look up from his study and he glared angrily.

A hulking form entered the room, dressed in a dark sweater, dark pants and even darker shoes. With his fur gleaming like fresh blood and his scarlet gaze vivid and alive, Rakinos entered the room and everyone, just for a fraction of a moment, stopped, his looming presence knocking them off guard, though they knew him well. They also knew enough about his temper and that of the man who studied the screens to not stop work for long and so returned to their tasks without so much as a word. Everyone was paid well here.

"Where have you been?" Dr. Harvey Madison snarled with venom at Rakinos.

Rakinos pinned him with a glare and Madison wisely shut up.

"I've been at Riley's. He contacted me for help, of all things."

Madison frowned. "After all this time?" Then dismissing the idea, he went on. "We've got bigger problems, such as who is leaking our drug? We still haven't made any headway in that respect---

"The drug is ready and I'm working on finding the leak." Rakinos nearly snapped at him. The years had not done much to change him. Sometimes, the man, for all his considerable intellect, he could be small minded.

"I've discovered something far more curious and if I'm right, it will change everything we've been planning." Rakinos told him bluntly, crossing the room and standing directly opposite of Madison.

"What the hell are you talking about, Rakinos? We've been working on this the past five years. I've invested so much capital into this that my company's shareholders are getting suspicious and I can't fend them off forever. When I decided to help you, when you first suggested the idea of the serum, it was because I needed something new, something beyond shock staves and collars! We could sell this to the military like you suggested in the first place. What in God's name could be more important than the project's success?" Madison demanded, throwing his hands up and sighing in frustration, putting his hands on his waist. Since his back was turned to Rakinos momentarily, he didn't see the tiny but deadly change in Rakinos' expression, the downward turn of his eyebrows, the minute curling of his lip and the slightest slip of a white fang. Before Madison turned back around, the expression was gone.

"Wolf's Bane will be work. It simply needs more time. We've tested it but this," Rakinos said, pulling out the DNA samples he had stolen from Raven's lab, holding them up before Madison, the tubes winking in the light. "This may change our avenue of approach entirely. We need to think bigger. We need to go back to the original mission of the Bane program."

"For God's sake stop calling it "Wolf's Bane". I hate that term. It's what a street thug will call it for lack of a better understanding. What is that you're so fond suddenly of waving about?" Madison saw the gleam in Rakinos' eye and recognized it. "Not the idea of a super-werewolf again. It won't work. The army never got it to work and that's why the Bane program was scrapped generations ago."

Rakinos moved over to a DNA sequence analyzer and opened its hood. Carefully he put in the samples from Brian and Max and shut the hood. Keying in a sequence of commands, he waited for the machine to do its work. It whirred, electric motors moving the samples in a circle as laser scanners pierced it, electric eyes seeing far beyond and deeper than even his own vision could. A moment later, the machine dinged and a result was displayed on the screen behind them. Turning around to the monitor, Rakinos directed Madison's attention to the screen.

"What is that, some kind of RNA scripting mutation?" Madison asked, pushing his glasses up on his face, the screen reflecting in the polarized lenses.

"Indeed. Watch. The one on the left is a normal human DNA strand when it gets exposed to the proteins in normal shifter saliva."

Rakinos keyed the simulation to start. They had already had this old simulation from years ago when Rakinos was chasing the original dream of the military to make werewolf super-soldiers using the bane as a catalyst.

It was ludicrous, Madison thought as he continued to watch.

On screen, the CGI DNA strand moved across the screen and merged with the protein from the normal shifter's sample that was already on file. In mere moments, the DNA began to unravel and in seconds, it was destroyed entirely.

He then keyed up dual sample from Brian and Max and replayed the simulation, watching Madison closely.

On screen, the DNA molecule moved and merged with unique protein and for a moment, the DNA shook and the base pairs seemed about ready to dissolve when they suddenly stopped, came together and realigned, turning instead into something totally new. Gone was the double helix DNA structure that every single living thing on the planet shared, shifters included and there, in its place, was a triple helix strand, like a set of triangular stairs twisting up and up.

Madison's eyes widened, his pupils registering the shock of what he was seeing.

"Is this what I think it is?"

Rakinos nodded, and with his voice low and powerful, deadly in its certainty, he replied.

"What you are looking at, is a protein that can not only merge shifter and base human DNA without the death or rejection of the receiving host, but rather, make something altogether new and unknown. Something stronger. More powerful. Something that we've been looking for, something that can withstand the toxic nature of Wolf's Bane and better, if the hypnotic effects of the drug remain in place, allow for total control of the new form."

Rakinos looked at Madison, his scarlet eyes shimmering.

"Where once you had dreams of profit, of selling a powerful new super drug to the military to make chemically enhanced soldiers, now we have something better. Now, we have a way to make our own soldiers. Our own enforcement teams. We hold the means to make ourselves God. We create them. We control them. We own them. We could take this city and bring it to its knees and that's just the start. This," Rakinos said, pointing at the screen, "is the future."

Madison stood back, his arms crossed, his face distended in surprise and shock as the impact of what he just saw would have on the future of not just his company if he could somehow market it, but the future of genetics altogether. Everything was going to change, the entire paradigm.

Triple helix DNA had been proposed of course since 1953. The problem at the time, Madison remembered was that the Van der Waals distances were too small, basically individual molecules were too close atomically speaking to be able to have a stable linkage. Furthermore, Watson and Crick hypothesized that the polarization near the axis of the strands as they wove together would simply repel a third strand.

The only known example of triple helix DNA, Madison thought as he watched the animation loop on the screen was in 1957, when *E. coli* was observed briefly to use triple helix DNA during RNA transmission between the DNA and the cells and genetic alleles, telling the cells how to form and the genes what to do but beyond that it hadn't been observed since and couldn't be recreated. If triple helix DNA could be created in the lab, on a large scale, it would advance gene therapy, cancer treatments, eliminate genetic disorders, the uses, he thought, almost giddily, were literally reaching to the stars. Rakinos and his dream of an army of mutated shifters was shallow, in his opinion.

"Where did you say this came from?" he asked, looking at Rakinos who pulled the sample from the analyzer, placed it back into its container and shut the machine down. Rakinos, an odd expression on his face, dodged the question.

"I need to verify it, test it, make sure the simulations are correct." he said instead.

"Indeed I—" Madison began before he was cut off.

A phone vibrated and the sharp shrill sound blasted out of Madison's lab coat pocket. Cursing he answered it and his tone changed immediately. He went into spin mode, Rakinos noted with disgust. It must have been the board he was talking to at Madison Genetics, otherwise the hawkish asshole would have come out, more like how Madison really was. Rakinos hated a mind made small by concepts of greed and fame.

Hanging up the phone, Madison glared at his partner.

"Damn it all. I hate board meetings. They want me to come in and explain the funding that I've been funneling into here. Apparently, one our accountants was too good at her job and raised questions. I can cover for us but it's going to come at a cost for me."

Madison turned and faced Rakinos.

"Right now, we need to focus on finding the source of the leak of the bane, and then we need to verify what you've found. We can use the current version of the drug to mollify them for now. If I bring something to them, sooner rather than later, I might be able to salvage this with my head still intact while we work on this idea of yours. I must be insane but even I can see the possibilities of this."

Rakinos growled low in his throat as crossed his arms.

"I already know who our leaker is. As for verification, leave that to me. I have my own methods." Rakinos paused. A thoughtful expression crossed his scarlet eyes. "In fact, I may have a way of dealing with both at the same time."

"I don't want to know." Madison held up his hand and shook his head.

He quickly made for the lab door, shrugging off his lab coat and revealing an expensive suit beneath it. A Rolex flashed on his wrist. "Make it happen. However you have to. We can't keep stumbling like we have been. I'm off to see if I can divert them."

Rakinos watched him stride off towards the elevators through the glass walls that made up the labs hallway bulkhead. His scarlet eyes tracked the motion of Madison's arms and legs and for a fraction of a moment, a part of him begged to hear the sound of them snapping, wetly, one by one, until Madison pleaded to be killed. Maybe Rakinos thought, he would grant the man his request. Maybe not.

Rakinos did not care for Madison in the slightest. He hated him and tolerated him as a necessary annoyance but if what he had discovered was true, then the man himself was about to be irrelevant.

Five years ago, finding the tide of culture and society turning more towards a peaceful merger of human and shifter societies, Rakinos had withdrawn from his public crusade and went underground. For years, he had been a controversial figure and proponent of shifter superiority, openly calling for militant action against groups and those who would deny him and his kin their rights, their freedoms.

People called him the "Werewolf Nazi". People called him a trouble maker, a violent minded activist with no thought or care about the methods he used and he thought, if the shoe fit, it was best to wear it. It helped you not step in so much shit that way. He had no time for labels. People thought what they wanted and it slowed him down as much as an ant would pushing against a boulder that was rolling downhill.

The world was full of viral waste sacks that called themselves human beings. They were wasteful. Shameful, uncaring, unfeeling creatures that destroyed their world, their cultures and societies and then denied that they were doing it while in the very process of doing the same. It was a unique failing of the human condition and it would be their extinction. Even as a child, he had known this and acted upon it, seeing no point in social norms. He supposed his parents had been unable to handle him, not that it mattered really in the end. The group home had not held him, despite years of suffering under its roof. When he was eventually released, it had felt good to track down his family, his mother and father, and dish out his own retribution for their weakness. A hot rush shot through his system as he remembered it from so many years ago.

In his memory, the scent of burning wood, propane and blood wafted through the halls of his mind, the falling snow and ash white against the raging inferno and he savored it. The sound of a scream echoed and then was gone, fading into the ghost that it was.

He stalked out of the room and headed to the right, moving towards the basement manufacturing labs, where the Wolf's Bane was made. Normally, he hated going into the area because the fumes were overpowering but he had a reasonable suspicion that he would find his leaker there. After taking a bite out of the drug dealer he had kidnapped after a week of surveillance, he had followed up on two more leads. They had both been excellent sources.

The police had pulled their bodies from the river not long after.

Rakinos could have sent someone of course. He could have kept his hands off of it but he was a hands-on type and he prided himself on it. Descending down the corrugated metal stairs that shook under his weight, he went down three flights and came at last to the manufacturing plant. Two guards, both shifters, stood at attention at the door, heavy rifles barring their chests. He looked at them, feeling a surge of pride. Not for rigid discipline, but rather the source of the discipline.

The one on the left had the coloring of a Doberman and the one on the right was a brindle colored man with a sneaky face like a weasel. Both of them were heavily built and their expressions were cold and cruel. On both of their wrists were metal cuffs with tiny injector mechanisms and there, in the reservoir was glowing blue fluid. Tiny amounts of Wolf's Bane.

For them, he supposed, it provided a euphoric high, a rush of hot strength and rage. In reality, the leaders of his squads all had the cuff injectors. They were, unknowingly, all test subjects. The Bane, while providing the benefits, also gradually allowed Rakinos to reprogram their brain in combination with subliminal audio pumped through the mandatory headsets every soldier wore, making them loyal to a fault and so far, the test had been a stunning success. Even with that, Rakinos wanted more. By now, he thought, they were probably too addicted to ever come off of the stuff even as the radiation slowly burned out their immune systems. In time, they would probably die but that would be months, if not years. It helped to have compliant addicted help, especially if you were the one dispensing their vices.

Whether it was their own weakness to addiction, their desire of fortune or their love of carnage, Rakinos' operation had attracted the attention of several shifter mercenary groups. Every community had scum, even shifters, Rakinos thought as he stopped in front of them. Some of them, just wanted to watch the world burn.

He'd just help them light the match.

Recognizing him immediately, the guards stepped aside and allowed him to key in his entry. The double doors slid aside with a hiss and Rakinos stepped onto the factory floor.

The factory floor itself was not as big as the word "factory" made it seem. Rather, it was the size of two large conference rooms placed end to end and perhaps a few feet wider. The floors were beige concrete, pitted with time. The walls were rock, carved from the granite foundation that was the under city. The ceiling itself was thirty feet from the floor and was reinforced with heavy steel girders from which hung modern LED lights, casting the whole room in a bright antiseptic light.

Four rows of tables filled the room, each staffed by a teams of workers in hazmat gear, mostly shifters. Plastic eye shields, heavy insulated gloves and the whispery crackling of their plastic suits filled the air. Each table had a separate stage of the process. On one were the basic chemicals, held separately, each carefully measured and counted before being dispensed further down the line to the next station where they were mixed gently into rotating centrifuges and so on.

At least thirty workers toiled ceaselessly, and Rakinos nodded with approval that so far, no further deaths had occurred. There were a few accidents in the beginning but dead workers make no product and so now protocols were strictly enforced. No deviations were tolerated. Above the manufacturing floor, a suspended observation booth of sorts had been installed into a room suspended above the entire operation. It was here that Rakinos headed, making his way purposefully up the stairs and when he entered it, he motioned for the security there to give him the room alone, sending them away.

The observation pod was slate grey concrete and steel, with a bank of security monitors and keyboards lining the front wall over which was a floor to ceiling size bank of windows that gave anyone in the tank a fantastic view of the entire process below. Nothing could pass without being seen. Standing over what he considered his world, Rakinos felt more alive than he had in years.

For a while, he stood, arms crossed, his red eyes taking in everything below, silently watching, his muscles motionless. Everything was happening behind his eyes now, in the shadows of his brain as his plan evolved and he was sure of the key he had found.

Rakinos had targeted Madison five years ago when the man's once powerful company was starting to lose revenue and he was desperate for something to jump start his company before it was taken from him. Madison had been riding the coat-tails of fame and fortune from cracking lycanthropic genome and now, years after it was done, his relevance was wearing out quickly.

Rakinos had been on that project as well and he remembered Madison, even if Madison in all his blind self-absorbed arrogance did not remember him entirely. Madison had been drowning himself and his worries into the bottom of a bottle, and he had been using the data he had gotten from his work from the Lycanthropic Genome Project to create new means of restraint for law enforcement. The first item were the shock collars. Then came the electro-staves. The things were like six-foot-long titanium cattle prods. What had marked him for death originally in Rakinos' mind, was when he had announced in a Fox News interview that Madison Genetics had potentially found a way to suppress the shifter gene in human parents who had a child born with an active shifter gene.

Rakinos had went to kill Madison but instead found a broken, drunken mess and that his announcement was premature grandstanding and nothing more. Madison, in his drunken stupor, had been raving like a lunatic to anyone who would listen about genetic engineering and black ops projects and it was that rant that he had caught Rakinos' attention and which had spared his life.

Rakinos was in the shadows of the club, sitting, waiting for Madison to step out into the night and had overheard his conversation or rather attempts at it with a man next to him in the next booth.

"I'm telling you...there are secret projects...hidden things..." Madison had hiccupped to the man. The man had the scraggly wild look of someone who never left his basement and in fact he was covered in American flags and responded with his own theories about the Illuminati and secret societies and plots by "Big Pharma" for years to control people through the fluoridation of water. Rakinos had rolled his eyes until Madison's response caught him entirely off guard.

"No, you ignorant buffoon. The Illuminati aren't real. World War 2. The Dog Soldiers. You ever heard of them, my drunken sod?"

That name made Rakinos' ears perk up instantly because he too had heard rumors of the Dog Soldiers in his work as an activist and history was one thing he knew quite a bit about.

The Dog Soldiers were a black ops group of the US military and fought on the side of the Allies against the Axis Powers. The Dog Soldiers of the Cheyenne were legendary fighters and given that the group in World War 2 had been very effective in routing out Nazis and was made entirely out of shifters, they earned the name Dog Soldiers, as well.

Their mission, it turned out, was to infiltrate and wipe out the enemy units' key locations from deep behind enemy lines, using their naturally enhanced senses and abilities while striking from the shadows. All of that changed when the fighting became particularly chaotic during a hellish engagement and the Axis powers began to target civilians. The Allies were losing the battle and the Dog Soldiers broke ranks and turned their abilities on the Axis line, surprising them and turning the tide of battle.

When they came home, it emboldened other shifters in the US to step out and begin to integrate more openly in society, to demand equal treatment and shifters the world over responded in the same way. Shifters became heroes, nightmares, curiosities, and friends and family at the same time in a matter of a short few years.

It was what Madison said next about the Dog Soldiers that made Rakinos decide not to kill him. Madison had continued to rant, his voice heavily slurred.

"Did you know that the Dog Soldiers had a secret plan to win the war...they were experimenting with drugs to enhance the already superior forces of the werewolves involved...tried to turn them into super soldiers...they almost managed it but couldn't quite crack the code...I have their research...stupid fools didn't know what they had...what they could have done...I'm one of the richest smartest men in our country and look at me....drowning in a goddamned bar because some pencil pushers don't get the numbers they like or because some product fails and injures someone. It's bound to happen...it's just math...I can make it work if they'd just listen to me...ethics be damned! It's science, profit even, that matters! I could change the world!"

A few hours passed before Madison had wallowed in his despair enough and had finally left the bar stumbling as he went. Stupidly he had taken a side street to get to his car which was actually parked off the street over from the dive bar he had somehow found himself in. He was barely conscious when Rakinos stepped out of the shadows and took him roughly, his eyes blazing in the dark.

Rakinos smiled.

He had savored the look of fear on the man's face, the music of his hammering heart, the blood rushing through his body and the scent of acrid terror as it wafted from his pores.

"What ...what are you...what-wh-what do you want..." Madison had stammered, trying to scream, his throat had refused to work. Rakinos yanked him in close and got nose to nose with him, holding him off the ground.

"I know you and you know me. It's been a while, Madison. You know about the Dog Soldier program. I want that information and maybe, if we work together, you and I, we can make something of it. Together. Maybe then, your company won't chew you up and shit you out like the maggot ridden piece of filth you are. Do you understand me?"

Now, five years later, Rakinos and a much soberer Madison had managed to save the man's career by coming out with various improved non-lethal restraints that the police were clamoring for, especially with the rise in violent crime involving shifters that they couldn't handle by normal means. Rakinos made sure the devices worked. He had plenty of test subjects, after all, he thought absently, eyeing the workers. Given that he was also responsible for the rise in crime, he had toed the line, playing both sides to profit his real agenda: the rise of own power base. It had all worked, chugging along like a machine for years. They had made progress, true, but it was halting, and for some time, has stagnated due to various bugs they could not seem to work out of the Bane alone as an enhancement serum. But now...

Now things had changed. He brought his attention back to the factory floor.

Rakinos let eyes fell upon a young male shifter, the one he had been watching now for days. Wolf's Bane was an amazing creation. Using the research from the Dog Soldier project that Madison had gotten his hands on from the Department of Defense, he and Rakinos had engineered a potent chemical capable of turning any shifter into a living weapon, incapable of feeling pain, changing them into a raging locomotive that was faster, stronger and more resilient than they normally were.

They were also loyal, forced into submission, keyed to responses that Rakinos and Madison had programmed into their minds via weeks of subjective therapy and the gravity bending, mind crushingly addictive nature of Wolf's Bane. The fact that it was a mild hypnotic also helped maintain control. Where the US military had failed, with time and technology, Rakinos and Madison had succeeded. And now, the young werewolf below him was selling out their creation to the public like stolen candy.

It enraged him because it bucked his control.

Control, Rakinos thought, as he turned his gaze to the far wall of the room. Control and discipline were essential and to have them flouted was not acceptable. Weakness was not to be tolerated. Studying the young man as he worked, Rakinos reflected on the Bane.

The drug burned out the immune system of the shifters in the large doses required to create the reaction that turned them into compliant weapons. After a series of tests that ended the life of at least ten shifters, Rakinos and Madison found that by making the mixture slightly radioactive with an oxygen isotope, the drug didn't burn out the system of the shifter's, since the radiation kept the immune system reaction under control, but ultimately, it consumed them nonetheless in a period of days. They died screaming, drooling on themselves, useless as a weapon or for any purpose, their DNA obliterated. Newer versions had been more effective and the dosing issue had been worked out but now they had hit a brick wall of development. They were so close. *No, I was so close*, Rakinos thought.

But now...

Rakinos pulled the samples from his pocket and studied them again. The one marked with Brian's name held his fascination the most, his red eyes thoughtful and calculating.

If DNA could be re-written into a triple helix then it would be stable enough to withstand the drug indefinitely, and furthermore, if Rakinos could create shifters from baseline humans, he could easily create his own army in a matter of weeks. Days, even. An army of supercharged super-shifters, obedient to him, unkillable, unfeeling, living walking breathing weapons with the cunning of their predatory ancestors and the cruelty of the human condition wrapped up in a neat package, all under his thumb. Madison and his bullshit desire to sell to the military would be irrelevant. *No one should have this power but me*, Rakinos thought, *where it belongs. With someone who can wield it appropriately.*

Naturally, the first thing he needed to do was set a list of goals. It was what the best minds always did, he thought. Prioritize.

First, he needed to test the DNA in a shifter. There was enough DNA here for that, maybe two shifters. Make sure the DNA would affect them. If it did, then he could test them using a full dose of Wolf's Bane. Assuming both worked, he could move on to testing on a human being, one he knew had no shifter ancestry at all. To do that, he'd need a subject.

Thankfully, a human subject had just sprang to mind, Rakinos made a note. As for the first shifter for the DNA recombination testing...

He looked back to the young shifter he had been silently watching this entire time.

He did have a leak to deal with, after all, and to waste a resource was pointless and bad form. Better repurpose it into something useful.

Stepping forward, he extended one of his index fingers and his black claw clicked on the intercom system.

His voice was broadcast over the work floor.

"Alex Hollens. I need to see you in the observation pod. Now."

Rakinos cut the feed. His voice was instantly recognized. The young shifter seemed to stiffen where he stood, paused and obeyed.

A satisfied expression crawled over Rakinos' snout. Discipline, was indeed, a beautiful thing.

#####

Alex Hollens was eighteen. His mom was a meth head and his father was an abusive drunk. After spending the last years of his time in high school under the old man's lash, Alex had finally had enough and struck out on his own, quitting school, leaving his wreck of a life behind. He didn't plan on ever going to college.

Neither of his parents was a shifter, but Alex himself was. He had learned that he was not long after he turned twelve and started hearing things he shouldn't. Of course, over the period of a year, other things had started to happen. His vision changed. He started to have dreams and then finally, one day in the bathroom, he found that he could change the shape of his ears at will. It took effort, and concentration but in time he mastered it. By the time Christmas had come that year, he had gotten good enough at it that he was able to fully transform into his wolf form at will. His mother, of course, when she found out, waved him off and told him his grandfather had been one of those wolf freaks, while his old man tried to get him to use his new skills as a source of income, primarily to be a look out during Ronnie's pill trades.

Forced to use his superior hearing and scent tracking ability to keep an eye out for police and fake product, Alex had spent his freshman year eyeball deep in his father's pill hocking schemes. He was arrested later for breaking and entering at a pharmacy and spent a good chunk of his summer in jail. The relationship between him and his parents eventually grew so strained that one night after scarfing down cardboard reheated pizza, he told them both to go to hell and get fucked and had left.

Gradually he had drifted deeper and deeper into the underworld of shifter prostitution, drugs and crime. One day, he had been approached by a tall shifter with blue black fur that had refused to give Alex his name but had made Alex an offer to come and work for a project that would make him rich beyond his wildest dreams and enable him to get some payback on the assholes that made his life a living hell.

Alex had taken him up on the offer and now, a year later, he found himself making one of the deadliest drugs in history, though he didn't know that. He only know that he was paid very well. Not that he had spent that money wisely. Crack was expensive. So was pot, and women were as well. He especially liked going after the human women who were into male shifters. He earned a good bit of side cash from that.

Gradually, he had learned from the guards that the drug they were making provided a short and powerful high as long as it was given in small doses, more powerful than anything on the streets today, something so strong that even shifters could get off on it.

Alex had asked a guard for a quick hit and it had been as if paradise had exploded in his veins carrying the sun behind it. For the next few hours he had been tripping balls essentially, high as a kite; he had felt like he could do anything, could beat anyone. He had felt strong for the first time in his life. Powerful. Unstoppable.

He had also found an opportunity.

Over the course of several weeks, unnoticed he thought, he had spread the word among the drug dealers on the streets, the 86ers especially. They controlled most of the drug trade in Dawson City. Finally, he had given a tiny sample to one of the dealers who had nearly died from the explosive high it had given him. Alex told him to keep the doses miniscule, barely more than a drop or it could end badly, to spread the doses out over a week or more.

He made sure to tell the dealers to fight the urge to increase the dose. Needless to say, it had become an instant hit, spreading into the underground club scene, passed off on laced ecstasy pills or even in its raw liquid form and for a while, it had gone well. Alex hadn't been caught and by taking small amounts of the drug out in the small vials, he had built himself a healthy network. He could approach his in deals human or shifter form and keep his identity a secret.

Then the people had started dying.

He knew that at least three people had died from overdoses in the last week. The news had been all over it, with the police conducting intensive investigations but the hospitals were stumped and couldn't figure out what the drug was, or where it was coming from. No one ever suspected it came from shifters since all the product itself was being fenced by the 86ers and the other human gangs, sold to them by a single low key 18-year-old kid with a knack for bad ideas.

The first three to die had died in the hospitals while rumor had it, a fourth had died in a police drunk tank, having gone insane and bashing his own brains out on the doors. Some of the cops were on the take, he knew and even though that would slow down the investigation, it probably wouldn't halt it.

Since then, Alex had tried to keep a low profile, even lower than normal. It was best to stop while one was ahead.

He had been processing the Bane as the guards called it when his name was called over the intercom from the observation tank, and the voice that had called it was nothing short of being called by the Devil himself. That deep resonant sound that caused his bones to shake had frozen him in place before he had forced himself to move, knowing that disobedience was lethal. He had looked up at the tank and the bright lights overhead cast the tank itself in dark shadows.

There seeming to float behind the glass was a dark living shadow, hulking and looming in the tank, red eyes burning out through the glass.

Swallowing his panic, Alex had moved quickly, mounting the stairs and stepping into the observation tank where the door behind him closed with a hiss and a click of the latch. In the sharp finality of the lock's clicking sound, Alex had the fleeting screaming fear that his own fate had perhaps been sealed.

Rakinos stood, towering in the room, his back to Alex, arms crossed behind his back, legs spread wide, his ears alert and his fur seeming to run with that strange blood color. With his dark clothes, he seemed to be living burning blood and that image sent a chill down Alex's spine.

Rakinos didn't turn to face him as he addressed Alex.

"Take that off. We need to talk, Mr. Hollens."

Alex was confused for a moment and then realized Rakinos was talking about the hazmat gear. His hands shaking, Alex did just that, unzipping it and pulling it off, a piece at time. Gloves, mask, shield, respirator, they all came away with a crackle of a plastic tarp and Alex didn't know where to put them so he just put them at his feet. He stood there, exposed now.

He was dressed in a pair of dirty blue work coveralls, old work boots with a white t-shirt peeking out from the collar of his coveralls. He was covered in tawny fur, and it was thin and patchy, and he realized he could smell himself and that he needed a shower. His tail hung behind him, trying to curl up from his unease and his ears had fallen to his head in deference to the walking mountain before him. His eyes were unique: one was honey gold and the other was bright blue; both were bloodshot. At least one of his incisors was growing back in. It had been knocked out in a fight a few weeks ago.

Alex felt very small and his thin frame only reinforced the feeling.

"Sir?" he asked, his voice surprising him with how much of the shake he felt in his body came out with his words.

Rakinos still didn't turn to face him.

"Mr. Hollens, in the last few weeks I've noticed several dips in our production numbers. Small, barely noticeable. You wouldn't know that something was off unless you knew what to look for. That piqued my curiosity so I dug a bit deeper. I found that someone, here, in this facility, was stealing entire vials of the Bane and sneaking it out. This was before I started making...inquiries...on the street. Street dealers talk so much under duress. They say the most amazing things and afterwards, to confirm their story, I checked our footage, our quality checks, your station in particular and what I found, profoundly disturbs me."

Alex felt his blood run cold. His mind began to race and his heart hammered loudly. He knew Rakinos could hear it and he mentally fought with himself, begging his tell-tale heart to calm down, to relax.

It didn't work.

Turning, Rakinos finally met Alex's gaze, his red eyes boring into the young man's. Alex felt his bladder nearly release.

"S-s-sir?"

"You wouldn't know anything about that situation, now would you, Alex? You know how seriously I take security.... discipline..." Rakinos growled softly, stepping forward with each word, his looming shadow falling over Alex's shaking frame like a corpse shroud. Rakinos was now inches away and Alex felt himself take a step back only to find that his back met the cold unyielding concrete wall.

There was nowhere to go. Nowhere left to run.

Alex felt the vials he had taken earlier touch in his pocket and his heart dropped as he heard the clink of the glass. He was nearly in tears from fear as Rakinos heard it too. Rakinos cocked his head and his eyes flicked down to the pocket on the right chest of Alex's overalls.

Deciding the game was up, Alex knew he could either stay and die or make a run for it.

Alex, once again, chose wrong.

He dashed to the right, bolting down the stairs and out the door, his feet flying, alarms blaring—

In his mind, that is.

That sweet dream of being able to run was knocked out of him the moment he made the move to run as Rakinos shot out his thick heavy left arm like a ram rod, his open palm, black claws flashing, crashing into the concrete wall, cracking it from the impact, sending up dust in the air, blocking his escape.

A screamed whimper of fear was ripped out of Alex as he fell back against the wall, knowing he was trapped like a goddamn rat in a trap. He buried his head in his hands, his tail between his legs, shaking like a blade of grass in a thunderstorm. The fear was making him sick. He was going to vomit, going to pass out

"Please...don't kill me...I'm sorry...I just...I... I...."

Rakinos lowered his massive head and brought his muzzle close to Alex's tear streaked face, a deep growl rumbling from his throat like a tiger. Without taking his blazing red eyes off of the boy, he reached up with his free right hand and slipped his fingers into Alex's pocket, taking out the two vials of glowing blue fluid.

When he spoke next, his fangs were within centimeters of Alex's snout and Alex could smell the coppery rotten scent of blood on his hot breath.

"Don't worry, Alex. I'm not going to kill you. In fact, you could say you're getting a promotion. I need help with a project and I think that you will be able fill that role quite nicely."

When Rakinos didn't rip his head off a second later, Alex dared to lower his hands and crack open his eyes to look up.

Rakinos shot his left hand away from the wall, slamming into the back of Alex's head and the young werewolf dropped to the floor instantly unconscious with a sickening thud. He lay there, crumpled, a trickle of blood running out from his ear and nose but breathing slowly, nonetheless.

Rakinos pocketed the vials and knelt, picking up Alex, throwing the young man's limp form over his shoulder like a sack of potatoes and carried him back down to the manufacturing floor. He felt the eyes of the other workers briefly look up, see who it was, and quickly resumed their work.

Fear was a powerful motivator and a valuable tool that Rakinos had mastered long ago.

He enjoyed it.

Moving quickly with purpose, he made his way down the corridors and into one of the subject testing labs that was unoccupied. The lab was spartan: a stainless-steel table with restraints and a rack of surgical instruments in a sealed sterile case. A single bright light hung from the middle of the room and a few cabinets with the proper drugs all neatly labeled lined the far wall. The floor was made of slick tile with a metal drain in the center of the room.

He roughly threw Alex onto the table and stripped him of his clothing, tossing it into a corner. He worked expertly, shackling the restraints around the young man's thin limp wrists and ankles. Another set of canvas straps with solid steel buckles were tightened around the man's chest and stomach. The restraints were made for shifters of course. Rakinos had designed them himself and provided Madison with the schematics. That had been a hefty government contract and Madison funneled a great deal of that funding into their project here.

Satisfied his charge wasn't going anywhere Rakinos stepped out of the room, sealing it with his private pin code. The door was solid titanium more than four inches thick. The room was also sound proofed. If Hollens did wake up and caused a commotion, no one could hear him and even if they did, they knew better than to open the door.

Rakinos was headed to his own private office of sorts, two floors up. In there, he would be mercifully free from fools and have a few moments of silence while he put his plans into motion. Now that he had shut down the drug leak and secured a test subject, he needed to test his theory on the DNA. The samples he had were small but they could be amplified and made to work but they wouldn't do in the long term. He would need a bigger source.

He needed Brian.

Of course, Brian was so far up Riley's ass that was going to be difficult now. He was surrounded by them. Jones, Mullen, there never seemed to be a moment when he wasn't alone. First, he needed to find out where Brian was staying. In fact, he needed to find out more about him in general and with that in mind, he knew his next move was to learn everything he could about Brian MacGregor.

The DNA tubes clacked together in his pocket.

Then there was Max Mullen himself. That was a thorn as well, mostly an annoyance. Several of his contacts had been beaten into pulps by Mullen's nightly forays into vigilantism but Rakinos doubted Mullen himself truly understood the importance of who they were. They were low level scouts who had gotten a bit too hands on when their urges got the better of them. As long as it didn't impact their service to him, Rakinos hadn't cared, letting them form their own little fiefdoms and he had let Max beat on them fairly regularly. But now, Max would need to be neutralized.

The only question that was looping through Rakinos' mind was a simple one and one that he would soon have a definite answer to while he waited for the DNA he had to be amplified for injection into Hollens. The question began to loop in his

Anthony Milhorn

mind as he set to work:
Who was Brian MacGregor?

CHAPTER 2

It had been a week since Brian had first met Draco Riley and now, altogether, it had been two weeks for Brian in his new life.

After the first night at Max's place, Brian had spent three days straight at Draco's house, desperately trying to learn how to shift his form and had, thus far, failed. Growing frustrated with it, even with Raven's guidance in her time away from the hospital, Brian had asked to take a break. He had taken some time to just explore the grounds of the manor and had thought about calling his mother to finally ask her the questions that had been burning through his mind, but so far, he had not worked up the courage to do so. He had heard from Ellie, however. She did finally return a call to him late last night and they had finally talked about what happened. While he didn't tell her everything, Brian did tell her that he too was attacked by the same gang and was recovering from the experience but that he was fine and they she didn't need to worry about him. She did apologize for losing her temper with him and for blaming him, and he said he understood, which he had. They were back on speaking terms for the time being, both healing in their own ways at their own pace.

Right now, Brian was outside on the well-manicured manor grounds, laying on a stone bench beneath a thick grove of trees in the middle of one of the grassy fields behind the house itself, on his back, his head in his hands crossed behind him. He was dressed in a pair of loose jeans Draco had found for him, slightly smaller than the too big pair Max had loaned him, but bigger than his old size, which was just about perfect. He wore no shirt, enjoying the warm heat of the sun as it warmed his thick fur, heating his skin below. It surprised him that he wasn't hot. Here, there were no sounds of cars, no rushing traffic, no horns, no people shouting, none of the sounds of the bustling city. Here, there was just nature and the layered years of history of the house and grounds. Peaceful and green, the warm pulse of life was almost palpable. His tail waved occasionally on its own in a lazy arc. He paid it no mind.

The summer had finally come into its own and the storms had passed, the season finally sliding into the warm days of hot dogs, grilling out, and about two weeks from now, the fireworks of July as the latter half of June settled over the world. On the horizon, the dark forests looked shady and inviting, with streamers of sunlight filtering down through the trees. Max had been busy at his shop as summer's arrival had brought on a few clients; mostly maintenance jobs but a few challenges as well. Brian had been splitting his time between Max's apartment and the room that Draco had allowed him to use at the manor. He had also been back to his apartment at least once more to get his computer and charging cord, to pay his bills and keep up the appearance that everything was fine. He had kept up the story Max had told his landlord and so far, she seemed none the wiser. Brian knew he couldn't keep up that charade forever, but for now, he wasn't worried about it.

Right now, his mind was occupied by more important thoughts.

Brian and Max had slowly begun to communicate over the last week or so. It wasn't much: A self-deprecating joke here, a few pieces of history between them about their respective experiences there, and slowly, Brian had begun to feel at home. Comfortable. Elijah was still there but he had become a memory that could be looked on with a smile now and remember the good times instead of sorrow. Brian was sure that if Elijah had lived to see what had become of Brian, that he would have wanted Brian to keep going, to live life. That was their motto between the two of them; you only live once. Enjoy it while it's here. By living and tackling this situation head on, Brian would honor his friend.

Brian also surprised himself by finding he didn't miss his security job as much as he had thought. These two weeks (if he counted the original four or five days after he was bitten and this week) away from it had been illuminating for him. He had gradually started to accept that he hadn't been happy where he was and that he was in fact, merely existing, tolerating life. It also occurred to him that he needed to acknowledge that the existence he had been living in was tied to never having gotten over the death of his father. The wound that had left ran deep and dealing with all the changes he had been through recently had caused Brian to do some serious soul searching. What he found is that he wanted more than a grind. In a way, he supposed, what had happened to him may have been a blessing; a kick start of sorts because now he was being forced to leave his past behind and face his future while considering his own identity and what it meant. One question kept floating in his mind:

Who am I?

The question had come one afternoon during a workout at the gym in the manor to ease his stress at not being able to shift yet and had rattled around in his head every single day since it had been born. The easiest answer to that question, he thought, as he let his right leg dangle off the side, the toe of his boot touching the grass, was simple: he was who he was. Sniffing once, he blew a gnat away from the end of his snout. But that didn't really answer the burning question. The real question was: *Who was the werewolf in his family?* Did he know them? Were there more? Was there an entire side of his family, a history with faces he didn't know? Relatives lost to time?

Brian's natural sense of curiosity came from his dad, and he tried for so many years to be like him, even after he had died, becoming a guard after not being able to become a cop, that Brian now realized that he had never tried to be anything else, despite that curiosity and drive to help others. He had surrendered to his depression. Now, things were changing.

I should have died there in that alley way.

I didn't.

Maybe there was a reason why all this had happened.

His mind drifted to Draco.

The man was a mystery. Not exactly in a bad way, Brian thought. He was just very private and reserved, but not in the manner Max was. Draco was old fashioned and kept his issues to himself. He had made himself available for Brian during any free time he had, which wasn't much, considering how often he was on the phone or answering emails, writing papers and seemed to genuinely care very much for the movement that he had helped spearhead. The man wanted a better world for everyone. Brian had seen nor found anything to suggest that Draco was anything than what he appeared to be: A good man trying to give people a good turn and in the process, maybe help heal some of his own pain and loss. He was very parental, and Brian did feel good around him. Draco was not Brian's father, but he was pretty close to what Jacob had once been for his son: a powerful force of calm in the storm. *It feels nice to have that again*, Brian thought.

He had met Roy Daniels, Draco's house manager. Roy, as it turned out, was the executor of the estate and kept the house and grounds in remarkable condition. Nothing escaped his notice. The man himself was smaller gentleman with a thin build and like everyone else around the manor, he too was a shifter and his accent was a thick Scottish brogue. Brian nearly made a grievous error of social etiquette by nearly laughing when he first met him and introduced himself on the grounds a few days ago. The man looked exactly like a black furred Scottish terrier, even down the thick mustaches. He had twinkling warm brown eyes and a mouth so foul, it would have turned a sailor red.

Brian had also briefly glimpsed Molly O'Hara, Draco's assistant as she went about her work. She was a human woman with a fit and trimmed frame, who seemed to see a dark pantsuit as a uniform and wore it with pride. She had a small simple golden cross on a fine chain on her neck and kept her red hair trimmed neatly to her shoulders and her blue eyes were always on point. Her smart phone and her Blue-tooth were never far from her and when she was around, Draco seemed to change. He seemed more relaxed, more open and Brian had even heard the old man laugh once, the sound rolling from his study. He suspected that Draco cared for Molly far more than he would have ever told anyone. Brian wondered if the feeling was mutual, since Molly also seemed to be more at ease around him, especially if no one seemed to be around.

The last person that Brian had finally ran into on his final day at the manor before taking his current break and subsequently returning, was Draco's technology expert and resident living IT department, Everett Benjamin Jackson, who told Brian his full name the moment they met. Jackson was considerably shorter than Brian and he was a shifter as well, though whether he was a full generation or a shape-shifter, Brian couldn't tell. Jackson looked like a beagle in terms of color with rich brown and white fur, as well as the shape of his face with his ears being just about as big. He had a medium build and his tail and ears were both constantly moving. Jackson also wore glasses with large round frames that he had strapped to his head since he spent so much time losing the things.

He was young too, Brian thought, maybe twenty-five or so and was friendly enough but *Jesus*, that kid could talk your ears off and not by intending to. He had the unfortunate habit of saying just whatever came into his brain and then realizing what he had said, backtracking and making it worse. Draco had been right about that, Brian thought with a chuckle to himself, remembering the first time he had met Jackson in the hallway after that work-out session that had started this whole line of thought.

Jackson had rounded the corner, not watching where he was going (admittedly, Brian hadn't been paying attention either) and they had bumped bodily into each other. The impact sent the much smaller shifter sprawling into the floor with a heavy thump. Brian had been shirtless and in need of a shower with a white towel draped over his neck. Max had lent him a pair of loose cotton workout pants that he didn't use anymore, and he was barefoot.

Jackson looked up at him from the ground, his mouth agape as Brian quickly tried to recover his own balance.

"Oh my god, I am so sorry I d---" Jackson had stammered, shoving his glasses back up on his snout, quickly grabbing his phone and then grabbed the hand that Brian had extended down to him, yanking him up to his feet. The ease with which he had been able to pick up the younger shifter surprised Brian. The kid must have been maybe a 130 to 140 pounds soaking wet and probably just under five foot seven.

"No, no, it's my fault, man. I wasn't paying any attention to where I was going. Are you okay?" Brian had asked, checking Jackson over visually for any signs of harm. The floors in the house were solid oak floors and had no give to them.

Jackson had dusted himself off quickly, looking rather sheepish when he looked up at Brian properly and his eyes had gone wide as they traveled up and down the bigger shifter's frame.

"Oh! You're the, uh new guy, the, uh medical marvel that Raven brought in. She said you were one of kind in the entire world and I said—"

Brian had felt his face flush under his fur and Jackson quickly shut his face.

"Yeah...you could say that I'm new." Brian had replied, rubbing the back of his head, a sheepish grin creeping up his face involuntarily as his face had burned.

Jackson tried to reverse course and instead drove straight into the awkwardness he had accidently created.

"Not that there's anything wrong or weird with being a medical marvel or that it's any of my business, absolutely none of my business. I, uh, I'm Jackson. Everett Benjamin Jackson. I do the computers around here." He said looking at Brian's arms.

Jackson had cringed and his ears pinned back as he groaned. "Do the computers? God I did not mean that to sound like that, I swear. I fix them, I make new ones, I do a little tinkering, I meant-- Jesus Christ..."

Brian had chuckled, his embarrassment fading a little. "It's okay, man. I got what you meant. Good to meet you. I'm Brian. Brian MacGregor and yeah, you could say that I'm the newbie."

"Awesome. You seem to be fitting in pretty good. If you need anything to do with a computer or electronics, I'm your guy or just have Max yell at me. He seems to be here a lot when you are. You guys make a-- "

Brian had felt his eyebrows go up and his face felt hot again as Jackson's words registered in his mind: *You guys make a.... A what exactly?!*

"I'm sorry?" Brian finally managed to stumble back out, the idea of him and Max together was ludicrous, and it made his face so warm his ears burned, and he laid them down on his head unconsciously.

"No.... I think you have the wrong idea." Brian said gently shaking his head.

"Oh. Oh. Oh God. I'm sorry. I didn't mean to assume." Jackson shut his mouth and nodded, holding up a finger and shaking it, as if suddenly reminded of something. "Um, never mind. I'm going to get back to work before I sacrifice what dignity I have left. Someone was messing with my program the other night and I'm trying to reconstruct what they did. People need to stop messing around with stuff they don't understand, I mean, seriously. This stuff isn't free to develop and the lab gear is sensitive as hell. Butterfingers, I tell you. Butterfingers!"

With that, the young beagle looking shifter had hastily made his exit and vanished down a hallway talking to himself. Brian thought he head Jackson repeatedly call himself stupid, but he wasn't sure.

They were all an eclectic bunch, Brian thought back in the present, kicking the grass a bit, smiling. More and more, he thought they were growing on him.

Thinking about meeting the little furball made Brian think about what Jackson had said or rather implied.

Max.

Brian thought back to all the times he had been at the manor the past few days and Max had in fact there nearly every day, never far from him. Of course, Max was his ride most of the time so that was a given but what did Jackson see that Brian didn't?

There had been moments in the car and then later in the lobby with Max and thinking about them gave Brian a fluttering feeling in his gut and it caught him by surprise by its strength, remembering the way Max's scent had affected him so powerfully.

One night, after a failed shifting session, Brian, exhausted, had asked Draco about the situation with scents, of course, eliminating the specifics of why he was asking, making it seem as if he was asking about how scents worked for shifters in general.

They had been out on the back porch of the manor, the afternoon sun had been setting and through the glass of the porch, Brian could see into the house and specifically into the gym. Inside, Max had been practicing, boxing with the dummy in the corner, stripped to the waist, driving blow after blow into it, occasionally giving it a kick so hard the entire thing rattled. He was a powerful man, and his fighting skills came with ease and flowed like raging water, landing expertly, the focus in his intense blue eyes absolute. Wherever Max mentally was in those moments, it wasn't where he was physically. Brian suspected he was in the past in those times.

Draco had offered Brian a glass of lemonade and had taken one for himself as he sat back in the white wicker chair. As the sun slowly went down on the horizon, Draco had answered his question.

"Well, my boy, that's an interesting topic. Humans, baseline humans, spend so much of their lives relying on sight that evolution eventually robbed them of their sense of smell. Do something for me. Take a deep breath, but inhale through your nose, not your mouth and tell me what you smell."

Brian had set aside his glass and exhaling, he closed his mouth and inhaled deeply, the warm evening air rushing into his nose. He felt it enter the end of his snout, course through the bridge of his nose and pass down his throat and instantly a barrage of information was there, images, information, thoughts and colors.

The smell of freshly mown grass.

The warm loamy aroma of turned earth, of hot rock cooling in the afternoon shade. The sharp bite of the lemon in the glass, the sparkling coolness of the water itself. He could smell the trees and their bark. He could smell gasoline from the lawnmower that Roy was riding. Each one was different and after a moment, it was overwhelming.

He breathed normally and opened his eyes.

"Wow...that was...intense. I hadn't tried that yet."

Draco smiled and laughed gently. "You got bombarded by images, and each image told you something about the visual input. The state of the grass, the temperature of those rocks, the water in your glass, the scent of your own body. You'll notice that last one was especially unique, I'll bet."

Brian had indeed noticed that. His own body smelled like hot sun and warm air, the same earthy scent that you get from being outside for several hours and then coming indoors. It was fresh and clean. That scent lived under the artificial smells of his deodorant and bath shampoo.

"I did." He said, intrigued. Draco continued.

"You'll find that scent brings with it a treasure trove of information and that until you learn to filter it to find what you need, it can be like being in a symphony orchestra trying to listen to a pin drop. It can be done, but it takes practice. Until you get the hang of it, I suggest breathing mostly through your mouth. It will help."

Draco seemed to consider Brian as the younger werewolf found himself watching Max in the gym and a wry smile came over his face as if he was amused by something. When he spoke next, it was warmer than usual.

"As for the scent of your own body, you'll also find that every living being has their own unique chemical makeup that gives them a unique scent. That scent can alter from time to time to give you information about the person, information like mood, general wellbeing, stress and more. Sometimes, you'll encounter pheromone-based scents, which are more often encountered among those couples who are engaged in the risky business of romance and courting, which is something I've not had the distinct pleasure, thankfully, of putting up with in a very long time. You will also find, perhaps in time, that beneath all those indicators, each person has their own unique scent identity that reveals who they really are. It's wise to pay attention to that information when you come across it. " He finished with a subtle grin.

Brian had been looking back at Max through the gym windows as Max grabbed a towel from the rack and dried the sweat from his face, his loose blue basketball shorts flashing in the glare of the sun, the shock absorbing bindings around his wrists hanging loosely. Draco's words had registered distantly but they had stuck with him.

Ever since that afternoon, Brian had been experimenting slowly with scent when no one was looking, since he felt silly just walking up to random things and sniffing them. Thankfully, no one had caught him at it and he had found that Draco was right. Everything had its own unique scent and with it came a ton of information. Brian found that sometimes, flashes of an object's recent history came with it, little glimpses into the moments that had happened. That was one thing, he thought, that he was getting good at. Scenting, apparently for him, came naturally, like writing.

Over the days since, he had gotten quite good at filtering out scents that he wanted and those he didn't. Still what Jackson had just assumed about Max and himself and what Draco told him about scents had Brian thinking quite a bit about those moments in the car and the lobby when Max's scent seemed to overpower him in a way that nothing else had.

So far, it hadn't happened again because Max was careful to put a bit more distance between the two of them in close quarters, more so than usual, like he was going out of his way to do it.

Could Max actually feel something more for me?

Did he scent something similar coming off of me?

Was that why Max was so stand offish and taciturn towards others, and or maybe the reason why he seemed to be more open with Brian than he was anyone else lately? *Frankly,* Brian thought, *it was confusing as hell.*

What if Max isn't the only one that feels that way? His mind asked him, and he shook his head to clear that thought out of his head and it did leave, but it left behind it the strong ring of truth that Brian couldn't quite help but to wonder about listening to. What if it was true? *Those moments...*

Nope. Not possible, he mentally told himself quickly. Elijah flashed in his mind. He felt strangely guilty but also, a part of him was intrigued and confused.

No, it definitely wasn't possible. It would be so...odd.

Shuffling his weight on the bench because the stone was digging into the small of his back, he felt his ears perk up and swivel towards the sound of approaching footsteps crunching on the grass.

Speak of the devil and he shall appear, Brian thought amused and for some reason embarrassed almost as if his thoughts were on display.

It was Max.

He was back in his standard uniform of white tank top, jeans and boots again. The boxing tape around his wrists was gone and as the breeze blew, Brian could smell him again. He radiated the scents of Old Spice (a different one this time, Bearglove maybe? Brian was familiar with that one and it reminded him of that scent) and the gentle masculine scent that he always seemed to give off. Brian indulged himself a bit and hoped Max wouldn't notice where he was still a good distance from the bench and inhaled sharply through his snout, unable to resist the curious urge in the back of his mind.

Instantly the world came alive in a world of sensory data, but Brian pushed through it, past the scents of grass and dirt and the forest, past the scent of the water of the lake, the smell of the fish under it, past the hot stone of the manor's walls and there, standing out like a search beam among all the noise was Max.

To Brian, Max's scent was utterly new when done this way, with intent. He had never experienced this side of the man before, not this completely. He smelled the hot sun on Max's gray fur, smelled his aftershave, his fur conditioners, smelled the hot leather of his worn brown belt, the cotton of the shirt he wore. He could smell the slightest bit of masculine musk there as well, and below that, was the fresh clean scent of icebergs and snow, of pine trees and long winter nights.

Max smelled like winter and fresh snow, Brian thought. There were also traces of fire wood smoke and something soft and clean, gentle, almost....

(A dark-haired woman with soft blue eyes and a warm smile)

Exhaling, Brian quickly sat up and made it appear that he had been yawning as Max arrived. That last image was particularly powerful and he filed it away. He knew the face. It was the woman from the photo in Max's garage, the one Brian strongly suspected was his mother, but that Max did not want to talk about.

He looked up at the gray werewolf as he came closer and realized just how similar his blue eyes were to the woman that had to be his mother.

"Hey." Max said, nodding slightly, dipping his chin just a bit. He came around the bench as Brian moved his feet out of the way and took a seat next to him. Brian scooted to the right to give him more room.

"Hey." Brian replied, stretching and popping his spine back into order.

"Heard your practice sessions went to shit the last few days." Max said, looking down between his feet, his hands hanging loosely between his knees. A bird tweeted in the trees and Max's ears flicked towards the sound unconsciously before coming back to them.

"Yeah. I can't seem to get the hang of shifting. I may not be able to." Brian admitted quietly, looking at his nails, flexing his fingers a bit to get the blood flow back into them. Max sat up a bit straighter and glanced over at Brian as he spoke, his blue eyes searching without him realizing it.

"Would that be a bad thing?" he asked.

Brian head the concern in his voice and as much as Max tried to hide it, Brian could also feel the apprehension.

He considered his answer and decided to tell Max the truth. He deserved it.

"Nah, man. I think I could live with it. It wouldn't be so bad. Hey, I've got friends now I didn't have before. When some of them aren't taking my blood and hey, the ears aren't so bad." He looked at Max again more seriously and before he knew what he was saying, the words left his mouth. "Some of them have turned out to be pretty good."

Max almost chuckled again and pretended not to hear the last sentence a Brian's face flushed hot under his fur. He pushed past it, pretending it didn't happen.

"Oh, come on. That ears and blood were funny. You can laugh, you know." Brian gently ribbed him, the corners of his mouth turning up slightly. As he did, he saw Max's grin try to form as well. It got about half way and stuck, but it was there nonetheless, no matter how hard Max tried not to let it be.

Max avoided Brian's gaze, but Brian could tell he was looking for Brian's reaction all the same.

"Yeah. I reckon it was funny. Anyway...I just wanted to come and check on you a bit...you've been down here a few hours and well...you know. They were uh...they were worried." Max said, his blue eyes catching the setting sun.

Brian found that he liked the idea that Max was checking on him and he had a powerful suspicion that no one had asked Max to come looking for him. He also strongly felt that no one was worried about him except one person.

"Ahhh. How was, um, how was work today? You said you had some customers lined up earlier before you headed back."

Max shrugged. "Wasn't too bad. Oil change. Spark plugs. Nothing major. Made a few hundred dollars. I just got back up here an hour ago. Been talking with Draco about some things. Needed to get my head straight."

Max didn't meet Brian's eyes when he said that last part and he paused for a moment, seeming to have a brief internal struggle before he seemed to dive into whatever he was fighting in his head. He sheepishly kept avoiding Brian's gaze as he asked his question.

"I, uh, was coming to see if you wanted to head back to my apartment for a bit. I know its earlier than usual. I... I can't stay here for too long. I worry about my shop." Max added at the end hastily.

Brian blinked.

The question had come out of the blue and was out of character for Max. Max had always let Brian come to him about whether he wanted to stay at the manor or not. It wasn't like him to come around looking for an answer. Truth be told, Brian did need a break and that was the whole reason he had come out here.

To get perspective.

Sitting here, as the sun was inching towards the horizon from its high position in the sky, throwing slowly growing shadows onto the ground Brian looked at Max and decided that for the first time since they had met, he really saw him for him, not just as a savior or a grouchy ass hole.

Max sat there, looking off into the distance, at something only he could see on the sky's limit, his blue eyes the same color as the summer sky. His thick gray fur lifted gently in the summer breeze and his tail hung behind him on the bench. His face, even with the barely noticeable scars on his snout was truly noble, refusing to give into the pain he carried with him on his back. He was slumped as he sat there, elbows on his knees, as if that emotional pain he carried had physical weight, his broad strong back bearing it all and Brian knew that the pain was heaviest in his heart.

Seeing past Max's powerful shoulders and arms, Brian saw the talented and scuffed up hands of a master mechanic, saw a fierce intelligence in his eyes. The fact that he carried more healing wounds than any other person Brian had ever seen, and he kept taking on more told Brian that Max cared deeply about people he fought for and that was despite his own losses and his anger. Beneath that rage and anger, was something more.

Something richer, something that smelled like freshly fallen sun kissed snow on the first welcome day of silent whispered winter.

Maybe I just GOT some perspective, Brian thought in that moment, surprised as his insight.

It was unspoken, Brian knew now but yes, it was there, after all. His mind was right.

Max was feeling a pull and he was not the only one.

Brian had no choice but to acknowledge it. He couldn't refuse it or ignore it this time. He felt it strongly behind his chest, in his gut and somewhere deeper and in those silent seconds, as Max stared into the azure orange sky.

What do I do with this? Brian thought, his heart racing. He had no idea and so, he decided for the time being, to say nothing and see how things went. He didn't want to say anything and jeopardize the fragile understanding that had developed between them the last two weeks.

Taking a deep breath, he blew it out casually and bumped Max with his shoulder.

"Hey."

Max came back to the field and turned to look at Brian. "Yeah?"

"Let's head to your place. I do need some space away from these nerds. Well, slightly nerdier than me anyway."

A small smile tried to be born on Max's face and this time, it was successful, his blue eyes lighting up in a way Brian had not yet seen them do. He wasn't sure Max was even aware of it.

As they stood up and walked back towards the house, their shadows grew long and at the far end, they merged together as one. Brian spoke up as they neared the house.

"We can order pizza. My treat."

"No anchovies. Those things suck balls." Max replied.

"Agreed. No pineapple either. You're bringing the beers." Brian added.

Then it happened.

Max actually laughed as he replied. A genuine small laugh. Not just a chuckle. It was a soft rich sound and it rolled easily in the summer air. It felt good on Brian's ears, and he had to consciously stop his tail from wagging, though he wasn't entirely successful.

"Deal." Max replied.

#####

For the first time since Brian had set foot into Max's apartment two weeks ago, the place felt like a home, a safe place where he could be at ease, even if it wasn't exactly his own apartment. It felt lived in and it didn't feel as if there were some black specter lurking in the shadows, hovering over everything. The night was hot outside, and he was grateful that Max's apartment had central air. When they had first arrived, Brian had seen a single motorcycle in the garage work space. Its engine was exposed, and several parts lay around it in neat orderly piles. *One of the customers Max had*, he had thought. Instead of going out for food, Brian had, as promised, ordered in for delivery. His appetite had surprised him, and he had gone all in for four large pizzas, two layered supremes and two bacon and ham and pepperoni pies.

Max brought the beer, and to Brian's amusement, the buzz he got from them was not half bad. He and Max sat on the sofa together, side by side, relaxed, feet up on the coffee table, and for the first time, there didn't seem to be any of the animosity or tension between the two of them that had been maintaining a constant presence.

Max himself was different. He was still gruff, but he was also more relaxed, not as dead serious and it was nice, Brian thought. It made the whole situation he was going through more tolerable and honestly, it brought back many good memories of his times with Elijah that seemed to push his failure to master shifting out of his mind for a while. It was like having a best friend again, though he could hardly call Max that, he supposed. It felt close enough in the little moments, so Brian didn't argue with it and instead, he simply let it be what it was.

The television was on and a boxing match was going down. Max had been deeply invested in the match, Brian saw, in the way his tail would twitch, and his ears would jerk when a jab or a block failed. Max tried explaining to Brian the different moves and was pleasantly surprised to find out that Brian knew a bit about the sport and soon they were both rooting loudly for their chosen fighter. The smell of hot melted cheese, tomato sauce and grilled vegetables filled the air.

The two of them had made their way through nearly half of the food and the beer was settling nicely when there was a brief lull in the moment.

"What's on your mind?" Max asked, taking a quick glance at Brian out of the corner of his eye, swallowing the last of the beer in his bottle.

Brian looked over at him.

"Ah nothing, man. It's just after two weeks of insanity it's nice to have a normal night with.... well...you know, friends. Reminded me of times with Elijah and Ellie, and my mom and dad before things went to shit. It's nice to feel welcomed...to feel like you belong somewhere." Brian told him with a contented sigh, stretching his large frame, popping his back and shifting his feet around, placing them back onto the floor, finding it oddly hard to meet Max's eyes, his face warm from the alcohol.

Max considered him and shrugged.

"Heh. I guess you're right. You've put up with my ass this long being a dick and with being poked and prodded at and even then, we didn't have much to tell you. I guess it is probably nice just to live." Max's dark eyebrows came together as a thought occurred to him. "Why are you still around? After the way I acted towards you, I would have thought you would have wanted to stay at Draco's." Max asked quietly, brushing crumbs off the front of his white tank top. The bread pieces fell onto his jeans legs and then bounced to the floor.

Brian considered that as he looked back over at the gray werewolf.

"Honestly, I can usually tell about people. It's one reason I was good at my job. I can read them. You guys all seem like you genuinely care about people and were there for me when there was nowhere else I could have turned to. You've all stuck by me and that counts for something. Most people wouldn't have."

Brian found himself tugging at his own shirt tail, his hands suddenly needing something to do. It was one of his old favorite navy-blue t-shirts, and now, it was almost too small for him. He had gotten it during one of his trips back to his apartment. He would really have to go clothes shopping as soon as he figured out this shifting business. He found that he was shaking a little bit and tried to hide it as the quiet moment extended between the two of them.

Max snorted gently and sighed.

"Hey, listen, I'm sorry for being such a cunt to you at first. I don't really know how to deal with people much and you're the first person who's really been up close to me in a long time. It honestly made me uncomfortable at first. But I guess you turned out to be okay. Not too shabby."

Brian felt his emotions burst out of him in a genuine laugh. "Thanks. I think. You aren't so bad yourself...not really."

Max seemed to take those words and nodded quietly, his face a mask of quiet contemplation as if he weren't used to thinking about the notion that he was worth someone's time and effort. Brian's stomach grumbled loudly, breaking the moment, and Max's eyebrows went up.

Feeling his face flush hot, Brian sat up and bent towards the coffee table as he grabbed a slice of pizza and scarfed it down, relishing the explosion of flavors and scents as he did. He chewed thoughtfully, a smile blooming on his furry black face. He looked over at Max.

"Dude that is one perk about this whole situation that I will not complain about..." Brian said through a mouthful, knowing it was rude but unable to help himself. Max raised an eyebrow and that cocky amused almost grin came back.

"What's that?"

"Food is fucking awesome now. I can taste and smell everything about it. It changes everything about eating."

Max shrugged. "Huh. I guess I never noticed since I've always been this way. I guess for you it's like being born again only able to remember and experiencing it."

Nodding, Brian swallowed.

"Yeah. It's been wild. I wish I could share this stuff with you because it's hard to put into words. Draco showed me how to scent and how to pick out individual scents from the background. I think I've got it down pretty good and it may be the one thing I think I may have down about all this."

Max toasted him with a new beer he had cracked open.

"Well that's something. Scents give most of us a hard time until we get older and can sort through them. It's good you're getting that out of the way. Shifting though...that's something I can't really offer much advice about but you said you were having a hard time?" Max asked, setting his new beer bottle down between his legs.

Nodding Brian did the same and tried to explain, his brain a little slowed down from his drink.

"Yeah. It's like I get what Draco and Raven told me to do, which is to just see myself the way I want to be and then just will it, but nothing's happened. The most I get is a weird tickle at the back of my neck. It feels like a muscle that wants to move but it's too weak. Gave myself a migraine trying so I gave up for a while. they keep saying 'see yourself' but I guess right now, I can't really do that."

"Damn, that sounds rough. I've always wondered what it felt like, though." Max said, looking down into the open eye of his bottle.

"What, the shifting itself?"

"No, not exactly." he replied, shaking his head, his blue eyes distant. "Just being able to put on a human face and step outside and blend in and no one looks at you like you're going to eat their face off. Just to be one of the crowd instead of sticking out like a sore thumb. Sounds like bullshit and it probably is but...it is what it is, I guess."

Suddenly the air in the room changed and Brian felt the seriousness return and in that moment, he realized Max was opening to him in a way that he probably hadn't done for anyone, if ever at all. Swallowing quietly, Brian turned to face him on the couch and felt his ears swivel towards him.

"I can see why you'd like that. It would be nice, sometimes, to just melt into the crowd. It was kind of hard for me to blend in though, even before this happened. I'm a tall bastard. Kind of draws looks from people."

Max nodded quietly and sat his beer on the table with a heavy *clunk*.

Brian pushed on softly, feeling suddenly brave in the moment that was slowly connecting them together it seemed, remembering the woman's face from earlier.

"Max, your mom. Your dad. Those images.... tell me about them. I feel like I know them, but at the same time, they're ghosts to me. I can't get the images out of my head. Who were they? What really happened to you?"

Brian's words caused Max to visibly stiffen and his ears fell towards his head, his blue eyes went far away, and Brian wondered if he saw fields of snow and smelled the thick scent of pine. Brian thought for a moment that he would sit back on the couch and not say a word or change the subject or tell him to piss off but none of that happened. What did happen, shocked Brian as much as anything ever could.

Max sat back on the couch, legs spread, arms not crossed, looking deeply into the open mouth of his beer bottle, and for that tiny eternity, he looked more vulnerable than Brian had ever seen him. Taking a deep breath, Max blew it out and without looking at Brian, he began to speak. His voice was calm at first, but as it went on, Brian noticed he was struggling to talk about it but couldn't bring himself to interrupt.

"I guess you have a right to know after all I've put you through so here goes: I was born in Juneau, Alaska, in the fall of 1979. My parents were good people. Kind people. My mom was school teacher at Donner Elementary and my dad was an oil worker for Exxon. He was a shifter, a full-generation like me, and he was proud of it too. My mom was human. They met when they were sixteen and fell head over heels for each other. Believe me; they had sappy pictures all over the house. Used to make me sick as a kid," Max said, attempting to grin but only half succeeding.

"We had a good life for a while. When I was in third grade though, things started to change. Things had been getting rough for me at school for a while and then there was a fight. A boy was hurt. Instead of punishing the kids who started it, the school board suggested I be transferred to another school in the area to avoid any more issues. They said there was an all shifter school not far outside of town and that it would be a better learning environment for me there. My mom said no, that I needed to be among kids, all kinds of kids but they pushed and finally, after it happened again in fourth grade, she pulled me out of school altogether and gave up her teaching career to homeschool me."

"What the hell....." was all Brian could say as Max continued. "That is fucked up..."

"We started getting threats in the mail, and some assholes tagged my dad's truck. Someone shanked his tires. Eventually, we moved to Nome, to get away from the city, to get a fresh start and for a while, it seemed like we had. We had a great hiking trip one year and after that I always wanted to go, every winter. I used to love snow. Sometimes it would be too dangerous, and we had to stay home but my dad would set up a tent in the living room in front of the fireplace and we'd have a little camp right there with marshmallows and graham crackers."

"Sounds like you all were very close." Brian said quietly, having turned to face Max, who had a small but sad smile on his face. In the background, the television sound had faded away.

"We were. They were my world, Brian. When everything else sucked, mom and dad were always there for me. Always. Like a rock. I never imagined I'd have to face...to have them taken from me." His voice almost cracked.

Brian's face darkened as he remembered all too well that feeling.

"I know what that feels like...I wish I didn't."

"Yeah. It's hell." Max sighed and continued, gathering his strength it seemed.

"It was one winter when was I seventeen, I had gone out on a hike not far from the house. By that time, I had really started to enjoy it as a hobby. I loved the outdoors, the adventure, the thrill." He looked over at Brian. "It almost a full moon, but not all the way. The ocean waves were dark blue with white crests that night, so blue they were almost black. Out on the horizon, I could see icebergs. The Northern lights were beautiful that night...red, blue, green and orange."

He looked down as he went on.

"I had this little spot that no one else knew that overlooked the ocean in a little clearing of pine trees. I could be up there and look down at the entire town. I had gone up that night because I was having a stupid teenager moment. I went against my mom's advice. She thought it was too cold, but I went anyway. It eventually did get too cold, and I had to turn back when it really started to snow and when I got back..."

Max stopped and for a few moments, he just breathed, his chest rising and falling slowly.

"Listen, you don't have to tell me anymore...it's okay. I'm sorry I asked." Brian said quickly, and Max shook his head. "No, I need to tell you. I do."

Taking a deep breath, Brian watched as Max relived his nightmares.

"A lot of this is fuzzy. Some of its sharp. Other parts, not so much. Sometimes, I wonder what parts are even real. Anyway, I got hit in the head pretty hard. The clearest thing I remember is that I smelled the smoke first before I saw the embers in the air. When I got into the yard, I saw men dressed in dark robes, like the KKK wear only black, like living shadows. I saw my dad. Somehow, they got the jump on him. There was so much blood. It turned the snow scarlet like fresh paint. I lost my temper and charged them. I was blind with it...so much anger and pain and fear...It was like I was drugged. I hurt one or two them bad before they finally got me down and beat me pretty good. That blow to the head I told you about. I remember voices and shouting, and something slashed me in the face," he told Brian as he unconsciously touched his snout. The four scars were there on his muzzle, barely visible in the light.

"I heard one of them, a big bastard, shout at someone in the house, but I don't remember what. They kicked me loose and dumped me and ran. I went over to my dad and tried to get him up, but he was gone. The house was engulfed. I knew it was a matter of time before the propane tanks outside became hot enough to blow and I could only think about my mom. I ran into the house and found her upstairs. She had been stabbed."

Max was shaking a little, Brian noticed, the liquid in his bottle sloshing.

"I picked her up and held her.... I could hear her heart slowing down and she looked up at me and she touched my face and tried to tell me something but she didn't make it and she just faded away. It was so fast. The next thing I know, I had woken up in a hospital in town, with my feet and hands covered in bandages from burns and my fur was scorched and blackened. My lungs hurt from the smoke, but the police told me what happened. The propane tanks had finally blown, and the explosion threw me clear of the house. The snow slowed down the first responders."

Sighing, he finished his tale.

"I never even got to bury my parents because there wasn't anything left to bury. The blast incinerated what was left of my life, my family. Everything I had ever known, everything that was happy, that was me, all of it, just gone in a single blow. The town tried to get me into a group home, but I didn't stay. I ended up running away, living from day to night, under bridges, in burned out cars, making my way down the coast and across the country. I spent almost all my twenties like a fucking hobo. I did things I'm still ashamed of. Draco finally found me a few years ago and helped me turn things around. If it weren't for him, I don't know where I'd be."

"But the mechanics shop.... how did..." Brian asked, stunned, trying to put it all together into a coherent timeline.

Max's shaking had stopped a little as he finally looked back up and the sad smile was back but with it, a hint of pride.

"My dad taught me from the time I could handle a wrench how to work on cars and see how things worked. I loved spending time with him working on the car and the snowmobiles." He smiled for real and chuckled. "One year, I got in major hot water for taking apart the snowblower motor."

He looked up at Brian.

"I just took what I knew, the one thing I had left from them and applied it. I couldn't fix my life but I could fix things and make them work again. It helped in its own way. Draco helped me get started with the place."

"Well, that's my story. That's me in a nutshell. An ugly nutshell but it is what it is."

Brian sat back, unsure of how to answer, what to say or what reply was good enough.

"That explains a lot about you, I think. So much of it makes sense now. What were their names?"

Max's blue eyes looked moist, but the tears did not fall. Brian could see talking about the past for him was the hardest thing he had ever done but he did it, faced it and came through it.

"Eric and Diane."

"You had no one. It's no wonder you didn't trust me or anyone else. I'm sorry you had to go through all that." Brian said, sitting forward, his tail hanging off the couch.

Max sighed and shrugged. "It is what it is. Working on cars, things I can fix, going out some nights and doing what I do...That's got me through a lot of shit and it still does. Still, not everything about me is depressing I guess. Favorite sport is boxing. Love beer. Pizza's good too." he told Brian.

Brian smiled. "Yeah I kind of picked up on that one."

Max gave him a sheepish grin. "I do have other interests you know. I mean, I'm not all hard ass fists and fury. Don't tell anyone but I'm a Trekkie, too. Not so much a Star Wars fan."

"Bullshit." Brian said flatly flabbergasted.

Max nodded. "Yup."

"I've never been a con or anything. Maybe one year I will, someday." Max added.

Brian shook his head and grinned, just floored.

"Max, why don't you show this side of yourself to others...Raven...Draco...hell, even Jackson. The real you isn't some grouchy gruff asshole, the real you is a pretty awesome guy." Brian remarked, standing up and popping his back again. Sitting still was causing him to get stiff and he needed motion.

"I have a reputation, you know. It helps to keep it up." Max said, seriously, putting on his gruff face again but it fell into bit of a half-smile. "Can't let anyone know my weaknesses. Might use it against me."

"We can't be friends if you're a Kirk fan. Shatner was the worst for over-acting.

Remember that time he was split in two?" Brian said with grin.

"I guess it's lucky for you I'm a Janeway fan. Just something about a captain and her crew, lost but always determined to get home. They made it, so maybe, I can too someday. Maybe."

"Janeway? I knew there was something redeemable about you. She's pretty good. Best captains get through the worst with coffee." Brian cracked back. He looked around the room and back at Max.

"You need some fresh air? I do. It's a bit stuffy in here and my tail has gone numb. At least, I think it's my tail. Need to move a little." Brian said, moving towards the garage stairwell door.

"Help yourself. Just watch out for the bike in the work area. That guy would have my head on a pike if anything touched his fucking bike. He really thinks it's some kind of prize winner." Max said sarcastically, standing up and heading off towards the bathroom.

Nodding, Brian made for the garage. Once downstairs, he hit the light switch and the overhead fluorescents flickered once, twice and then held their steady electric brilliance. He noticed they didn't flicker anymore. The bike in question was right in the middle of the work bay just as Max had said. Its frame was a faded maroon with splotchy chrome accents. Its handlebars swept up and back and its body had seen much better days. Brian wondered if the owner was restoring it. It didn't look that impressive if he was honest.

Instead of going outside or to the roof, carefully avoiding the bike, Brian moved over to Max's private gym area, where his recently patched up punching bag hung like a dark sentinel from its metal frame and there behind it was the photo of Max's family.

Eric and Diane Mullen, Brian told himself as he looked at them, finally able to put faces to names. Here among the detritus of life, Brian truly saw Max's private space for the first time. He saw a thick beat up old brown leather wallet, thick with cards and receipts. A pile of blue spiral bound receipt books were stacked off to the left and there next to them, sure enough, was a small poster from *Star Trek: Voyager*. Brian smiled. How had he missed it the first time? Maybe he wasn't really seeing Max for who he was, and only instead, what he appeared to be.

With no one around, Brian, unsure of what else to do with himself, took a few swings at the punching bag.

The swings were clumsy, and he realized how much he was out of practice. Simmons would have had his head. Strictly speaking, the only training they were supposed to call on at work was non-violent restraint, but Simmons had always made sure they had a few more tools in their tool box so to speak for the rowdier hospital clients that got rough with the nurses and staff. Brian also had taken tai-kwon do for several years. He had stopped just after his dad died, not having the drive to do it anymore.

Taking up a stance, Brian decided to give the bag a few more whacks, to see if he still had it.

Thunk

Thunk-thunk.

Thunk.

Definitely rusty, he thought. It felt good to be in motion. It always did. For Brian, motion was like therapy. It helped him think. It helped him write. In those moments, motion removed any external thoughts, removed him from the flow of time and he could just exist free in his mind.

He never heard Max's footsteps come down and enter the garage nor did he feel Max's eyes on him as Max stood, leaning in the doorframe, watching him box badly and he never saw the tiny grin pull at the corners of Max's mouth.

"Your stance is off."

Brian jumped. Max's gruff voice surprised him and he nearly yelped. Perhaps feeling more embarrassed than he should have he stopped what he was doing, turned to face Max and stammered.

"Oh well...you know...just trying to work out some kinks. I'm a bit rusty."

"Is that what that was?" Max asked, coming across the room, his hands in his jeans pockets, tail flowing behind him, his ears alert, his eyes holding none of the gentle mocking that was going on in his voice. His eyes were warm.

"It's been a while since I've been at the gym, you know. Two weeks now at this point." Brian defended himself, blowing a lock of fur out of his face, which given his muzzle, he felt, was an achievement.

"Let me show you a few things," Max said gentler than Brian was used to as he stepped closer to Brian. "Start here." He said as he grabbed Brian gently by the shoulders and turned him around to face the bag. Brian felt Max's large powerful hands fall upon his him and that scent was suddenly back, the smell of pristine snow and cool sunlight on pine trees. Brian felt Max's hands move from his shoulders down to his biceps and then to his forearms.

"Lift your arms up like this...one a bit higher than the other.... always guard your face....no matter what. Your head is your top priority. Never let a blow land there." Max said, adjusting Brian's forearms up in front of his snout. "Especially now that you have a muzzle. If you thought a broken nose hurt before, well, it's best to

73

avoid being cracked in the snout. Trust me."

"Right..."

Moving behind Brian again, Brian felt Max's body press against his and an electric charge shot down Brian's spine. A hot rush flooded his brain and he felt his lower jaw begin to tremble. Max's body felt hot, like fire, even though the clothes. His scent of aftershave and winter was overpowering. Brian could feel the power in the muscles of Max's chest and stomach as Max breathed, could feel the thick leather of his belt and the rough texture of Max's jeans pressing against him and felt their fur rub together as Max guided him.

Brian felt himself begin to tremble as Max's hands and thick arms found their way around his waist, adjusting his stance. He felt Max's right leg shoot between his feet and push them apart.

"Now," Max said quietly, his snout in Brian's ear, his voice low. "Brace your weight on your hips and knees. Stay loose. Never go rigid; if you go rigid, your center of gravity will pull you down. Use your shoulders to direct your throws." As he talked, Max's hands moved up from Brian's waistline and up to his arms, pistoning them out one at a time, rotating his shoulders as Max put him through the slow motions of a proper right and left hook.

"Okay. I think it's coming back to me."

For a moment before he pulled back, Brian felt Max pause, his jaw and snout hovering over Brian's neck, his nose nearly touching Brian's skin. Brian felt that hot wave that washed over him before hit him again and this time there was no doubt about it. As Max's warm breath caressed his neck, lifting the fur there, Brian shuddered like a horse and felt the shudder run down the front of his stomach coursing lower and lower into his legs and he felt himself becoming more than nervous. He felt himself becoming very much aroused in a way he didn't understand or fully comprehend. It was deeper than a physical response though the sudden extreme tightness in the front of his jeans told him it definitely had a physical component. This went beyond anything he had ever felt before, so powerful it was without description.

He suddenly felt the need to move, to change the subject, to do anything yet a part of him, longed for, no, *needed* Max to stay there. It was a deep primitive part of his brain and he felt within himself the stirrings of something more powerful and primal then he had known himself to ever possess. Deep within him, that strange eyed dream stalking beast began to growl low in the shadows of his mind, and whether it was protective or approving, he couldn't tell.

Before he could do anything, a sharp electric trilling noise broke the moment into a thousand pieces and Max stepped back. Not turning around fully, wanting to hide the very obvious erection he was now sporting, Brian busied himself by walking behind some of the weights on the bench, his heart flying a million miles an hour as his pulse rushed so hard he could hear it in his ears.

The sound, it turned out, was Max's phone going off. Sighing, Max pulled it from his jeans pocket and the blue glow from it lit up his grey furred face. Brian watched his face crumple into a scowl as he read a message on it and then with a sigh, Max clicked the phone off.

"Man... it's late. Didn't realize how late it actually was. We should get some rest. I'm gonna call it a night. You're welcome to the couch."

The sudden transformation in Max's mood and his mannerisms threw Brian for a total loop and once his personal problem was gone, he stepped out from the bench and nodded towards Max's phone.

"Everything okay?"

"Yeah. It's all good. Just stuff with a customer. The asshole with the bike. Wants it done tomorrow but not gonna happen. I still need to call CJ at the parts store and see if I can even find the throttle for it. It's at least thirty years old." Max told him and Brian got the distinct impression he was being lied to about what was bothering Max, but unable to give any evidence as to how he knew, did the only thing he could which was to shrug and roll with it.

"Sounds like an asshole. The bike owner." Brian said, flashing Max a disarming grin. It was like Max had his shields up again and the taller werewolf was unphased.

"Yeah. He is. I'll be up in a few. Gonna work on some things down here before I come up." Max replied. Nodding, Brian turned and trotted up the stairs, his mind racing down so many tracks and roads mentally speaking, that he felt like he needed some downtime in all honest truth. Maybe sleep wasn't such a bad idea.

When he was alone, and the garage door had closed with a click, Max pulled his phone back up and clicked on the screen. There, in the messages was a single message in a green bubble, the one that had just shattered the quiet between them. He read it, feeling a heavy sense of duty call to him.

Raven: "Another dead tonight. It's been a week. Please find out where this is coming from. No more dead bodies. Please, Max. Remember what we talked about."

Sighing, Max looked up at the closed garage door and thought about Brian. There was something truly special about that guy. He felt like he should tell him what Raven had asked him to do back in the lab. He had been neglecting his street patrols, lost in the confusion of his own conflicted feelings about Brian and this whole situation. Closing his phone down, he shoved it into his pocket and crossed the gar-

Anthony Milhorn

age to his lock box and entered the combination, opening the metal lid with a slight squeak.

Reaching in, he came out with a glowing blue vial, the same one Raven had handed him last week at the manor when they had brought Brian up to talk with Draco. Raven's soft voice came up out of the shadows of his mind as he thought back to that conversation they had after Rakinos had left.

"I don't want Draco to find out what I'm about to ask you for because he would try to stop it, but there's no other way."

"Raven, what are you talking about?"

"I need your help, Max"

"On what?"

She had held up the blue vial.

"People are dying. My lab techs can't figure out what this is or where it comes from. Its killed too many already. Humans so far. It's some kind of hyper-amphetamine, custom made for shifters. I've never seen anything like it, Max. You know the streets better than anyone else I know. You can find the source of it then we can have the cops move in and clean it out before anyone else dies. You and I both know it won't stay contained to the gangs. It will spread."

"That's a big maybe, Raven...How would I even begin to track it down?"

Raven had cracked open the vial and the smell of the drug was nauseating, making his eyes water. "You can smell it. You've got the best nose out of any of us. The most experience out there. Just don't do anything stupid, just find it and come back. That's all. Can you do that?"

Max closed the lock box lid and slid the vial into his jeans pocket. He hadn't been out on the streets since Brian had shown up and it looked like that was about to change. Raven had never asked anything of him before, but she had always been there for him unconditionally. It was risky but there was nothing wrong with just scoping things out and gathering intel. *Don't engage just get it and come back. Simple.*

He would wait, he thought until Brian was fully asleep and then he'd make his way out across the rooftops where he could get the best scent profile. For now, he made his way back upstairs and made a show of being tired and thoroughly full. Having some small talk with Brian, Max tossed off his shirt and helped put the food away before collapsing into his bed, his back to Brian, still in his jeans, with his right hand covering his right front pocket.

An hour or two passed and gradually, as Brian lay on the couch, his mind racing, he found himself dozing off, the carb overload from the pizza and beer catching up to him and before long it legitimately took him down and sleep claimed him as well.

CHAPTER 3

In the darkened apartment, Max's ears perked towards the sound of Brian's breathing and they listened carefully to the slow rise and fall of that rhythm. Carefully, Max turned over and sat up in his bed, his bare feet touching the floor, the thick pads on the bottoms of his feet muffling the sound. Glancing at the nightstand clock, he saw that it was going on two in the morning. In the darkness, his eyes glowed amber yellow and in the blue-grey of his night vision, he saw that Brian was indeed passed out, his left arm hanging off the sofa, his long legs dangling off the other end, his tail sticking out from the blankets, twitching.

Yanking his phone out of his pocket, Max cut the volume off of it and slid into his nightstand. Standing, he quickly pulled on his boots and moved carefully, placing his heel down before the balls of his feet, walking heel to toe, effectively canceling out any sound he would have made as he walked. He deftly avoided the step up onto the kitchen as that board always squeaked. He fingered the vial in his pocket as he stepped up to the door that led out of the apartment and into the connecting hallway. For a moment and he didn't know why, he glanced back and looked at Brian's form as he lay sleeping peacefully.

A part of Max desperately wanted to stay here and another part of him, the loudest part, the scars from the past that drove him, the sense of penance, finally won. For a few hours today, he had almost felt normal. Felt a connection. Felt something warm, but then real life kicked him hard and it always goes for the balls. Deeply torn between his own desires and his sense of duty and obligation, Max turned away.

"I'm sorry." He said simply and left the apartment.

Heading for the roof, he stepped out onto the gravel and cracked open the vial, inhaling its contents deeply, before closing it and shoving it into his pants pocket. Instantly he felt the smallest of euphoric highs hit his system, as a billion stars wanted to suddenly be born in his brain. His arms and legs tingled, despite the odor of the stuff.

It was noxious, almost sulfuric and there was nothing like it in his experience or in all his time in the city. That meant tracking it down would be somewhat easier. Closing his eyes, he began to breathe deep, slowly inhaling and exhaling, in through his nose out through his mouth, tasting everything the air had to offer. Car exhaust, rut, blood, motor oil, stagnant water. Tears and joy. The burning hot scents of late-night grease shacks and filmy scent of late-night laundromats.

There it was, hovering like a poison fog. First, he visualized it as the information came to him, flooding his brain. His apartment, his garage. Draco's manor, Raven handing him the vial. No, deeper, he pushed.

There.

The scent led offer deeper into the older part of town, deeper down near where the old coal power plant was, near the river, the docks and the warehouses. Straight into drug gangland territory.

Mentally measuring his steps, Max backed up and took off at a run, his powerful legs pumping and propelling him into the air as he reached the edge of his rooftop. He soared through the air, touching down with a crunch of gravel and leather before standing and moving again, running off into the night, hunting down his quarry.

In his dreams, Brian was not alone but now he was no longer human. He was now in his werewolf form.

The hulking shadowy wolf beast from his nightmares was with him again and it walked in the shadows, stalking him, though it was not hunting him, he realized. It was simply watching him. It lurked, breathing and as he walked down the empty hallway of the dark building he was in to get closer to it, the dreamscape shifted and this time he was in a strange place, a dark void. It was featureless, and he could not hear his footsteps. There, standing in the dark right in front of him, was the dark shadow, powerfully built, gigantic and with twin green eyes that gleamed in the dark studying him. Reaching out a hand, he touched its muzzled face and felt hot fur and a low rumbling curiously gentle growl was sent through the shadow form into his arm. It blinked, its eyes blazing white again in that second. He no longer felt no fear from it and instead moved closer to see its face and—

He woke up.

Blinking owlishly, his own eyes gleaming green in the dark, Brian felt the leather couch beneath him squeak and he remembered where he was. The room was dark, but his eyes adjusted quickly as the blue-grey night vision he now possessed settled in and he found that he appreciated it. It was good to not be totally blind in the dark like he had been before all this. He was shirtless, his silver blaze on his chest gleaming in the streetlights from outside. His shirt and socks and shoes lay on the floor next to the couch. He never could sleep in socks; it always made him too hot. Throwing the thin blanket and sheet off of himself, he sat up and rubbed his stomach absently.

Max's apartment. *What time is it?* Why had he woken up to begin with? Scowling with his sleep swollen face searching out a clock, he saw the one next to Max's empty bed.

It read 2:20 AM.

Damn it was late, he thought annoyed. He was about to go back to sleep when he suddenly realized the importance of what he had just skimmed over.

Max's bed was empty.

Getting to his feet, Brian hit the lights on the table next to the couch and instantly the world was flooded with a warm amber glow. His vision returned to normal and confirmed that Max's bed was indeed empty. The sheets and blankets were barely disturbed, he noticed as he got closer, the hard wood floors creaking under his feet. He looked off towards the bathroom and saw the door was hanging open and the light was off. It was empty.

Frowning, Brian went out and down to the garage.

Empty and the truck was still parked.

Now thoroughly perplexed, he returned to the apartment and stood, in the living room, confused, arms crossed, wondering what the hell was going on since Max's truck was still here. Even though it probably wasn't any of his business, something wasn't right, he didn't like it. A sinking feeling was settling in his gut, a feeling that always meant trouble. As he walked through the apartment looking for any clue that might tell him where Max had gone, Brian found a part of his mind was wandering back to what had happened downstairs between them in the garage.

There was no denying it now, he thought. *I have feelings for this guy. I feel something powerful and strong when he is near, and I can't explain it but I like it. It feels good and I don't feel the huge emotional hole inside as much anymore but what do I do?*

Brian was fairly sure that Max felt it too and he wondered what might have happened if that phone call or text or whatever it was hadn't come through.

The phone.

An idea blossomed in Brian's mind as he quickly hunted for Max's phone, feeling guilty for going through the man's belongings. He turned out the pockets on a pair of pants, found nothing and then heard it. A quick rhythmic vibrating buzz.

A phone on vibrate.

He swiveled his ears around like radar dishes, searching for the source and he found it a moment later.

Brian yanked open Max's night table and found his phone in its orange and black case vibrating in the drawer among the detritus of Max's life: coins, old coupons, nail clippers and a bottle of personal lubricant next to a small baggie of weed.

Feeling his face flush hot, Brian picked up the phone and was glad that Max didn't seem to take security that seriously because the text on the phone was still visible:

Raven: Be careful out there. Keep this between us until we know more. Thank you.

There were other messages but Brian couldn't get past the fingerprint sensor. The message was barely two hours old. What in the world did Raven mean by "*be careful out there?*"

Sniffing, Brian caught a whiff of something he had missed before. It was an acrid chemical odor, strong and noxious that made his stomach want to come up and he recognized it immediately.

It was the same drug that man had been on in the emergency room. He hadn't smelled it since but even then, as a human, it had stunk to high heaven and here it was again.

Pulling on his shirt and shoes, Brian followed the scent out of the apartment and surprisingly found that it did not go down into the garage but rather turned left at the stairwell and down a hallway that led up to the locked roof door. He had never been up to the roof of Max's building and mounted the steps two at a time. At the top, a simple steel push door was all that was between him and the outside and Brian nervously saw that it was unlocked. Pushing it, it opened with a click and he stepped out onto the flat unadorned roof of Max's apartment building and garage.

The roof was layered in black shingle and gray loose gravel. A series of small vents poked up near the far-left side next to an aging air conditioning unit. A pole led up to the power lines and the telephone transmission wires but otherwise the roof was spartan. There were no lights and Brian was soon seeing in the blue-grey of his night vision.

"Max are you up here?" He called, his voice sounding oddly small in the early morning darkness.

No answer.

Scowling, he sniffed again and found that the scent trail of the drug led right to the edge of the roof which made no sense at all. Back tracking, Brian tried to put it together.

Then he saw them.

Boot tracks. Big boot tracks. Work boot tracks.

Max wore work boots, just like he did. They had displaced the gravel and were plainly visible in the blue grey hues of his vision. Frowning, he followed the tracks back the roof access door and then turned back around and followed them to the edge of the roof. He saw that their depth and spread changed as they got closer to the edge and it dawned on him why.

Max had not taken his truck or any conventional means of leaving the apartment because he didn't need to. He had taken a running leap and was using the rooftops to make his way to wherever it was he was going. Wherever that was, it was bad enough for Raven to tell him to be careful. Whatever that business was about, Brian didn't care but what Brian did care about was Max being out there in the city alone involved in God knew what. Raven knew something and she hadn't told him. That miffed him that he was being left out of whatever loop it may be, especially given that it may have to do with himself. The fact that Max was out there alone made it worse.

Brian made up his mind on the spot.

The only logical answer as to what to do came to his mind in a single moment of glorified insanity:

Follow him.

Max had risked his life to save Brian and now he was out there, and he may need help. He would deal with the fallout from whatever Raven was hiding and he was sure it was something and whatever it was involved that drug that started this whole mess. Making up his mind, Brian knew what he had to do. At the moment, he didn't know if he could trust Raven anymore but he did trust Max.

Closing his eyes, Brian inhaled, in through his nose and out through his mouth, seeking not the drug's scent but rather, Max's unique smell, and after a moment of struggling, he focused his mind enough to find the trail and it did indeed head out and over the rooftops.

That's where I'm headed then, he thought and quickly mentally evaluated the distance between this roof and the building next door. Max's apartment building was only three stories tall, mostly from the garage, and the building next door was about the same size. The alleyway between the two of them however, looked precipitously far below, Brian thought as he stood at the edge and looked down. Heights had never bothered him exactly but then again, he had never contemplated actually doing what he was about to do. Swallowing down his apprehension, he went back far enough (he hoped) and lined himself up with the edge of the roof. Taking a deep breath, he steeled himself and then charged into an open sprint.

He had never run before in his new wolf form and thus, when he ordered his legs to move, they not only moved, they exploded with speed.

He was moving too fast but it was too late and the edge of the roof loomed ahead. Planting one foot on it he boosted himself off it, launching himself into the air. Swinging his arms wildly he crashed down hard on the opposite roof, slamming hard on his ass, coming up in a roll that scraped his knees and elbows bloody, driving the wind from him.

Groaning from the pain, he got to all fours and then, gingerly made his way to his feet, testing to see if he had broken anything.

Besides my pride...

No, everything seemed more or less intact and the small scrapes were already healing. He hadn't known how fast he was in wolf form but now he knew that he was not just fast but he was *blazingly* fast. And he could jump. Just like Max did that night when he took a multi-story fall only to land on his feet unharmed. After the initial pain began to wear off, Brian began to feel the tug of adventure, the promise of finding out that he could do much more than he ever thought possible. Shaking his head, he tried to focus.

"Ok, I can do this.... I got this..." Brian said, psyching himself up as he looked at the next building which was slightly higher by a good ten feet. That was where the scent was and that was where he had to go. The building was flat sided except for a wrought iron fire escape. *If I could make it to the fire escape and boost myself up...*

With another charge and a yell, Brian launched himself with a running leap at the fire escape and with a loud clatter that rattled his bones and dangled him a good four stories above the ground, he managed to snag it and pull himself up onto it. Gasping with pride and a bit of irrational cockiness, he made to move towards the next building but quickly found those hopes dashed.

The building he had landed on was a good two stories higher than the one he needed to leap to and between them was an entire street, not just a side alley. He walked to the edge of the building's railing and looked down. Below him the street lights glowed amber and a car honked as it drove past a hooker on the sidewalk. The distance between them was at least forty feet of open air. If he missed it and fell, he thought he might just end up killing himself.

"Fucking hell..." he snarled, panting, aggravated as he stood back from the edge, unsure of what to do or how to proceed as he ran a hand over face, trying to think.

The idea that he could make it began to germinate in his mind like a weed while his rational brain argued that it was a suicide run. *That didn't stop Max from leaping down into gun fire to save me*, he snapped at himself mentally.

His heart hammering in his chest, Brian took one final glance at the edge of the roof and the open black space beyond it. He couldn't even see the other roof from here. It was a leap of faith. He threw his hands up.

"This is crazy..." he told himself but dropped into a running stance anyway, this time more mindful of the power he actually had in his legs. He hoped it would be enough.

In three, he told himself.

One....

Two.....

Fuck it.

He bolted.

His feet hammered the rooftop, tossing up gravel as it crunched under his weight, his tail flying, his fur lifting, his green eyes blazing, the rail was coming up faster and faster the railing was there he was vaulting over and then—

He was in open air, flying through space itself, gravity having lost its hold on him as he sailed like some mutant bird towards infinity. Gravity of course found him and it angrily snatched him out of the air, yanking him fitfully towards the earth. The rooftop of his target building was rushing up at him fast and Brian realized in that split second that he hadn't thought of exactly how he was going to land. Instinct again told him what to do and he listened to it.

He loosened his knees and ankles and when the ground slammed into him with enough force to make him cry out, he tucked and rolled twice, coming up to a skidding stop into a crouch, slowly standing up.

Brian felt his heart was going to explode with adrenaline, as he looked back at the leap he had just made, a wild grin on his face as he panted. He trotted over to the edge of the roof and looked over.

This...is cool as fuck. He looked at his hands and then at himself and back to the sheer size of the leap.

"Holy shit...I'm like a goddamn superhero..." he said out loud, giddy with the adrenaline rush, laughing as the words left his mouth, despite the seriousness of the situation.

Exhilarated and confident now, he wasted no time and began lining up his next jump. He ran and for the first time in his life, Brian felt pure joy as he escaped into the moments in the dark morning light, discovering the simple ecstasy at moving at speeds so fast a human being could barely track him even if they wanted, making leaps of ten feet or more, shaking off impacts like they were nothing. This was beyond his wildest dreams, his wildest expectations. These things simply didn't happen to real people yet here he was and it was happening to him.

This was what he was now. This is my reality.

As he ran, he lost track of time, flowing into his instinct and heartbeat. He simply followed the scent, leaping from building to building, gradually getting more graceful as he went, falling less, soaring more and finding a connection with his new body that he never knew was even possible and in that moment, for the first time since he had been turned, Brian accepted his new form and found a joy in it that he couldn't explain as he set off into the night after Max. A single powerful thought rocked the foundations of his sense of self:

This is who I am now.

#####

The scent led to the old warehouses near the docks and there, Max crouched alone, perched like a gargoyle on the edge of a concrete roof, looking down at just one of the buildings, his eyes blazing golden yellow as shadows moved below from the water's reflection on the docks. The crates and containers that were stacked up like metal firewood. Old street lights lined the docks but half of them didn't even work. This part of the city, though vital to its survival, had been neglected. He watched quietly, keeping his ears forward listening, watching, because he saw that he was not alone here.

Not by far.

Below him, people milled about and in his blue-grey vision he could see that they were humans, humans toting assault rifles and gleaming pistols. Most of them appeared to be street thugs, low level dealers and each of them, Max noted, was branded with a dark black tattoo on their left forearms. A twisting infinity eight with a Roman numeral six and a snake binding them together. Others had a similar snake with a pentagram and snake, while the remainder had the Roman numeral for 86: LXXXVI.

The 86ers. Different tattoos but all the same gang.
Lots of low-level trash and some high-ranking ones, too, it seemed.
Their tattoos are what separated them but each was just as mean as the last.
The warehouse must be either a distribution or storage site, he thought.

These were the same pukes who had tried to kill Brian two weeks ago. Brian did say that he and Elijah had stopped one of their dealers in the emergency room and that had led to the two of them being jumped later that night thanks to some corrupt cops who leaked the information to the enforcers. Max didn't understand why Raven cared so much about these assholes, the ones who overdosed. If they wanted to die by overdosing on some hot new drug let them.

One less piece of trash to have to clean up honestly. On the other hand, his loyalty to her and his connection to Brian had compelled him to go along with this stupid idea. Besides, the drug wouldn't stay contained to the gang territories; Raven was right. It would eventually spill out into families and kids.

He watched the scum milling around below, talking, but he didn't see any shipments moving in and out, nothing that would have indicated a steady flow of a drug onto the streets. In fact, it looked like everyone was mostly relaxing, waiting on something or someone. He could smell them from up here, smell their sweat, their rut, their weed and their crack. Trying not gag, he squinted as a darker shadow suddenly moved from the far edge of the pier and made its way across the dock. Max quickly made himself smaller as he watched.

Whatever the shadow was, it was massive, huge. It walked with a purposeful grace and it gave Max the willies as his fur stood on end even as he frowned at it. There was something about it that was familiar and it took him a second to realize what it was.

The eyes.

The eyes were glowing red.

He had only met one shifter in his entire life that had red eyes.

Rakinos.

"What the fuck are you doing here..." Max snarled quietly to himself, a low growl erupting in his throat. The slanted roof below him was made of corrugated metal sheets and he thought if he rode it down just the right way, he could jump at the end and make it behind a series of crates without anyone seeing him. This whole situation had just gotten much worse and far more interesting, he thought darkly, navigating his way down from his perch, deftly stepping out onto the edge of the slope. If Rakinos was here and he was involved in this new drug, that bore looking into far more than any drug pushers or low-level enforcers. This little outing had just turned into much more than an intel gathering mission.

Double checking the patrols, Max leaped out, stepping off the edge, his boots hitting the corrugated metal, the sudden sound lost in the night. He slid crazily but he maintained his balance and at the end of the makeshift roof ramp, he leaped into space, coming to a hard stop landing in a crouch behind a stack of huge metal shipping containers. Now on the ground, he could get a better look at just what was going on in that warehouse.

Sliding between the shadows, Max moved as silently as a predator, ducking once as a patrol of thugs went by, talking loudly, the scent of the gun oil in their weapons rich in the ebony air. They missed him as he melted into the darkness.

He crouched low and stuck his head around a corner just enough to see what was going on.

Rakinos and the gang members met and after a tense moment, Rakinos seemed to gain the upper hand. He motioned the gang members inside and followed himself not long afterward. The thugs closed the warehouse doors behind them with a metallic clang.

"Fuck..." Max cursed as he looked for a better vantage point. The warehouse building itself was flat with no fire escapes but there was a series of broken and cracked windows that had yellowed with age along the top rim and there was a stack of shipping containers that were stacked up against the wall....

Perfect.

Slinking over to them, Max crawled and clambered up the containers until he was at the top and there, the light from the inside of the warehouse spilled out through the ancient glass.

Below, in the warehouse itself Max felt his heart skip a beat.

The entire warehouse was filled with thugs, and a quick count told him there were easily twenty of them, each heavily armed. Rakinos, it seemed, was alone and he was dressed in an open black leather vest, a dark shirt, black fatigue pants and black combat boots.

Old machinery lined the walls of the warehouse and a few druggies leaned against the walls twirling vials of blue liquid.

Voices drifted up from below.

On his hands and knees, careful to keep as low as he could, Max leaned over the edge of the windows and looked and listened.

####

"...You mean to tell me that this stuff is yours? What did you call it again?" the lead thug (at least Max thought from above hidden on his perch, that he looked like a leader) said as he swaggered forward, an assault rifle slung over his shoulder causally, stopping just in front of Rakinos who towered over everyone in the room. The thug was tall, bulky. Definitely a dangerous threat.

"Wolf's Bane. It's a hyper-amphetamine stimulant. Only I know how to make it and I know that someone in my crew leaked it to you for profit. I see that the profits from those sales," Rakinos said, eyeing the new weapons in the hands of the thugs, "have been well spent. Needless to say, I took care of my problem but now I'm here to address a new one, mainly, you."

The lead thug snorted, his bald head gleaming in the light. He too, was tall, powerfully built, dressed in jeans, a dark red shirt and a black vest. A silver ring glinted on his right hand. He had the air of someone who was not to be trifled with and did not seem to be intimidated by Rakinos in the slightest. He faced the giant werewolf.

"The only one here who's got a problem is you. If you've got security issues, not my basket, not my nuts. What do you want from us? A cut? Not happening. We aren't here to run drugs for you and we don't make partners. We were supposed to be making a deal tonight and you are in the way."

Rakinos studied him carefully, his red eyes calculating.

"Who do you think made that offer? Your gang should be more careful of who you deal with." Rakinos told him.

The thug's eyes narrowed at the truth and Rakinos went on.

"Money is not my concern. I need volunteers. This drug is only part of an equation. There is so much more. Power. Strength. I can give them to you but I need humans, one's that aren't afraid and already have some combat skill. All you need to do is come work for me." Rakinos finished, appraising the thug in front of him with a raised eyebrow. "Come with me, and this gang that you run for will seem meaningless. This isn't true power. I can give you that. Beyond your wildest imagination. Of course," Rakinos added, "You and your gang have been thorns in my side for a while, rivals as it were for the city's turf and the theft and sale of my drug did put my operation at risk, so the alternative, should you refuse, is that you die. Your choice."

The thug in charge laughed. "You have got some big balls, fur-face. Big old balls, I'll say to come in here, and threaten me and my guys. We outnumber you, ten to one or can't you count?"

Rakinos calmly looked around him and when he turned his eyes back to the gang member in front of him, a chilling predatory glaze settled over his scarlet vision.

"And yet, you're still outclassed and don't even know it." Rakinos said quietly, standing neutrally, his arms at his sides, but his red eyes never leaving the thug's pacing body, the gun metal gleaming in the overhead lights. Max recognized the stance Rakinos was in and knew that he was about to witness a blood bath.

"Sounds like you need a lesson in manners, dog." A second gang member snarled and as the new guy stepped forward, he brought around his rifle and ratcheted the slide back. He got between Rakinos and the hood Rakinos had been talking to.

Rakinos smiled revealing his long fangs

"I agree. I'll go first." With that the red werewolf whistled sharply.

The smaller upstart thug shoved his boss backward and pulled the trigger; gunfire exploded but the bullets never reached Rakinos.

A hulking dark form had appeared out of the shadows faster than even Max's eyes could track. The bullet slammed into it with wet *thunks* but despite the spray of blood and gristle, the hulking form showed no sign of pain. Standing on two thick powerful legs with a ragged tail, its broad back was double the size of Max himself with its arms as big around as his torso. Large hands splayed out into long curving claws and a thick neck led up to a huge head, a head that was wolfish in form and shape with torn ears, bleeding snarling gums and a pair of strange mismatched eyes, one yellow and one blue, both glowing with animal hatred.

Some kind of metal bracelet winked on its right forearm and Max saw a glint of blue fluid inside of it, feeding through a short tube into the creature's arm.

Wolf's Bane.

Max felt a strange breed of astonishment and fear explode in his chest as he took in the strange creature. It growled with deep resonant sound that Max could feel even from his high position on the crates. What his eyes refused to register, his brain screamed at him and the reality was too horrifying to contemplate. The beast was taller than Rakinos, closer to eight feet in height. Rakinos was making monsters.

That thing that had moved between the gunfire and Rakinos and not even flinched as high-powered rounds ate into it was some type of shifter or had been and, it had been warped, mutated, changed into a hulking *thing*. Max felt sick as he watched it shoot out a hand, its black claws flashing, as it punched squarely through the thug's chest. A violent red spray filled the air with scarlet mist and the thug spasmed, jerking once, twice, hanging on the thing's arm impaled up to its wrist like some kind of god-awful fish. Blood ran down from the thug's mouth in rivulets and his eyes roamed crazily as his brain died, but very much aware of what was happening to him as the monster literally crushed his beating heart in its hand.

Grabbing the man's twitching body with its free left hand, the monster ripped him apart, tearing him into twin bloody chunks before dropping his steaming entrails onto the warehouse floor, the man's dead eyes staring up at the ceiling, his gun useless.

The beast stood still as Rakinos stepped forward.

"As you can see, I didn't come with empty promises and vague words. This is what I offer you. I can make you into walking weapons. Invulnerable. Unstoppable juggernauts. The only thing I ask, is that you work with me. We can own this city and make it bow. Believe me, if I wanted to, I could snap my fingers and this creature would tear you apart so fast you'd be dead before you realized it. Take this power and become more than you are. Decide now. Evolve."

Before anyone could answer there was a struggle from above, the sounds of fists hitting flesh, a snarl of anger and rage and then an explosion of glass. Rakinos, surprised, stepped aside as a grey furred form was knocked through the windows high up on the warehouse wall and came to a slamming stop at his feet, rolling in the dust, blood running from his snout.

A moment later, a thick set werewolf with blue-black fur dropped in behind him and his eyes were blazing with yellow hatred.

"John. You seem to have caught an eavesdropper." Rakinos said addressing the blue-black shifter who stood before him, panting, his yellow eyes furious as he met Rakinos' gaze. John Carrey stood a free man, just over six foot eight and all of 450 pounds of muscled fury, his tail lashing side to side.

The blue-black werewolf nodded as his yellow eyes faded slowly to brown.

"That bastard was listening in upstairs." He told Rakinos, not even bothering to look at the human gang members who had surrounded them in shock, none of them thinking it too wise to raise their weapons with three werewolves among them, especially given that one of them was like something out of a horror movie.

Rakinos appraised John.

"I'm so glad I got you out of prison. You did well with the library. I knew I could count on you. Always have. It's good to have you back in the field with me." Rakinos turned his attention to the crumpled broken form on the ground between them that was covered in blood and dust. "Now...who do we have here..."

Max had tried to get up and was on his knees. He saw Rakinos and lunged, teeth bared but Rakinos back handed him so hard in the temple that Max rolled like a rag doll, crashing hard into a set of crates, throwing up dust as the wood splintered.

A bored expression crossed his red-furred features as Rakinos recognized him.

"Max Mullen. Imagine finding you here. I think I preferred you on your knees."

Rakinos launched a savage kick, and with a wet meaty snap, four of Max's ribs broke like twigs. Coughing up blood, Max tried to stand and failed.

Rakinos motioned to those gang members who stood around him.

"If you want the power I've offered you, then you can meet me in two days' time at the coal plant administration building. Those who don't want my offer, I suggest you run and don't stop running until you've left the state because I will find you. If you want to prove your sincerity, you can start by killing him." Rakinos snarled, jerking his head towards Max.

Rakinos, the blue-black werewolf and the hulking monster made for the doors and as they stepped through, Rakinos looked back at Max. Max was on his knees, his mouth oozing blood, his eye swollen and his chest heaving. Blue eyes met red eyes.

Contemplating the fallen vigilante, Rakinos shrugged.

"Kill him slowly. No guns. The first one to bring his head to me intact gets my personal favor. Make it hurt."

With that Rakinos and his men vanished into the night, leaving Max crumpled in the middle of a throng of well-armed and now very enticed men who had seen power and wanted that power. Going through one lousy werewolf was going to be easy in their minds.

Dragging himself to his feet, taking a good look around him, Max knew that he may have gotten in over his head this time as thugs cast aside their guns and stepped forward with bare hands, iron rebar and anything else they could get their hands on.

Fuck, he thought as the first blows began to rain down with vicious certainty. He blocked one blow with his forearm, pain singing out in waves. Swinging wildly, he threw a vicious roundhouse, splintering a jaw and while his attention was focused on that creep, another man came up behind him and slammed a piece of board into the back of his skull.

Seeing stars, Max stumbled forward and charged the man, ducking under his improvised weapon, delivering twin punches to his chest and stomach and throwing him bodily aside. Two more went down but they got back up and now, Max saw, they had surrounded him, cutting off any escape routes. There were simply too many of them. The lead thug, the one Rakinos had been talking to, led the group, his cold eyes telling Max he was going to be the most trouble out of them all.

Goddammit, he snarled to himself and raised his hands to protect his face.

#####

WHAM!

Brain landed heavily, the corrugated metal roof cracking loudly with metallic thunder, bending his knees, quickly finding his tail came in handy for balancing, his chest thumping, his blood hammering hot in his ears, exhilarated and high on adrenaline. Rising from his crouch, he had no idea how far he had come but it had to be at least a mile, maybe two. The buildings had evolved in their challenges, some had been higher, others had been lower and still others were adorned with antennae and satellite dishes. Thankfully, all of them had been mercifully free of people. He sniffed the air and smelled water. He was near the docks then.

The thick fishy scent of the river and its unique Dawson City brew of waste confirmed what his eyes saw a moment later, looking over the edge of the building he was on. This part of the docks, he thought, was older, disused and generally looked considerably more abandoned and derelict than the new modern sections with their cranes that he could see in the distance. Those areas were well lit; this area with its two huge warehouses looked like something out of an old noir movie, just begging for trouble.

Breathing hard, he ducked down fast.

He wasn't alone.

Three figures were moving out from one warehouse, the big one with the row of broken windows on the upper floor. One of them looked familiar and squinting Brian had to suppress a gasp.

Rakinos.

The same giant guy from the manor last week. *What the hell was he doing here?* Beside him walked a similarly large werewolf with blue-black fur and snarling yellow eyes that looked familiar but Brian couldn't place him and there, behind them was something Brian didn't know what to make of. It was bigger than Rakinos himself yet walked slowly, almost with a shuffle, like it was having a hard time to moving its massive legs.

The three of them entered the shadows around the dock side and vanished, melting away as if they had never existed.

A moment later voices came from the warehouse. Brian could hear them, muted and distorted from the distance but they were definitely people in that building. He also heard snarls of rage and pain.

Something whistled through the air and impacted something soft with a disgusting wet squelch. The sharp whine of pain that was distinctly canine made Brian's heart jump and the fur on the back of neck stand up. Someone was getting beaten in that building and a horrible realization sunk in that he knew where Max was because he had heard the grunt of pain before.

Something angry stirred in him, something that had until now lain dormant. It squirmed in him like a dragon, moving after eons of slumber, locked inside of him for too long and it wanted out. Badly.

Deciding to throw caution to the wind, Brian leaped over the edge of the building, hitting the roof, sliding down its metal sides, his boots scuffing and catching a bit on the edges until he was over the edge and landed on the flat asphalt of the dock yard. The landings were becoming easier he thought as he stood and bolted for the shadows, his black fur and dark shit melting him into the obsidian darkness, in effect, making him invisible. His green eyes flared in the darkness and he realized he couldn't do anything about that.

For the last time that night, his rational mind tried to argue with him.

He was a security guard, not a street fighter. He only had basic combat skills and pretty rusty ones at that. It had been years since he was in taekwondo class, yet here he was, about to charge into a building full of god knows what. This was insanity. He was going to himself killed. He should call for help.

No phone, he reminded himself. Even if he did, who would he call? They'd never get here in time. Cops? Cops in this city were corrupt. Not ever again. That meant that he was in fact, going to have to go in there and do something. No one else could or would. There was no one else to rely on. Max hadn't waited when it had come to helping him.

Swallowing the last of his fear and anxiety, Brian closed his eyes and pushed everything else out of his mind. He had abilities he didn't have before. He could hear for miles. He could scent for just the same. He could see in the dark. He was stronger than most humans, faster. He just had to try to fall back into the old flow-motion of the old drills from the classes, to trust his body and his instincts. This time, he wasn't the one who was going to be caught by surprise and cornered in an alleyway. This time, he had had the advantage.

I can do this...

"HEY! What the hell are you doing here?!"

The surprised voice cried out from behind him and he whirled, his eyes shining in the dark to see one of the thugs had come up behind him. The black metal of the assault rifle in his hands shone in the dock lights. That rifle was quickly lowered and pointed in his face and in that moment, Brian let go and simply moved. Moved without thinking. Without hesitating.

Just move. Don't stop to think. GO!

As the rifle lowered down to his chest, everything seemed to slow down. Brian charged the thug, ducking under the barrel, using his shoulder to shove the gun up and away from himself, grabbing the man's weapon arm in a hard grip, digging his claws into the soft pink flesh.

With a grunt and cry of pain, the man angrily sprayed off a round or two, the sound painfully loud in Brian's ears, nearly deafening him. Snarling Brian held onto the guy's gun arm and threw him out to the side before slamming a powerful right hook into his jaw bone.

The sound of his knuckles hitting the man's skull was loud and the sound of his jaw bone breaking was even louder.

The thug dropped to the ground, blood pouring from his nose, completely unconscious as the gun skittered away.

Panting, Brian knew that the gun fire had probably alerted whoever else was in the building and moved. He couldn't stay here. With a two-step leap and a bound, he found himself at the front edge of the building and thankfully the doors were open. Kneeling, he peeked around the corner.

The warehouse itself was full of old machinery and tool parts. Stacks of wooden crates took up most of the space and the only lights were a series of dim yellow things that hung from the roof, leaving pools of dark shadow and ponds of light. His eyes narrowed as he saw the source of the sounds he had heard outside.

There was a ring of about twenty men, all of them surrounding a single person, all of them taking their turns beating on that person with makeshift melee weapons. Crowbars, fists, broken bottles. Brass knuckles.

Brian's heart sank and his bile rose as he caught a flash of silver fur.

Max.

Max was in the middle of the circle, standing on his feet and barely managing to keep his feet at that, Brian noted. He was totally outnumbered. Blood poured from half a dozen open wounds and even as his body tried to heal them, Brian knew that it couldn't keep up with the damage. He looked like he was nearing exhaustion.

Max was crouched over, hunched over really, his breathing ragged. To his credit, he still managed to land a solid blow on one of the thugs with the brass knuckles, sending him sprawling.

He got a crowbar to the back of the knees for his trouble.

With a cry of pain Max went down on all fours, blood leaking from his snout and ears.

"What was that? Someone's fired off a round outside." One of the larger men with a bald head and a silver ring said, stopping midway in his beating. He motioned at two of the others. "Go see what that was. We'll finish this up."

Brian noticed that none of them had guns and he quickly found out why. All of their guns were lain up against a table. They had set them aside to torture Max and make it as slow as possible, to inflict as much pain as they could.

That thought caused the thing deep inside him to stir, much more aggressively. He felt a change slowly come over him and he saw red.

Rage.

Unbridled unchained rage.

All he had to do was let it loose. To trust it. To take it off the leash.

The two men that had been sent to check out the gunfire made for the gun tables and Brian knew he had to act now. Glancing around, he found no weapons of his own but a second glance revealed a ten-foot piece of steel rebar propped up against the wall.

Perfect.

Snatching it, he crouched low, closing his eyes as to not give away his position, his ears swiveling in the direction of the foot falls, relying on the blackness of his fur to keep him hidden. The two men cocked their guns lazily and were about five feet from Brian when he sprang.

Swirling the rebar like a staff, he laid the pole into the side of one man's skull sending him sprawling, his gun clattering away into the water with a wet splash. The other man had more of an advantage and ducked Brian's reverse swing over his head, ducking the deadly metal bar.

Going low, Brian swiped the man's feet out from under him and brought the metal bar down hard across his head in a single sharp rap. Whether he had killed him or not, Brian didn't really care as long as the man stayed down where he belonged, which he did.

His mind argued that taking a life was sickening but the monster in him was now in charge as it reminded him survival outweighed morality.

The sharp sounds of metal on flesh drew the attention of the others and they turned. The lead bald thug looked at Brian confused, and kicked Max aside.

"Who the hell are you?" he snarled. He looked over the newcomer, sizing him up: A tall powerfully built werewolf, covered in jet black fur with a silver-gray blaze down his front that stuck up a bit out of his dark shirt and angry glaring hot green eyes armed with some kind of makeshift staff.

Brian said nothing in return but charged into their midst with a single goal in mind. He knew his efforts would be clumsy from not practicing in so many years, and he would have to make each strike count, no mistakes. A mistake was going to end up with him dead.

"GET HIM!" the bald guy with the ring belted out.

Brian knew he had to keep them away from the guns and thankfully, the staff was one weapon he did at least sort of know how to use. In addition to taking tae kwon do, he had also found in his time taking martial arts that he had a natural affinity for staff weapons. He had channeled that when he was younger, becoming quite adept with them. As he moved now, he wished he hadn't given it up but what he had managed to retain would come in handy now. He may have been no boxer like Max, no street fighter but he wasn't defenseless. Far from it. As he met his opponents in the battle, he felt the old muscle memories kick in.

Ducking a blow that came at his head, Brian whipped his makeshift staff left and right in two quick snaps, dropping two of the men into bloody unconscious piles. His staff found three more bodies in quick succession, the rebar sinking hard into soft meat and bone, cracking both with savage efficiency. Grunts and cries of pain he heard but ignored as he continued to drop them. He moved in a flurry of motion he didn't know he was capable of, channeling his new enhanced speed and strength. He soon found his reflexes were faster than he'd ever thought. Combined with his enhanced senses the thugs couldn't touch him even with his own out of practice form.

Their numbers whittled down slowly until finally just four of them remained. Bloodied bruised semi-conscious bodies lay on the dirty floor. Brian watched the four pieces of remaining human trash that were somehow still on their feet, panting, watching each of them as they circled him, his vision and sense of smell on overload, seeking any kind of early warning from them. They smelled like fear and testosterone. They stank. None of them had been able to get to their guns so far and that was what Brian thought had kept Max and himself both alive. However, now that it was just four of them on one, it was going to be harder to keep them away; they were no longer going to get in each other's way. The guy with the ring, the leader Brian assumed, was pissed.

As they circled each other, the only thing that Brian wanted was Max.

Max at this point had fallen completely to the floor, unable to even get onto all fours, and his body lay worryingly still. Brian could see his chest rising and falling slowly so he wasn't dead. Not yet.

The biggest of the still conscious thugs, the leader, the bald one with the ring and a cut going up the side of his face that bled profusely, shouted at Brian in blind rage.

"What do you think you're some kind of hero?! You're nothing! This isn't the movies, kid. This is cold hard reality. Eventually, you're gonna get tired or fuck up." He snarled and waved his own piece of broken rebar, a three-foot-long chunk of heavy steel he had managed to grab hold of. He spat a blood clot out of his mouth. Brian had tagged him with the edge of his rebar earlier in the melee. The thug looked down at the blood he had just spat and then he glanced up at Brian.

"You owe me for this. Mark my words. I will collect on it. You don't know what you've messed with tonight, you and him. I never forget a face. I swear to you…" He finished with a growl.

The three remaining thugs moved behind him and as Brian moved to turn and counter them, the lead thug charged, his makeshift club of rebar whistling through the air. Brian spun to block it, bringing up his staff and the two metal weapons met with a bone jarring thud that sent shudders running up Brian's arms.

Brian realized his mistake the moment it happened. He had left himself open.

The three other thugs took the chance and railed him from behind with a series of violent kicks to his kidneys, his spine, and a heavy blow from something hard slammed into the back of his skull. One of them slammed their foot down onto his tail, grinding their full weight onto it. Brian yelped in agony as the bone fractured. Shards of hot pain ratcheted up and down his body and he nearly threw up but stopped himself. Using the distraction, the bald bastard in front of him suddenly grabbed Brian by his shirt front and dragged him to his feet. He was much stronger than he looked.

The lead thug laid a terrific blow across Brian's sensitive snout, his silver ring slicing open Brian's muzzle.

Crying out, Brian went down on his knees, his rebar staff falling from his grasp. His face felt like a bomb went off in it. The guy with the silver ring kicked Brian's rebar away angrily as the other three men moved behind him and snared him, holding him in place for their leader, their thick arms wrapped around his arms and neck. The boss stood in front of Brian, his eyes swimming with hate, his silver ring stained with blood.

"See…in the movies…this is where something, someone comes to save you but in real life…that kind of shit doesn't happen." He panted, trying to catch his breath. "You get yourself in too deep and well, boy, you die. It's just that simple. So," the gangster said, picking up his broken rebar again. "Here's what's going to happen. I'm guessing that piece of shit there is someone important to you. I'm going to kill him in front of you, make you watch him die. Then, I'm going to take my time with you. We just got an offer we can't refuse, and we are gonna tear this city a new asshole.

This gang? It's finished. A new dawn is going to rise on this city. I'm done being mid-level. You just won't be around to see it."

The thug moved towards Max, the heavy rebar glinting in the light as the man held it like a baseball bat over his shoulder.

Seeing that glint, Brian remembered how it felt to have a blade slice into him, cutting him up like a piece of meat. The searing hot pain as he had bled out in that dirty alleyway.

Snarling he growled and something like a strained whimper came out of him as he fought against his captors, unable to break their hold on him. The grip around his neck only got tighter. Brian felt his anger and adrenaline surge beyond the red zone.

That thing inside of him stirred again and this time, it did not go back to sleep. That lumbering growling presence that had haunted his dreams was now with him and for the first time, it was fully awake.

And it was angry.

Green eyes in the blackness of Brian's mind flashed white.

Time seemed to slow down and sound faded away as Brian watched the man with the ring raise the rebar above Max, preparing to bash his brains out with it, forcing Brian to watch while the other three goons held him down. Brian could hear his own ragged breathing and that monster inside begged him, whispering in his brain to be let loose, to let it run wild. It seduced him in a way that was almost sexual, whispering with its power, begging him to trust it. Straining, his teeth bared with the effort, Brian tried once again to break free and reach Max and failed.

The rebar come down.

In that instant, Brian gave in to the whispers and everything changed.

A hot shudder ran down his body, cascading from his head down to his feet and he felt himself begin to tremble. He seemed to fall away and become something else, something far from the action, like he was drugged. It was similar to how being put under felt like just before surgery, a feeling that he was not connected to his body any longer as something else rose to take his place.

The three thugs were so intent on holding him in place that none of them saw what was happening as Brian's bright green eyes began to burn away, losing all their color instead turning a silver white, his irises and pupils vanishing in the white glow that had replaced his eyes.

None of them saw as Brian's body began to change, his hands growing larger, his fingers longer, his claws lengthening, coming out of their sheaths, exposing reinforced black blades of bone. By the time the thugs began to feel the change it was too late. Brian's torso and arms had swollen, muscle layering upon muscle, the silver blaze in his fur burning away to a black that was blacker than any black hole in the darkest depths of space as his torso tore apart his shirt.

"What the hell!?" The smaller man holding him cried as his hold was broken by Brian's now swollen neck, but that was wrong because Brian was gone and in his place was something entirely new. Something far larger, darker, more primal and infinitely more lethal.

Snarling, not getting up from the crouch he had been forced into, the hulking black form knocked the one man aside on his right, sending him careening headfirst into a crate. He collapsed and didn't move. With motions so fast and fluid it was hard to see, the living darkness in the form of a wolf swung its curving claws around and up into the torso of the man who had been holding him in a choke hold. Blood sprayed as the man yelled in surprise and anger. He was dead before he dropped to the ground. The third man went down just as easy.

With a roar that was deeper than any animal on earth that shook the air itself, the monster that had been Brian heaved himself up to his feet, glaring at the sole remaining threat before him.

The lead thug with his rebar and silver ring stared in horrified shock as he tried to process what he was seeing.

Gone was the human sized werewolf and in its place, rising like a living shadow with blazing white eyes was instead an eight-foot-high monster with a long wolf's snout lined with black fangs, curving black claws that walked and moved like a living tank. Seeing the last of his still conscious men be swatted aside like pests enraged the man to the point of reckless insanity. He too was a big man, standing will over six feet himself.

"YOU WANT SOME? COME ON!" he bellowed and kicked Max aside, dropping into a fighting stance facing the beast with his raised bar.

With a snarl, the monster lashed out with a vicious swipe of its right claws. The man brought up his rebar and slapped its massive hand aside, the sound of metal clanging on bone echoing loudly as the beast bellowed with rage.

Seizing his chance, the man charged in and drove the rebar down in a vicious arc at the beast, intending to knock its head clean off.

The rebar suddenly stopped as the beast snagged it with its other hand in midblow, the force sending shock waves through the man's arm. Yanking the man close, the monstrous shadow-beast bared its teeth in his face and squeezed the bar.

The metal groaned and bent like a spoon.

Furious and surprised, the man let go of the rebar, dropped into a better stance and pulled a large blade from behind his back, slashing it down violently across the beast's massive chest, drawing blood.

Screaming in a canine rage, the beast looked down at itself, surprised it had been injured. The man moved in again, drawing his arm back.

The shadow wolf moved, ducking under the blow and went to claw the man's chest open but the man was no longer there.

He had taken the chance as the monster ducked to leap upon its back and began to rain down blows with his blade, stabbing the beast over and over in its meaty shoulders, his free arm wrapped around its rippling neck.

Roaring in rage, the beast clawed at him but could not shake him and in desperation, did the only thing it could.

It brought its head in as far as it could, loosening the man's grip and as he tried to move his arm for better purchase, the beast brought its jaws down hard on his meaty forearm, driving its black teeth deep into the flesh. The man let out a howling scream, the knife falling away and using his pain as a distraction, the shadow wolf bucked him off, throwing the man heavily to the ground where he hit hard, rolling several feet, his arm a bloodied mangled mess.

Standing, panting, the black beast considered his opponent carefully. Though smaller, the human was obviously a clear and present threat. It was suddenly cautious.

The man, groaning in agony but still enraged, the fight not out of him yet, rolled to his feet and staggered for his dropped knife.

With earth shattering force, the black werewolf stomped its right foot down hard on the discarded blade, crushing it's housing, driving the metal into the cement floor with crack and spray of dust.

Now, defenseless on his knees before the titan, the man looked up at the angry god-beast and stared, his body refusing to allow him to do any more.

"What...what are you..." he panted, forcing himself to his feet, wobbling in place, his face full of confusion and hatred even in his defeat.

The space black beast considered him for a moment, looked at the crumpled gray form on the floor and down to its own bleeding but healing chest.

With a dismissive growl, the creature lashed out with a violent kick from its left foot, catching the injured gangster full on in the chest with a sickening thud. The man didn't even have time to make a sound as his body flew backwards, smashing through the stack of crates as they collapsed onto him in a crash of wood, metal and splinters.

He did not get back up, and his arm hung limply out of the debris, his silver ring glinting in the lights.

The sudden silence in the battle ravaged warehouse was deafening, the only sound was the groans of pain coming from the men who were still alive and the sharp heaving panting of the giant black monster.

The beast stepped forward and fell to its knees, groaning and began to shrink, its form collapsing in on itself, its arms and legs trembling. The form continued to fade away until finally, Brian was back to himself, on his knees in the middle of a room full of bodies and bloody carnage, the silver blaze on the front of his chest streaked scarlet.

He groaned in pain as his head wanted to explode and when he opened his eyes, they faded slowly from the burning white back to their iridescent green. Looking around, he saw that there were no more thugs, no more threats. He did see that his pants were shredded below the knee and that he hurt everywhere, his shoes ruined and pieces of his shirt lay torn apart across the floor. He could feel his body knitting itself back together and he looked up, confused, seeing the only thing that mattered to him as his mind reasserted itself.

Max.

"Max!" he yelled, his own aches forgotten as he dove forward and came up beside Max on his knees. Reaching down, he grabbed the bigger shifter by the shoulders and turned him over gently. Brian's heart sank at what he saw.

Max's thick gray fur and silver blaze were stained red, the deep wounds on his arms, legs and chest looked ugly, weeping but they were already starting to close. At least, they looked like they were trying to. His breathing was slow his pulse was thready.

"Come on...I need you to stand up...we can't stay here.... gotta move...." Brian pleaded with him, shaking him gently. Max groaned and cracked an eye open. Brian saw recognition in those blue eyes and felt a surge of protective energy come over him.

"We've got to get you home. Can you stand up?" he asked Max gently, his own throat raw.

Max nodded and pushed himself up only to collapse back into the dirt with a heavy exhausted grunt.

Seeing he had no choice, Brian summoned the strength he had left and scooped Max up with a strength that surprised even him, and laid his friend over his shoulder, just like Max had done for him two weeks ago. He grunted under Max's weight and Max moaned in pain, whimpering in a way that wasn't normal for him, but he didn't struggle.

Calling upon whatever reserves he had left, Brian moved, carrying his friend out of the bloody mess, bounding into the shadows, and was gone a moment later, leaving the carnage behind.

As they left, several of the men began to move again, consciousness returning to them in painful headaches of bright lights and sounds. Many of them were nursing broken fingers, shattered hands and parts. Broken, bruised and battered, unsure of what hit them, the men were quickly coming around to find that not all of them had made it out of the battle alive. Some of them were angry. Some of them were already wanting payback.

Some of them began to think on what that big red furred werewolf had offered and then and there, the majority of them who had survived, decided that yes, they would take his offer as they limped out of the warehouse, the drug operation they had been working out of that building compromised beyond repair. Their gang bosses would be furious but it no longer mattered.

Their allegiances had changed and the power balance in the city was about to change and they, the survivors, would be on the vanguard. The only one who would have paid for the failure of tonight, for the loss of the drug storehouse, well, the surviving thugs thought, spotting his unmoving bloodied arm poking out from the debris of shattered crates with its distinctive silver ring, well, it looked like he wasn't going to have to be worrying about that anymore.

Hours later, long after the last surviving gang member had left, in the shadows of the ruined warehouse, buried under the shattered crates where he had been kicked, the man who had went toe to toe with a monster and had been bitten and broken lay in crumpled bloody heap. He suddenly stirred, groaning as an onset of shivers took over his body while he came to. An electric burning sensation cascaded over every nerve he had, sending him into a brief but violent set of seizures. This passed and a moment later, his breathing stabilized, his wounds began to seal and with a groan of pain the man's eyes flew open as he sharply inhaled, his body coming to life in new in ways he couldn't even begin to comprehend. Death fled from him and he knew he had survived even as his body burned from the inside out.

As he lay there, the weight of the debris on top of him pinning him down, the man realized he had a promise to keep and he would keep it, no matter how long it took. That understanding kept him alive, focused his rage and with the thought, his eyes, once dull olive brown, blazed a hateful and fiery scarlet red.

CHAPTER 4

By the time that Brian managed to get them both back to Max's apartment and inside, the door safely locked and bolted behind them, the sun was beginning to peek over the edge of the sky, burning away the darkness with a line of orange pink light. His shoulders ached and the webbing in his back burned. Half way into the garage, he nearly fell under Max's weight and with a snarl of determination he fell to his knees and forced himself to stand back up. Max tried to squirm and get free to try to walk on his own but Brian refused to let him, instead carrying him laboriously up the stairs.

Crashing through the kitchen, Brian knocked a stool over and it clattered loudly across the floor and finally, he lumbered into the bathroom and finally, he collapsed under Max's weight. Unable to hold him any longer, Brian set him down as gently as he could, propping him up against the bathtub. Brian snapped on the light and moaned.

Max looked far worse than he thought at first. Max stirred and he tried to open his eyes but couldn't. Brian told him to be quiet and sit still as Brian ripped off Max's bloodied pants and shredded shoes. Tearing off what little remained of Max's underwear, Brian lifted his friend up and with a grunt, eased him down into the bathtub itself, nearly slipping on the blood pool that had formed under Max's limp body.

Brian had not seen so much blood in such a very long time. He had, of course, seen car accidents and injuries at work, but to see someone you cared for, weak and reduced to wreckage was something different. Two of Max's fingers were broken, sticking out at odd angles. His left ear was torn badly, his left eye swollen shut. Vicious slashes cut left and right streaks up and down his chest and stomach, revealing wet red flesh beneath. His tail also stuck out at an odd angle, near the base where it connected into his spine. One of his teeth was broken.

Brian saw that Max's body was desperately trying to mend itself. Even as he watched, the flesh was knitting itself together and the blood flow was slowing but it wasn't enough, he had to try to do something, to help Max heal. He wasn't even sure a shifter could take so much damage and live. The risk of infection was high, he thought, given the filthy state of that warehouse.

"Hang on, Max....gotta get you cleaned up..." Brian choked out as his eyes stung, surprised at how much his own voice was trembling. He felt himself shaking and knew then it wasn't just his voice. He was running on adrenaline, trying not to think about the blackout he had experienced. Reaching up, Brian spun the hot water handle and a cascade of warm water rained down, and in moments, Max's thick gray fur was drenched. Grabbing a washcloth, Brian did his best to gently clean out the wounds, gingerly but quickly moving, trying to mask the trembling in his hands.

The water turned copper red in moments and soon the entire tub ran with blood. Brian tried to wake Max up, talking to him, shaking his shoulder, anything.

If he had a concussion he shouldn't be sleeping. He may never wake up.

"Max....come on...wake up...please..."

Brian ran the warm cloth over Max's broken face, gently dabbing away the blood from under his split eyelid. As he did, Max's blue eyes slid open, briefly and they looked at Brian with the most curious expression before seeming to accept his ministrations and closing again. Brian watched as Max's ear knitted together and sealed off the wound but his breathing wasn't getting any better. In fact, it was getting raspier. The time between breaths was becoming more and more spaced apart.

Brian realized that even though the minor wounds on Max's body were healing, Max, on the whole, was fading away and that he had extreme internal injuries. Grabbing his wrist, Brian felt Max's heart begin to slow. The damage was too much. It was burning out his immune system.

Max slumped forward and stopped responding entirely.

"No, no no no!" Brain cried, shaking Max harder, desperately trying to get him to wake up. Max's crumpled body simply slid lower into the tub. Brian had no idea what to do. Totally at a loss, a thought struck him.

He knew that when Max had bitten him, it had caused him to heal very quickly. He wondered if the same action would work on someone who was already a shifter. Having no idea how it worked or why it might, hoping that whatever was weird about him could be of use, Brian decided.

"I'm sorry, Max."

Brian desperately sank his fangs into Max's forearm, his own blood mingling with Max's.

For a moment, nothing happened.

Anthony Milhorn

Max's eyes shot open and he groaned low in this throat, unable to speak and for a moment, his body went rigid before he collapsed again. Brian withdrew, spitting out the blood in his mouth, the coppery taste almost nauseating him. He looked at Max again expectantly and this time felt relief begin to flood into him.

Whatever the process was, however, it worked, Brian thought, it was working. That weird protein that apparently saved his life was now working on Max's wounds as they began to seal up, melting away without so much as a scar. His teeth repaired themselves. In moments, there wasn't a wound left and Max simply lay sleeping in the tub, soaked and drenched in the bloody remains of the night, his breathing deep and regular, his pulse strongly threading.

Doing the only thing he could, Brian washed Max off, cleaning his fur as best as he could manage and half way through it, Max woke up and looked at Brian.

"What...are you doing...Brian...I.... Rakinos...." he asked, his voice weak.

"Max....none of that matters right now..." Brian said, relieved to see his friend up and talking again, smiling a bit, hoping Max didn't see how wet his eyes were. He shook his head. "We can talk about it later. Can you stand up? Gotta get you into bed...."

Max nodded and groaned as he tried to stand and failed. Brian reached out to try to put an arm up under Max's shoulder to boost him and Max tried to shove him away but Brian pushed past it.

"Stop it. Let me help you goddamn it. You don't always have to be so stubborn. I'm here. Let me in."

With a growl, Max gave in and Brian managed to get Max onto his feet. Stumbling, he managed to walk Max into the bedroom area of the apartment and gently sat him down. Moments later, Max was unconscious, sleeping deeply on his back, his body mending. Brian draped a sheet and blanket over him and made sure he was as comfortable as he could. Brian stood watch over him for a while before sheer exhaustion finally hit him, driving him back over to the sofa. Brian looked out at the rising morning sun and crashed down onto the couch, landing heavily, not even bothering to clean himself up, too tired to move or think about it.

Images flashed through his mind of the fight at the warehouse and after a while, he realized he didn't know how he had beaten those men only that they were beaten and that he and Max were alive. That blackout scared him but something during it had saved him.

There were disturbing visions in his head. Visions of a monstrous shadow wolf with white eyes, black claws and teeth flashing, blood spraying and screams but none of it felt real to him. It felt disconnected. That feeling of being dis-

104

connected felt so heavy that Brian's eyes closed and he too passed out into a dream-less sleep.

#####

"Hey..."

A quiet gruff voice intruded into the deep dark space of his dreams where he walked but not alone. Something was with him.

"Hey...Brian..."

A gentle prodding on his shoulder became more insistent and finally much harder, until Brian woke up, his eyes thick with sleep.

"Huh.." he grunted.

He blinked, sitting up, the mid-afternoon sun blinding him for a moment to the silhouetted figure that stood over him. Focusing his eyes, Brian saw that it was Max. He stood before him, dressed at least in a pair of black and red plaid pajama bot-toms, his tail hanging behind him. Its tip, Brian noticed was moving side to side ex-pectantly, gently. The thick gray fur on Max's powerful chest was clean without the slightest hint of blood and the only thing remaining of last night's battle were in fact, some very small scars that themselves were fading away. He had showered again, Brian could tell, based on the sharp clean scent rolling off of him.

"Max....You're alive..." Brian said relieved as he sat up and fell back onto the sofa, rubbing his head. It throbbed and ached in a way that was begging for Aleve.

"Yeah. I am. " Max replied, coming around and sitting down next to Brian thoughtfully. He looked up at Brian. "Thanks to you."

Brian had a million questions, dozens of thoughts rushing through his sleep addled mind. "What were you doing out there.... why did you go...what...?"

For a moment, Max wouldn't look at him and finally, he did, his blue eyes looking deeply into Brian's green orbs.

"Raven asked me for help. She wanted me to help her track down where that drug was coming from.... it's the same one that was in your druggie in the ER. People have been dying from it and no one can figure out where it's coming from or what it is. Raven did. She found out it's some kind of hyper-drug made for shifters. She just wanted me to find the source and then let the cops handle it. She wanted put an end to it before any more people die. She was worried it may have a connection to what happened to you."

Brian shook his head. "You could have told me. I would have come with you. Helped you. Why didn't you?"

Max frowned, his face darkening with shame and a little defiance. "I'm not used to having anyone else here, Brian. I've spent my entire life on the streets. I can hold my own. I didn't need a babysitter."

Waving that off, Brian turned to him, his temper rising a bit at that last remark.

"Max, it's not about babysitting you. You could have used back up—"

"Back up?" Max asked stunned. "You're a security guard, Brian. The real world doesn't play nice with passive restraints, man. I know how to fight."

"That's why you were laying in the bathtub dying last night, then?" Brian snapped at him, his relief at Max's survival quickly turning into anger over his friend's brash stupidity, of his unwillingness to understand, to see, that people cared for him.... that Brian cared for him.

"Why didn't Raven tell us all? Why did she hide it especially since it has something to do with me?" Brian asked and realized immediately why she hadn't told anyone but Max.

"It's because she didn't trust me not to go out there and sent you instead because you're the vigilante."

Brian saw Max's ears fall and felt a pang of guilt and tried to dial it back a bit. Max however dug deeper.

"Brian...this is my life. This is how I've lived for so many years I've lost count. I go out there every night. I get beat up. I heal. I do it again. I've kept the whole lower east side safe as I can because no one else gives a shit about the people who live here. I have experience out there. It's why she asked me. It's my burden. It's my--"

"Punishment? Is that it? For what? Your parents, Max?"

Max said nothing and had turned away from Brian, looking out the window at the bustling afternoon city. Brian went on.

"You can't beat yourself up over something you cannot help or change. You nearly died—"

"But I didn't!" Max finally snapped back, standing up, towering over Brian, his voice raised and directed at Brian for the first time in two weeks. He was more defensive than Brian had ever seen him and he could see thoughts whirling behind Max's blue eyes.

Brian gave it right back to him, meeting him toe to toe. Enough was enough.

"You did! If I hadn't followed you, you'd be dead and we'd have no idea that Rakinos was involved in this. I saw him leaving the docks just before I came in. He was in Draco's house. He's too close to us all and now we find out that he's involved with that crap and you walked right into it without saying a word!" Brian snarled.

"BRIAN! ENOUGH! I do this every night. This is who I am! This is all there is to me; I'm nothing more! I can't separate it from me any more than you can about your dad! You want me? You have to accept all of me or none! I can't pick myself apart!!" Max roared, his blue eyes vivid, his chest heaving.

Max's words caught Brian completely off guard and the instant silence in their wake left oceans of distance between the two of them until Brian crossed that distance and resolved it with a simple question as they stood face to face.

"What did you say..."

Max growled in frustration. "You're different okay?! You've gotten past my fucking walls in ways no one else ever could. I don't know how and I couldn't tell you in words. It just is...."

"Why didn't you say something..." Brian asked softly, the full impact of Max's revelation hitting him in the stomach like a tractor trailer.

"Because," Max said the fight gone out of him as the truth finally spoken laid him bare. He collapsed heavily onto the sofa, his heavy body thumping hard on it. He sat there, his head lowered, hands between his knees, shaking. When he spoke next his voice was broken and quiet.

"I was afraid."

Sitting in stunned silence, Brian took up the space next to Max on the couch and this time, there was no distance between them. Max swallowed and his next words were so quiet that Brian almost missed them.

"You? Afraid? Of what?" Brian asked as Max refused to look at Brian, focusing on a spot instead on the floor.

"Of you saying no. I've got nothing to offer anyone. Look at me. I'm a broken mess and you don't even know the half of it. You're the first person I've ever felt this way toward. I never realized it until last week when you were gone and all I could think about was you."

Brian reached out with his black furred palm and took Max's head in his hands, gently below his jaw line and lifted, meeting Max's blue eyes which to Brian's shock, were moist.

When Brian spoke, his voice trembled as mini earthquakes ran through his body.

"I told you on that rooftop last week that I wasn't going anywhere. That I would always have your back. I meant it."

Moving closer Brian kicked away the last of his reservation, the last of his apprehension and doubt, and holding Max's head gently in his hands, he closed the distance between them with a deep kiss.

Instantly the sun exploded between them, waves of hot and cold racked his body and Brian felt gravity lose its grip. He felt Max simply sit there stunned until a moment later, Max returned the kiss, his tongue moving gently, meeting Brian's as they danced over each other. Sparks and lightning flew as thunder exploded in Brian's ears and Brian realized he loved how Max tasted, like fresh clean water from the deepest purest mountain spring. He drank in that taste, swam in it and went for more and when he finally pulled back, he and Max sat facing each other, inches apart, both of them breathing hard, volumes unspoken between them and now no longer needing to be spoken. Light headed, Brian blinked as he looked into Max's blue eyes.

"Wow. You're good at that." He told him a tiny smile growing on the edges of his mouth, his tail wagging behind him beyond his control. He didn't care.

Max nodded, unable to speak and he seemed to hesitate but instead he frowned and shook his head, turning on the couch, moving over to Brian, leaning into him, meeting the smaller shifter's lips to his own, instinct and drive taking over and a moment later, he lay on top of Brian, their bodies entangled, the heat cascading off of them. Tails flew, ears were down and eyes closed. With a small grunt of pleasure, Brian pulled Max onto him more so that Max was squarely straddling him.

When they broke and came up for air, Brian's eyes had taken on a glazed look as he took in Max. The man was surprisingly handsome and now he felt no shame in admitting that. No apprehension. He ran a black furred hand up Max's ridged stomach, his fingers slipping into and out of the canyons of his abdomen, coursing up through the silver-gray blaze of fur there, feeling Max's scars and the hardness of Max's nipples.

He tweaked them gently and Max let out a low growl. The sound surprised Brian, seeming to enter his ears and run up and down his spine, vibrating his bones with its deep resonance, like a tiger. It rumbled and shook yet the sound itself wasn't that loud. His brain told him the answer without thinking: subsonic vibrations.

For the first time, Max put a hand on Brian's body that wasn't in defense or anger and simply rested it there, on Brian's stomach, enjoying the sleekness of his fur, and the simple joy that blossomed within him at the rise and fall of Brian's breathing, of feeling his heartbeat. Max felt his own heart speed up, thumping in a way that didn't come from the thrill of a fight but rather the thrill of true existence, of a peace he had not felt in a long time slowly coming over him.

Hot blood rushed through his ears and he could hear his own pulse. Brian felt a pleasant shudder run up and down his side as Max came down and nestled his snout into Brian's neck, kissing and biting him there, gently yet powerfully, causing Brian to buck gently on the couch with a groan, both of them breathing hard. Brian heard a sound come from himself and it was alien yet familiar.

It was a low rumbling growl of pleasure, egging Max on, the same kind of rumbling subsonic sound that shook the air a moment before. Max's scent was over-powering this close, so much more so than in the lobby or even the truck. Brian let it wash over him, dance in his nose and glaze the back of his throat, cascading like an avalanche that drowned him in sensation, sight and smell mixing in a way that was impossible for a human, forming an ecstatic electric synesthesia.

Pushing Max up, Brian sat up, stood up and came together with Max, moving across the room, leaving the couch behind, both of them falling onto the bed, not caring what they knocked over or what got broken. He ended up on top of Max this time, straddling him. Brian could feel how hard Max was in his pajama bot-toms, and Brian felt himself throb just as much.

Kissing gently over Max's chest, his whiskers and chin fur tickling him, Brian moved lower, working his way down the hard V of Max's groin, just above the waistband of his pajama bottoms and with a final look at Max, Brian moved, sliding the pajama bottoms off and out of the way, shuffling off his own clothes in the pro-cess and for the first time, the two of them were laid bare before the other, naked, with no barriers, no walls. Brian drank in Max's body, his eyes and sense of touch, the warm fur, the hot skin beneath, the musk that was quickly filling the air that only the two of them could smell. It was turning into a churning storm threaded through with psychic lightning pulsing to the sound of their heartbeats.

Max was powerfully built, thick but lean at the same time, his body covered in layers of scars, his thick fur hiding most of them, but they were easy to feel. Like Brian, Max had a blaze of silver gray in his pubic region and there, stand-ing at full attention was Max's penis. It was fully rigid, harder than stone. Unlike Brian's which was black, Max's was a bright pink color, and like Brian, Max too was uncircumcised, the velvety sheath visible there as it pulled from back from the mushroom head of Max's cock, which glistened wetly with a single drop of clear fluid leaking from the tip.

Max was not small and was in fact nine inches or so and had the thick-ness of Brian's wrist. His balls hung low as well, heavy and round, covered in that same velvety gray fur. For a moment, Max seemed to grow shy, and Brian didn't need to be told why. The scarred over nature of his body was making him uncomfortable and Brian removed any doubt in that instant by running his snout into Max's belly, moving lower, the tip of Max's cock bouncing under his chin until finally, it was poised before him like a ship's mast in a hurricane.

Without hesitation, Brian took Max inside himself, careful of his sharp teeth, sliding all the way down to the base, using the length of his new muzzle to his advantage, burying his snout in Max's fur where he caught the slightest whiff of masculine musk. It encouraged him and Brian went again as Max arched his back on the bed, growling and grunting in surprise and pleasure. It was like running and jumping off of those buildings earlier; exhilarating as gravity let go, losing its eternal hold only to grab him and slam him back down but he never hit, rather, Brian felt like he was rising again, flying through the moon-scarred obsidian night. He wrapped his long tongue around Max's shaft as he moved, gliding with hot moisture, the musky taste of Max and his own breath mixing in a hot cloud.

Panting, Brian came up and moved up Max, kissing him deeply, relishing the clean slightly musky masculine taste of his body and Max returned the kiss, losing himself in the reality that this was happening and it was real as Max grabbed the back of his head and held him, his tongue moving in Brian's mouth passionately. For him, there was nothing but this moment in which everything fell away, all the weight he carried on his broad shoulders. Brian felt Max's arms come around him in a deep embrace, felt the hard bulging of Max's thick biceps, pulling him down onto Max's chest as Max whimpered, not in pain but rather with the monumental release of a pain long held onto being let go and set free, unchained.

For Max, this moment, this exploration of his feelings, of his heart, felt like aloe on a sunburn: it stung but in the best ways, like a cooling balm.

Brian felt Max's right arm come free and felt his hand hunting and Brian raised his hips, allowing Max to work his hand under him and then gasped as Max gripped his cock, squeezing it firmly, working his hand up and down, with Max using his own pre-cum as a lubricant to stroke Brian. He felt rocking sensations travel into his groin and up his stomach, causing his muscles to contract repeatedly, each wave making him groan.

Brian growled in approval, not needing words any longer, the sound vibrating the air between them, kissing Max's neck, and soon found the urge to bite him there unbearable and so he did, roughly but not hard enough to break the skin. Max bucked and held Brian tighter, growling with pleasure, nuzzling the side of Brian's face, drinking in Brian's scent, the scent of fresh earth and grass, the scent of hot searing sun-kissed life itself.

They each moved in concert with the other, motion and meaning, emotion and instinct blurring into lines that were crossed and new emotions, new feelings exploded into supernovas. As new galaxies were born, both of them felt the surge in their drive increase into a percussive beating of their hearts into a single driven rhythm until finally there was no longer one or the other but rather at last, they were together. A bond formed in those moments. Walls fell. Barriers crashed down and a few moments later, as they climbed the peak of their mountain, both of them removed the last locked doors keeping the other out.

Brian felt Max throb in his mouth and felt Max's grip on his shoulders tighten significantly until it was almost painful. He felt and saw Max's thick powerful leg muscles go hard as stone and there it was; with a deep throaty growl, Max released, unable to hold himself back any longer. Brian immediately felt the salty yet smooth warmth flood his mouth in gush after gush, expertly swallowing it down as it came before Max was finally spent but Max was not finished with Brian yet.

"Lay down...I want you." Max grunted softly in Brian's ear, flipping him around and pushing Brian down onto the bed onto his back, moving up and around to straddle him. Brian did as he was told as Max placed his cock and Brian's together, in his gray furred hand and began to ride, moving, grinding up and down, sliding the moist hard flesh between his fingers, lingering over their mushroom heads, the sensation at once almost too much and leaving Brian craving more. Brian loved the heaviness of Max's weight, the solidity.

In a few moments, Brian felt the pressure that was building in his groin hit a peak and he looked up at Max, meeting his blue eyes, knowing his ability to restrain himself was quickly abating.

"Max..."

"I know..."

Max moved down and placed Brian in his mouth.

A second later, the world exploded as Brian bucked on the bed, his legs going rigid as if he had been hit with an electric shock but the most pleasurable electric shock he had ever known. The waves came, cascading over him in hot rounds, running from his balls to his forehead, the fur on the back of his neck standing up as he clenched the sheets in on hand and with a hearty deep growl of his own, he finally climaxed. He felt the ropes of hot liquid blast out of him at least six times, each shot sending a new wave of contractions through Brian's sweat soaked body. Max took it all and finally, when it was done, collapsed next to him on the bed, laying on his back, panting.

Both them were exhausted as the sun set outside, and for a time, Brian was unable to move and didn't try. When he did move, he turned his head to see Max was lying with his eyes open, staring at the ceiling, an odd expression on his face.

"Are you...are you ok?" he asked him.

Max nodded and grinned. "Yeah...that was.... unexpected.... that's all."

Brian nodded and blinked.

"Was it bad?"

Max shook his head. "No...not at all. I'm glad. I can't describe what I feel right now...I want to...but I can't."

Brian nodded understanding fully, a warm happiness blooming in his chest.

"Me too...."

After a few minutes had passed, Brian got up and grabbed a towel from the bathroom cabinet and came back. He cleaned off as best as he could and Max didn't resist when Brian did the same to him, running a towel under his balls and around the base of his penis. Instead he actually laughed a bit. The same small chuckle.

"That tickled."

"Sorry." Brian said, grinning and then frowning a bit.

"Hey, I just noticed...your eyes are glowing yellow. You ok?" he asked as Max looked up at him from the bed. Brian tossed the towel on the floor as Max nodded.

"Yeah. Sometimes, after a really intense emotional experience, our eyes will do that, have a little night-shine to them even during the day." Max chuckled. "Yours are glowing to. Really bright green."

"Oh hell," Brian chuckled back. "I guess that makes the walk of shame harder, huh?" he asked a little sheepishly.

Max nodded his head and grinned. "Yup. Come lay down."

With the world outside and Rakinos forgotten for a while, as the sun finally slipped below the horizon, Brian lay next to Max on the bed, both of them stripped bare, Max laying on his side, facing Brian, looking thoughtful and far away. Brian noticed and looked up at him, his green eyes gleaming in the soft light.

"What's on your mind, Max?"

Max shrugged and after a moment, found the words. "What now? Where do we go from here? I don't know the first step to take."

Brian considered and cocked his head. The effect was like a confused dog.

"You mean with the Raven situation with Rakinos and the drug?"

Max shook his head. "No... I mean...we'll get to that but...I meant....

what about you and me...where does this go?"

Brian turned over and faced Max, lying on his side with barely an inch between them, their fur lifting with the breath of the other. Reaching up, Brian stroked Max's cheek, before cupping his chin in his hand, the short claws on the end of his fingers scratching slightly into Max's fur there.

Max growled with pleasure and Brian thought that had caught Max by surprise that Max had liked that. Brian filed that away for future reference.

"Where do you want it go? I want it be more. Now that we've said it and we both felt it, we can't go back to how things were."

Max nodded and grabbed Brian's hand.

"I don't want to go back. I want to be with you. That's all I know right now. It feels right...it feels good." He said gently, smiling.

"Then we take it a step at time. One day. One step. I want to be here with you the whole way. All of it." Brian said, realizing as he said it the words were true. His old life was gone and there, in that quiet night with Max lying next to him, he didn't care if it was. He felt content on a level he couldn't explain. Max was the one thing he was sure of in all the chaos. He had been sure of it for longer than he had let himself feel.

Max only nodded and closed his eyes, exhaustion quickly taking him. In a few moments, he was snoring softly as he leaned against Brian's shoulder. Smiling, Brian turned around gently and backed up to Max, spooning gently as the moon rose. Brian felt a movement and a moment later, Max's arm was draped over him and had pulled him closer.

Brian himself wasn't long for the world and after a few moments, he too, slowly drifted into a sleep that was like slipping into a warm bath and outside, the world continued on. For him and for Max, for this moment, there was no more Rakinos. No more druggies. No more stress.

Just peace.

CHAPTER 5

The sun fell through the big windows in gentle rays, falling upon the bed, the intense afternoon heat from the light tempered by the polarized glass. It fell upon Brian's sleeping form, covering his shoulders, neck and the back of his head like the luminous touch of an invisible seraphim: warm and energetic. The light beams formed a spotlight as dust motes swam in them like plankton, warming his bare back, heating up the carbon black fur there, making his skin tingle as he began to stir slowly stretching. His ankles popped gloriously and he went from a partial stretch into a full-on lazy cat stretch, arms reaching up, fingers splayed, toes wide, his claws popping out just slightly, eyes tightly closed, tail stiff for a moment.

The stretch over, he collapsed back into himself and his hands fell onto the empty side of the bed.

His fingers and then his hands moved, seeking and finding nothing but warm sheets and blank space.

With a grunt, he slowly opened his sleepy eyes, the light dancing in his green irises. Washing away the sleep with a few blinks, Brian looked at where Max had been most of the night.

He was gone.

No... he thought, panic beginning to rise and disappointment along with it.

For a moment, he felt his heart speed up and he fully woke up, his brain finally engaging on all gears and he settled down just as fast. He could hear Max moving around and with a sniff of the air, found that Max was indeed in the house and that Max wasn't the only thing he smelled.

A warm relief flooded through him, warmer than the sun.

He smelled crispy greasy meats, spiced with pepper and warm seasonings. He could practically taste it dancing on the air in tiny excited bubbles. He felt his ears perk up towards where he knew the kitchen was and instantly the sound of cooking hit him. The sizzling of bacon and sausage, ham and the buttery cheesy scent of eggs; the gentle but flurried scraping of a spatula and the hiss of a gas-powered stove were like music moving in a symphony he hadn't heard in a very long time. It was a music that tugged at him behind his breast bone and a moment later, he felt and heard his stomach rumble madly.

Shortly after the relief hit him, he slid his eyes towards the foot of the bed and into the open kitchen.

Max was in there, shirtless, barefoot and in his plaid pajama bottoms, hustling around, stirring and whisking madly, trying his obvious best to be quiet and efficient at the same time and failing miserably. His ears were laid back against his head but Brian could tell it was in concentration, as if he hadn't cooked in a long time. Based on the way his thick dark eyebrows were furrowed and his tongue was sticking out of the side of his muzzle, just a little bit, that was very likely the case, Brian thought, a tiny smile tugging at his face.

As Brian watched him, he felt a pang of guilt for assuming that Max had ran away, wondering if that made him instead of Max the one who had something to be ashamed of. Shaking his head, he felt a yawn come and tried to stifle it, wanting to simply watch Max in this moment he was having without walls, or barriers, when he thought no one was watching, to see the real man behind the pain, the real wolf behind the scars.

Max turned to get something off of the bar behind him and had to whirl back around as a bit of black smoke began to pour up from an unseen pan and he cursed under his breath, nearly sliding on the hardwood floor.

The yawn was back and this time he couldn't swallow it down or hold it in and he let it out, his long jaws opening wide, his lips pulling back involuntarily exposing his long fangs and sharp teeth. The yawn passed and Brian closed his mouth, smacking his lips together carefully. His mouth felt dry as bone.

At the sound, Max's ears perked up and he looked over at the bedroom area.

"Oh! Jesus! Um. Hi. You're awake." He stammered as he was forced to quickly return his attention to his cooking.

"Well hey there..." Brian said, sitting up in the bed, running a hand through the fur on his head. It didn't help. It was currently sticking up like a goddamn cowlick, he thought and grimaced. Sliding his feet out of the bed, he stood, naked in the sun, drinking in its warmth, stretching his back one final time, his tail wagging on its own as it seemed to wake up. He saw Max sneak a glance out of the corner of his eye and so, he lingered a bit, taking his time.

After a moment he felt foolish and quickly bent over, rooting around in the discarded clothes for something to wear. He found his trunks and quickly pulled them on, working his tail through the loop in the back, the fabric snugly hugging his body, holding everything in place. Crossing the room, Brian dug around in his duffle bag and found a clean shirt, a navy blue one and hastily pulled on. He frowned as he realized it barely came to his belly button anymore. Sighing, he knew at some point he would have to go out and shop for clothes but now was not the time. *Procrastinator*, he chided himself.

Pulling his shirt down as far as he could, Brian moved into the kitchen and bar area, his thickly padded feet moving almost silently on the warm wood floor. He enjoyed the smooth gel like feeling the polish on the floor boards transferred to the pads on the bottom of his toes. It felt like the world's smallest air conditioner.

Sauntering his way sleepily around the bar, Brian stepped into the kitchen and for the first time saw that wasn't as big as he has previously thought. It was formed out of a rough oblong rectangle with a small set of counters and the sink connected by a curve into the stove, dishwasher and trash compactor. Over head the glass cabinets he noticed weren't as new as the rest of the kitchen and were in fact hand restored. The lights hanging from the ceiling Brian realized were actually bulbs inside of a set old Mason jars.

It gave the whole kitchen a strange feeling, mixed between the modern appliances, the older countertops and the home-made light shades. It spoke volumes about the owner of the home, he thought, watching Max's powerful back as he moved quickly to finish the food. Apparently, Max was more creative and handier than he let on and it wasn't just with cars. Brian smiled. The man was a walking mess of contradictions and it made him appealing in a way Brian couldn't quite describe.

"How long have you been up?" Brian asked sleepily as he came up beside Max, the scent of peppered sausage and smoky bacon, even burned a bit, making his stomach curl in expectation.

Totally focused on his work, Max glanced up at Brian with one blue eye quickly.

"A bit. Few hours really. I didn't sleep well but I rarely do. Got up, showered and fucked around with that stupid bike downstairs. Goddamn throttle is stuck in it."

Brian nodded pretending to know what he was talking about.

"That...sounds bad."

Max glanced at him again as he killed the gas and shut off the stove. Seeing his ignorance, he actually smiled a bit.

"Think of it as the gas pedal. Part of the intake system, though it doesn't actually control the flow of fuel but air so the fuel can combust."

"So, the bike is choking essentially?" Brian attempted, moving out of the way so Max could pull the searing skillet over to the sink counter. Max nodded as he moved, his tail flicking from side to side.

"Pretty much. Damn thing is stuck at twenty miles an hour. Going to have to order a new one. The upside is this guy pays well so I don't mind too much. Go sit at the bar and I'll bring you plate."

Brian hedged. "Is there anything I can help with?"

Max smiled and shook his shaggy grey head. "Nah. Sit. I haven't done this in a while and it feels good to do it."

With a grin, Brian made his way out of the kitchen around the bar, planting his furry butt onto a bar stool, his tail dangling behind him, inches above the floor. A moment later, with a clink of porcelain and a clang of metal silverware, Max appeared in front of Brian, and plopped down twin heaping plates of scrambled eggs, bacon, seared moist ham and thick peppered sausage.

"Wow. You put in a lot of work. Damn. Thanks." Brian said, stunned by the plethora before him.

"Well," Max said, pouring them both a glass of orange juice into thick tumblers, the glass frosting over from the chill. He set the pitcher aside with a soft thunk.

"I don't normally cook like this. I've spent so long living on take-out and delivery that when I do cook it feels like a major event. I just felt the urge this morning....and you're welcome." he finished. Brian laughed and jerked his head towards the huge windows in the living room, his ears flopping gently.

"Afternoon. It's gotta be after one by this point." He said gently, his face grinning as he bit down into a sausage patty. Max nodded, acknowledging the truth with a shrug, digging into his own food.

A few minutes passed as they both ate in silence and Brian noticed that Max never looked up from his plate. Brian did think that Max had done a bang-up job as the meats were juicy with just a hint of char on them, the eggs were smooth and rich and seasoned perfectly but he couldn't shake the feeling that something was up with Max this morning. After trying to let it come on its own, Brian realized he was going to have to push to get it and how far he would have to push made him cautious as he started.

"You said you didn't sleep good last night. You looked pretty knocked out after...well...you know." He started and watched as Max stopped stuffing his face, swallowed and looked up at Brian, his blue eyes thinking. Brian could see the wheels in his mind turning with warp speed.

"For a bit I did but I had dreams. Always do. Every night. The same ones."

"Of what?" Brian asked gently, taking a swig of the orange juice. It exploded on his tongue like a citrus iceberg. It felt and tasted sweet and bubbly. He noted the lack of pulp. That was another thing he was glad to discover he and Max shared in common. He hoped there were more.

Max hesitated but he did answer, as he pushed his food around on the plate with his fork.

"Of that night. The fire. My folks. The winter wind. It's always so sharp...it sounds like screams."

Brian felt the weight in that admission and the unspoken and deep trust it had taken for it to come out in the first place. Max would have told him to piss of just two weeks ago.

"Every night they come and every night I usually end up going out. You know. Come back in the morning bloodied up and pass out. Rinse repeat. It's been all I've done for so long that when I woke up this afternoon and you were here and I was here...It was surreal." He continued thoughtfully.

"You didn't go out at all?"

"Nah... I stayed in. I blame you." He said, looking up, his blue eyes holding the hint of a smile. Something about that smile felt off and Brian tried to figure out what it was but he couldn't. Max was good at hiding his feelings when he wanted to and it was so far the only frustrating thing about him that Brian could really find.

Brian decided to not push any further for now, deciding it was best to go slowly. Max was opening up to him more than ever relatively and he didn't want him to shut down again. He deftly changed subjects.

"I didn't know you could cook. This is actually really good."

"Thanks, man. Sorry about the crispy parts." Max replied sheepishly. Brian took a huge bite out of a seared ham slice, his sharp teeth shredding it into ribbons. He chewed loudly on purpose and swallowed with gusto, showing his genuine appreciation.

"Not a problem. I like it like that. Grilling out is one of my favorite things to do."

"Raven and the others usually do a cookout at Forest Glen on July fourth. Sometimes I go. Maybe we could go in a few weeks." Max suggested, his voice quietly hopeful.

"I'd like that." Brian replied, for some reason imagining the extremely awkward and clumsy Jackson on the grill, fighting like mad to keep it from exploding and feeling that he had made the right decision not to dig deeper. "I also noticed," he added, finishing off his eggs, "That you restored those cabinets and those lamp shades look handmade. Your work, too?"

Max actually coughed for a moment and cleared his throat, swallowing nearly half the tumbler of juice in the process. He was embarrassed and it struck Brian as cute.

"Well, yeah. I sort of had to. This place wasn't exactly the best. I fixed it up. Most of what you see I did over time. Smashed my goddamn fingers more than I can count." He told Brian, finishing off the rest of his bacon with a few light snaps.

"You seem embarrassed about it."

"No one's ever noticed."

"Hey, you have a talent. You should be proud of it. I hate when people read my writing even though I have to let them read it otherwise it would never be finished. I think we tend to be our own worst critics." Brian told him cleaning his plate like a pro.

"I don't read much but I wouldn't mind reading some of your stuff sometime...if it's okay." Max said sheepishly. Brian chuckled, his face burning hot.

"Um, sure. I'm not responsible for your eyeballs bleeding but sure."

Max gave a small huff of humor. Brian wondered if he would ever actually laugh and made it a point to remember it when it finally did happen. The chuckles so far and little ones were big steps for Max it seemed.

"I do have two questions for you though," Max began pushing his plate away, looking over at Brian at his side.

"Shoot."

"One: Did you bite me the other night?"

Brian started to ask if he meant what he thought he meant and Max gently cut him off.

"Not during sex. When you had me in the tub and I was a bloody mess." Max corrected him.

Brain felt his ears flatten and a hot wave of guilt rushed over him.

"Yeah. I didn't know what else to try and it worked on me when you did it. I didn't know if it would have worked on you in reverse because. You started healing super quickly. Even some of your older scars went away by the time I had tucked you in. I really don't know why I did it; something just told me it was the right thing to do. Is that normal?"

Max nodded thoughtfully. "Nah, it's not. There should have been no effect at all. Raven's going to love that little nugget. Thanks, though. I mean it."

Brian scowled though not at Max. "She and I need to have a talk about some things before she gets anything else from me."

Sighing, Max agreed. "Yeah. I guess she does. For what it's worth, I'm sorry I didn't tell you. I should have. It was about things that affected you. I'm not used to not being alone...you know...having someone there. I'll try to be better at that in the future. "

Brian's scowl softened and his reply was hopeful without meaning to sound it as he grinned gently.

"Future? You sound like you see something..."

Max looked over at him with a halfhearted glare but it wasn't malice but instead warm gentle humor and honesty that Brian saw in the expression.

"Don't get ahead of yourself there, pup. Maybe. Just maybe." He told Brian.

"Pup?" Brian shot back a bemused expression crossing his face at the term.

"Did I say that?" Max acted innocently as he got up and began moving his plates to the kitchen sink.

Brian followed suit. "You did."

"Hmm. Maybe I did." Max said with the tiniest of grins. He and Brian made quick work of the dishes and food mess and standing back, the counters gleaming proud of themselves, they stood side by side, arms crossed, surveying their work like master artisans.

"You know you're not that much older than I am, right?"

"I'm old enough. Second question, when are you going to call your mom?"

That one had come out of left field and Brian felt for a moment that his brain just went into the driest, tiniest, most pitiful explosion as it collapsed from the monumental fuckery of an *oh-shit moment* that just slammed into its place. He had forgotten in all the chaos entirely that he had not once called her since the night at the hospital. She never pushed him but two weeks without a call or text was odd for him. He had originally had so many questions for her especially about the family that could illuminate his present condition. He suddenly felt a twinge of guilt.

"Damn...You really think I should?" he asked Max. Max promptly goosed him with an elbow in the ribs for his question. He replied as Brian rubbed his ribs from the elbow poke.

"Yes. I do. Don't ever take your mom for granted. I know we've been busy and it's been rough but, you only have one and when she's gone... I'd kill to be able to speak to mine one more time. We can go see her if you need to. I don't mind. Might help ease her shock if you aren't alone, plus you've got some big changes to tell her about." Max finished, looking pointedly at Brian's ears tail and muzzle.

Brian sighed. Max was right of course.

"Fair enough. I'll give her a call in a bit. See what's what. We should probably keep the whole vigilante fights drug business off the table though. She's cool but I don't know how she would take that." Brian said, moving into the living room. He began rifling through his duffle bag for fresh clothes and finding some of Max's loaned ones that fit better, he tugged them out and headed towards the bathroom.

"Hey, you cleaned up the blood!" Brian called from the bathroom, his voice hampered by the walls.

"That's one thing I'm good at."

Brian's whispered comment rode the air like sprites. "Among many others."

"What?" Max called back as he headed towards the couch, his stomach pleasantly full and feeling relatively relaxed for a change.

"I didn't say a word!" Brian called back suddenly loud and a few moments later, the door closed and Max heard the rushing of water.

Settling back onto the couch, Max looked around at the apartment and saw how messy it was and decided he didn't care. The sun felt great on his gray fur, and with good food and he had to admit, good company, life wasn't bad today. It was different, that was for sure. He wasn't used to being around others as much especially around someone with whom a connection had formed like the one he and Brian seemed to share. Whether or not that was due to some kind of weird genetic intermingling due to him turning Brian in the first place or something more, Max didn't know, but he suspected it was something more and not the former. Whatever it was, he secretly admitted to himself that he was thoroughly enjoying it, exploring all of its corners.

Normally by this point, he was still asleep (given the dreams, if he could even call it sleep), bloodied from fights on the street, smelling like gunpowder and normally several new smashed up bullets had been pulled out and filled the ashtray on the coffee table. Looking at the ashtray on the coffee table, he studied the rounds in it. Each one was a melted bent slug stained maroon. There were different calibers, mostly handgun size rounds. Each one had been a blistering, white-hot shock of molten agony and each one, he thought, he deserved for letting his family die or rather, not dying with them that cold winter night. Each one was a round taken trying to protect someone with his own life, to make up for failing.

Considering the bullets made him consider the truth of the thought he just had, and he toyed with the idea that maybe he was wrong about that last part. That perhaps there was nothing he could have done back then, but he refused to let it continue. That was unknown territory and any unknown territory made him edgy. Being around Brian the last two weeks had upset and upended his entire life, but in strangely positive ways he couldn't have ever imagined. The night before was the first time he had hit the streets in that time span.

He had spent most of the time in that span of two weeks away from Brian at home or in the garage and had found his mind was occupied by a singular loop of thought that simply would not go away and it wore Brian's face like a mask. Any time he was around Brian at the manor or just hanging out was what he started looking forward to, and he found that he started missing that time early on.

And so, he had tried to suppress it, ignore it, shut it down but it came back late at night before the dreams hit, and finally, that argument with Brian last night had brought it out and once he had said it, he realized he could not "un-say" it. Did he really want to unsay it? What was so bad about this afternoon, about last night, at having a life for a moment, at the prospect of a future? What was so bad about that?

Still, something felt wrong and he couldn't pin it down and instead kept coming back to the thought he had before. He was blaming himself for not dying with his family that night and with an internal shock, he realized that thought was a new one. Any time he had allowed himself to think about the past, any time he had been drunk off his ass at the bar, being beat up by a thug or even the rare times he had held a gun in his hands, looking down the barrel's black enticing eye, wondering if he would be better off fixing that situation permanently, smelling the gun oil as he pointed it at his own head, it was in those moments, he always blamed himself for not saving them but now...that new perspective had caused him considerable pause.

Was he really blaming himself for being alive? Survivor's guilt? He frowned as he absently scratched his stomach fur, not even aware his hand was doing it.

Is that why this situation with Brian felt strange? He thought probably, yes. One on hand, if he was honest with himself, in the quiet of his mind where no one could hear, he desperately wanted things to work between himself and Brian. There had been something about the kid (*I shouldn't call him that. He's not a kid*, he chided himself) that had been different from the start and ever since that first meeting, their lives had been intertwined so intimately that not having him around felt strange. To lose him would be a wound that he didn't think would stop bleeding and the idea scared him.

On the other hand, the oldest part of his psyche was railing against the idea, the survivor part of himself, the part that was raw and angry, that hurt and told him that he didn't deserve to be happy, didn't deserve anything but the nightly penance he paid for his crime, his sin of being a survivor, that it would only end badly, that he was a cancer to those around him. The internal pull between the two thoughts was what drove him daily, allowed him to make the hard decisions he needed to, gave him the strength of will he needed out on the streets. *What would I be without that? What would peace bring?* Max thought and that scared him too, and the hand on his stomach had stopped scratching and had simply stopped moving, buried in the thick fur on the ridges of his stomach.

He had gotten up this morning in part because of the dreams but also because he felt restless in a way he couldn't identity. Waking up next to Brian had been wonderful and terrifying at the same time. Here he was, being given what a part of him had always wanted and balking at it. It made no sense at all and Max knew it perfectly well but he was unable to change the way he felt regardless. Not all of the scars he carried were physical and some of them ran very deep. Could he stand himself for dragging Brian into his world and chaining him down to the wreck that was himself? Was that fair?

Over the past two decades, Max had never once been given the true prospect of healing and having a real life, and now it was on his doorstep, being handed to him. All he had to do was reach out and take it and bring it into himself and for some reason, that idea made him tremble because suddenly the future was not the routine he was used to but totally unexplored territory with so many potential pitfalls.

He genuinely enjoyed making breakfast for them this morning (*afternoon* he corrected). It was a real moment, and it felt great, like an ointment on a burn. But was that balm addictive like a drug? If it was, was that a bad thing? Was that drug just covering up the underlying problem or was it really changing it?

The banter with Brian felt natural. It felt good. The apartment seemed to be more alive when he was here, the ghosts were quiet.

Sighing, Max flicked his tail hard, unaware that he was doing it and decided that for now, he would do what Brian said. Take it slowly. Try to see where this new path might lead, to see if any of the scars started to fade and if any of the wounds would try to close. For now, he would take the drug. It felt good. It felt real and he needed real and wanted real and the idea that he was locking Brian down with him and all of his demons was momentarily quieted as Brian himself came out of the bathroom, dressed in that long sleeve button down brown shirt, the sleeves pushed up to his elbows, a clean white shirt underneath and jeans that fit reasonably well. The smell of deodorant and soap washed over the room and Brian's carbon black fur gleamed in the light and the cowlick on his head was gone, his green eyes shining.

Max felt something in his stomach wiggle like a fish and a warm flame bloomed in his chest.

Brian came over and plopped down next to Max after digging his phone out of his bag.

"You okay? You look about a million miles away." Brian told him, adjusting himself, pulling at the scrunched jeans fabric. Max shrugged, his blue eyes moist a bit as he blinked them back to normal.

"Yeah, I'm good. Just thinking I guess. Gonna call your mom?" he replied.

"I reckon. I can't keep putting it off." Brian sighed, turning his phone on and pulling up the dialer.

Max nodded. "I guess I'll give you some privacy. Need to head down and work on that bike anyway. Lemme know when you want to head her way. Carsonville isn't far. You good?"

Brian nodded.

"Cool then. Holler at me when you're done." Max said, slapping a heavy powerful but gentle palm on Brian's thigh, reassuring him, standing to his feet.

Brian watched him leave and frowned. Something about Max felt off, like he was wounded in a way that couldn't be seen and he was fighting with something. Brian knew that he had an astounding amount of emotional trauma and he wondered briefly if it was wise to pursue this course with him, not because he was afraid of trauma but because he was afraid, in part, that when time came, Max wouldn't let him in enough to help carry it.

Brian did feel a tiny leap like a minnow in his chest as he watched Max's behind move in the loose pajama bottoms and felt his eyes travel up his broad back and smiled mischievously.

Shaking his head, he forced himself to focus, to actually dial the numbers and call his mom. Mentally he was doing hoops preparing himself, psyching himself up as he brought the phone to his ears and the distinct electric chime of a ringing line flooded his senses. There were a million questions, a million ways the call could go. He could spill his guts or freeze up entirely. The minnow turned into butterflies and for a good six seconds, the longest six seconds of Brian's life, he felt like the phone would ring forever until finally, with a click, the line went live and for the first time in two weeks, he heard his mom's gentle light voice.

"Hello?"

For that small eternity, Brian felt his throat lock up and then when it finally let go, he hoped his voice hadn't changed much as his heart began to patter harder and the blood began to rush in his ears.

"Hi, mom...its me."

There was a moment of surprise in her voice that made Brian wince guiltily. He swallowed it down and tried to pretend nothing was wrong.

"Brian? Well hey honey. It's been a bit." She said happily.

"Yeah. I'm sorry about that. Lot of crazy stuff's been going on and I've been so caught up lately I've..." he stopped as he found his mind wasn't providing him auto-words anymore. The truth instead dangled temptingly in front of him, all of it and it caused him to pause, his jaws locked, tongue refusing to make words. This seemed to go on for an hour but in reality, it was merely a second, maybe two.

"Brian?"

"Sorry. I've lost touch with what's important these last few weeks. What's going on up on your end?" Brian shuffled, switching the subject quickly before it could begin again. Why was he so nervous? He grew angry at himself and felt guilt sink in a bit deeper, like a twenty-ton weight tossed into a mud pit. Every second it sunk inexorably deeper. His mom, to her credit, didn't give him hell, didn't fuss at him. She never did. She always tried to understand, even when she couldn't.

"Oh, not much, hun. Works been a little crazy. Crazy tickets, you know. Had a few bans I needed to lay but nothing too out of the ordinary. A few item dupers and speed hackers."

He smiled. His mother was one of the only fifty-six-year-old game masters he knew of. She got to work from home and that made it easier on her since in later years she had gotten a bit more nervous about driving, and she would never explain why exactly. She worked for Blizzard, the company behind the massively popular games like *World of Warcraft* and *Overwatch*. Her job specifically was to handle incoming tickets from players, handle any disputes and track down cheaters. She was surprisingly technically savvy and in some ways, she excelled Brian in that regard. It made it easy for them to communicate most of the time since they spoke the same generational language.

She did have a game account of her own that was for personal use and played often with a few friends from all over the country in her own guild. Brian used to be a part of that guild before his bigger computer crashed. It now sat in a heap in the back of his closet at his apartment, buried under god knows what. Her position as a work at home moderator was one of a few thousand across the country with Blizzard attempting a new hiring and work model. She was lucky and found the opening a few years ago and took it. So far, it had been a godsend for her, both for income and keeping her occupied since Brian himself was no longer living close-by, something he did worry about from time to time.

"Those crazy hackers and bots, huh?" he said, a smile forming on his mouth and it only felt half fake.

"They never learn. They never understand that we can see them in real time. Had a really good raid the other night for our final Antorus push and we managed to get the achievement we were working on. I think we are through for now though, until

August."

That idea made Brian flinch internally. The guild kept his mom company, *(something I should be doing)* and if it was going into a quiet period, especially with all that was going on with him on his end, he worried he might be out of touch more than usual.

"What happens in August?" he asked absently, his green eyes far away from Max's living room. Downstairs, through the floorboards and masonry, he heard the distant sounds of mechanical work, the clanging of tools, the ratcheting of wrenches, the scrape of metal on concrete and occasionally, he smiled, the growled curses of a very frustrated werewolf mechanic.

"New expansion comes out. Honey you've got to get your computer fixed. You'd love this new stuff!"

Brian felt a tug behind his breastbone. He used to play all the time with his mom and her friends when he wasn't working or at the gym or off with Elijah. Hell, even he played from time to time, too. There were some fun memories they had all made and right now, the ghost of them from years past bubbled up as tiny echoes that he could almost hear. The sounds of abilities being fired off as his druid was kiting around the edge of the battlefield, casting destructive beams of white light or throwing fireballs. The cheers of the guild over voice chat as a particularly hard boss on heroic difficulty bit the dust or the crazy improv and insanity that just seemed to surface with any group of people that were highly caffeinated or in some cases, intoxicated. The ghost of laughter floated through his mind and he smiled for real this time.

"Maybe I will, but hey, um, can we talk real for a moment?"

The sudden change in tone made the air in the room feel tense even though his mom was an hour away, he could still feel the change on her end as well.

"Sure honey. What's going on? Is everything okay?"

Brian hesitated. *What do I tell her? Or rather, how much*, he corrected himself. He decided he would give her a fraction of the truth now and when they inevitably met in person, he would have no choice but to give her everything.

"Well," he said swallowing, looking out the afternoon window. His phone buzzed and he pulled the handset away from his face and looked at the display.

Raven. She was calling him and for a moment that puzzled him. Then he realized why. *Max wasn't answering her calls either, he realized.* He confirmed this a moment later when he looked over onto the coffee table and saw Max's phone in its orange and black case with four missed calls lighting up the screen. Max had turned his phone on silent.

With a frown and at the moment, regretting giving Raven his number, he stabbed the REJECT button and went back to his mom.

"Sorry. Telemarketer tried to call. I was saying that some stuff has happened to me lately and it's some pretty major stuff. I had to take some time off work. I don't know if I can tell it to you over the phone because," he paused and looked at his paw-like feet, his claws, and ran his tongue over his large fangs. "Because it's a lot."

"Well why don't you come down and see me. Stay the night. Tell me in person. I was off yesterday and today so there's nothing really going on especially since the raid nights are shutting down for a while."

Her idea, as usual, leaped past his defenses and stabbed right at where he was the weakest and most afraid: The concept of him seeing his own mother in person and looking nothing like the son she knew. *How did moms do that?* He wondered.

"Well...um..."

She interrupted him gently. "Brian, I know in the last few years, we've gotten on better since you were a kid...since your dad passed. We've reconnected like we used to and I'm sorry that it ever happened any other way. I love you son, so much. You have always been able to tell me anything, and if that means coming home and doing it in person or a thousand miles away on the phone in the middle of Egypt, you do it. I'm right here, baby. Always have been. It's up to you but I'm here and honestly, I'd love to see you hun."

Brian felt something rise up in his throat and it suddenly made his throat and jaws hurt. For some reason, the corners of his eyes were blurry and for few seconds, he sat there, those words stung the old wounds.

"Yeah I know..."

"So, come on down. Stay with me for a night. We've not done that since you moved away after college. I'll make us your favorite."

His stomach betrayed him and that surprised him as he smiled and laughed a little, a genuine laugh.

"Orzo spaghetti lasagna? God I've not made that in so long..." he said.

His mom laughed. "You and your dad's favorite. Just one of my amazing creations." She put on fake haughty air and it was, for a moment, like no time had passed between them at all and that bothered Brian. It made him realize just how much time was passing and that it slowed for no one. *Well....that wasn't true anymore*, he thought. It would pass for his mother but not himself any longer.

He shook his head and decided for the better for a change.

"I think I will do that. Would it be good if I brought someone along? He's..." Brian hesitated.

"He's a good friend. Helped me out with all this that's going on and he's a good guy." He finished.

"Sure hon. That stuff always makes for plenty. Any friend of yours is a friend of mine. You always had good taste in friends anyway. You have a knack for getting people."

"Ok um, how does in the next few hours sound? Have to see if he's free since he's a mechanic and he's got a customer's ticket at the moment."

"That sounds fine, Bri. That gives me time to thaw the meat out and get prepared and get things straightened up around here."

"Awesome but don't over-do it…I mean…it's just me. No need to go all out, I'm just coming home. Nothing special." He said gently.

He could hear the love in his mother's voice as she said her next words and it once again had that same aloe on sunburn feel.

"No, Brian. You're my son and you're coming home to visit me and that is something always special. Gimme a yell once you're on the road. I love you, Brian."

They said their goodbyes and as Brian clicked the phone off, he sat on the couch, feeling dazed and emotionally exhausted. He hadn't told her any of the important details and he felt like he should have, cursing himself for it. What good was it going to do to show up and just give his mom a heart attack at the sight of him.

Running his hands down his face in irritation, he stood up and paced the room, nerves jangling, surprised at the butterflies in his stomach. Not only had he told her nothing, not only had he agreed to go and see her tonight, but he asked her if he could bring Max, Max Mullen, with him.

In his head the interaction played out:

"Hi mom, this is Max. He's a mechanic werewolf who bit me to save my life and turned me into a werewolf. Oh, and he's a vigilante…."

"Goddamn I'm an idiot…." He said in hushed tones to himself with a groan.

"What could have I have told her? I mean, "Oh hey mom, by the way, I've got ears, a tail, big teeth and I'm covered in fur now. I might even be able to roll over and play dead on command, who knows! Oh, and the guy I may or may not be dating is a vigilante who breaks people in two for therapy." he said to himself.

"Fuck!" he snapped at himself, at the air. He felt like a goddamned idiot for not just being able to say it. Absently he circled the coffee table three times, having no clue he had done it.

"Hey, everything okay?"

Brian turned to see Max, still in his pajama bottoms, with large grease streaks across his chest and belly, wiping his oil and grease covered hands with a rough cloth. His broad body took up a good section of the hallway and he stood there, with his head cocked to the side just in the slightest.

Sighing, Brian told him.

"Talked to my mom."

Max winced. "Didn't go well?"

"Well, not exactly." Brian replied, walking over to him. "I told her a lot of shit has happened and she asked me to come down and stay tonight with her and tell her in person."

"I kind of figured that might happen, but we had planned on going to Carsonville anyway to see her, so, I think I'm confused. What part went wrong?" Max replied as he moved over to the kitchen sink, bent down and dug around in the cabinet under the sink, coming up with an orange bottle of soap. He shot a few bits of it into his furry palms and the scent of orange citrus and rock wafted into Brian's nose. Using his marginally cleaner wrist, Max flipped on the water and began scrubbing his hands and wrists, using his claws to get deep into his undercoat.

"I didn't tell her that I'm a six foot plus bipedal walking wolf man complete with ears, fangs and a tail."

Max's eyebrows rose and his blue eyes widened even as he had a sardonic grin try to show up on his muzzle.

"Ah. I think I see your problem."

"Exactly and there's more. I told her about you," Brian added, plopping down onto a stool at the bar. Max's eyebrows went up at that and Brian quickly added to his statement.

"I didn't tell her about us...as in us us.... I told her you were a good friend and helped me a lot through all this. Asked if you could come and she said sure. So now she's expecting us both to show in a few hours and tonight we're having orzo spaghetti lasagna like nothing is out of the ordinary. Jesus H. Christ...." Brain said, flopping his head down hard to rest on his crossed forearms on the bar, a tiny groan of frustration coming out from him, his tail lashing behind him and his ears pinned flatter than a pancake onto his skull.

Brian peeked out over his arms and to his right when he felt a heavy strong but gentle hand fall upon his shoulder. Looking up, he saw Max standing there, looking down at him with his ice blue eyes and a kind but rueful smirk on his face.

"So, you mean to tell me the idea of confronting your mother with the truth scares you and stresses you out more than facing a whole warehouse full of thugs to save my sorry ass?"

Brian growled at him, but only half-heartedly. "I don't think it compares. I'll take the thugs."

"Seriously," Max said, giving his shoulder a squeeze. "It'll be okay. I'll get cleaned up and we can head that way. The bike is in worse shape than I thought anyway. Be good to get out of the house. We got this, pup."

"There's that nickname again." Brian said muffled from his arms.

"Get used to it. It's better than what I originally wanted to call you two weeks ago."

As Max made off towards the bathroom to get cleaned up, Brian raised his head, suddenly intrigued and confused. Looking at the bathroom door, he called over.

"You had a nickname for me two weeks ago?"

There was a small chuckle from the bathroom, that same quiet sound.

"Yeah," Max called back loudly.

"Well don't keep me waiting. What was it?"

A moment of silence and then Max's voice echoed across the living room.

"Asshole."

That made Brian smile and he chuckled to himself, his worries momentarily forgotten.

"HEY! Fuck you!" he called back good naturedly with a laugh of his own and he heard a sound that he hadn't heard from Max before but it was so muffled through the bathroom door so that Brian couldn't be sure he had heard it.

To him, it sounded like a laugh.

#####

Carsonville itself was a place that would have vanished onto the map of the United States. It wasn't a small town nor was it a large city. Composed of about 56,000 people as of the 2010 census, give or take a few hundred, its claims to fame were the Carson Chemical Plant and the Komtar Paper Mill; the latter, the chemical plant, was a major competitor to Eastman Chemical located hundreds of miles away in Tennessee. It provided the city with its more urbane aspects while at the same time, it kept the town in a sort of stasis. Its jobs had provided at least two generations of families work and it had in fact made a few major contributions to medical plastics and prosthetics. Nearly the entire town revolved around the chemical plant.

The crime rate in the city was fairly high, consisting mostly of the usual vices that medium sized cities possessed in the usual high rates: meth, pills and of course, Jesus. The usual drugs of the people.

The Atorak River cut the city in two, with the chemical plant located on the far end of Long Island, a thin narrow strip of land that split the river, and the city on the opposite banks. In addition to being home to the chemical plant, Long Island was also home to a public park and a memorial to the fallen Wampanoag people, who had stood strong in the face of the invading forces of Captain James T. Wilson. In 1834, he led a bloody assault on Long Island, driving the native people off the island itself, which they considered sacred.

A large swinging bridge painted dull green connected the Long Island Park to the parking lot on the other side, but the park itself was usually empty; mostly because the crime rates there were higher than normal compared to the rest of the city. Locals said it was the curse of Chief Namumpum, who died cursing the armies of Captain Wilson, stating that the white man will never have peace on that land. Others, more pragmatic, simply knew it was the curse of humanity and the crush of urban life.

From the air, Carsonville's downtown was laid out into a neat grid with a northern section that turned into a spiral resembling an amphitheater. It was in this amphitheater that the local library, board of education and other public works were located. From there, the urban sprawl gradually thinned out as you left downtown behind and moved out into the suburbs and finally, the more open areas with distance between houses gradually becoming measured in miles instead of feet. With two high schools that both had competing forensics drama teams, a Catholic private school and twin medical campuses that rivaled Wade Johnson Memorial back in Dawson City, Carsonville was more like a small city trying desperately to be a big city but never quite reaching its potential.

Max's black well-tuned Ford quietly roared down the highway towards Carsonville, the tires bumping occasionally over the pot holes in the road. The drive itself didn't bother him, he thought, as he kept his eyes on the road, enjoying the thrum of his engine, the rush of acceleration as they rounded curves, the slight loss of gravity as they crested hills and came down. The drive was maybe an hour, hour and a half south of Dawson City, the opposite direction from Forest Glen. It wasn't a trip Max made often; in fact, he thought, he had never actually been to Carsonville, only knowing it by association.

He and Brian had left not long after he had showered and made himself presentable. The grease in his fur had given him a harder time than usual, but maybe,

Anthony Milhorn

he thought, it was because was trying to hurry. He had scrubbed himself so hard he felt like his skin was raw but he felt clean. Max thought he should do his best to look casual and as comfortably as possible: a pair of loose cotton Under Armor warm up pants and a blue t-shirt that shockingly had sleeves. The clothes weren't snug on him and in fact were looser than most of what he owned, hiding some of his large physique, which he thought was wise. *Make good first impressions and all*, he had thought. He didn't want to be intimidating. He had changed out his boots for his only other pair of shoes, a pair of high-top black sneakers.

Brian wore what he had on when they had left.

"So which exit are we getting off on?" Max asked taking a curve carefully as a semi-truck plastered with a Barke Trucking logo on it pulled up alongside of them, swelling in the mirror and then looming larger than life out of the window before passing them, rattling their truck slightly.

Brian looked over at him and then out of the windshield. A bright green road side sign flashed by showing the upcoming exits and towns.

"Oh. Exit 4."

Nodding, Max nudged the accelerator a bit more as the sun moved across the sky, sinking closer towards the edge of the horizon. It wasn't dark at all yet, but instead, the world was in that warm golden stage of the late afternoon that lit the everything with a soft orange red glow like the sun had been dimmed ever so slightly.

Max looked over at Brian in the silence and found his gaze distracted. He found his eyes tracing the contours of Brian's thick neck, the rise and fall of his furry chest with the little bit of his silver blaze that stuck out over his collar and went up the front of his neck, and most of all, his eyes that seemed to be far from the cabin of the truck.

"What's on your mind?"

"You keep asking that." Brian said, half-jokingly.

" And I'll keep asking until you tell me." Max told him bluntly but not unkindly.

"I'm just thinking about what's about to happen. She's my mom, Max and I'm not sure I'm the son she remembers anymore. I'm not sure I am who I remember anymore."

"Why do you say that?"

Brian raised an eyebrow at him like it was the most obvious answer in the world.

"I feel different lately. I feel like I'm getting close to remembering my-

132

self but at the same time the face in the mirror doesn't look like what my brain says it should. But it's not just the physical side, Max. Look at what I did in that ware-house...that's not me. That was something else, almost like it was someone else. I still don't remember much from that." Brian sighed.

Max looked back to the road and then back to Brian.

"You saved my life, doesn't matter how. They were thugs...and hon-estly," Max said, his muzzle forming into a grin.

"You look pretty good to me."

"Thanks. That makes me feel better considering that the person you seem to have fallen for looks nothing like what...what I think, what I feel, I look like in my head." Brian glanced at his reflection in the glass. "In my head, I still see the human me."

Max swallowed and thought about that for a bit. Cars shot by outside, one of them was missing a muffler and the mechanic inside of Max cringed.

What Brian had said stuck with him in a way he didn't like. Not because it was true (*it wasn't*) but because it reminded him of something and a moment later he had what it reminded him of.

Himself.

Max shook his head and when he looked at Brian again, his blue eyes glinted in the sun.

"Brian. You're the first person to ever truly be there for me in ways that no one else has. You stuck by me and risked everything to come after me. I don't' care if you were pink with purple ears, you're special to me."

Brian smiled a bit. "Thanks, Max."

Nodding, Max turned his attention back to the road. Up ahead the exits began to tick down as they passed the signs at seventy-five miles an hour. Exit 10. Exit 8. Exit 6.

"Exit 4." Max said, mostly to himself, slowing the truck up and taking the right ramp down and off the highway, sliding the big vehicle around the bend and finally bringing it to a stop at the intersection.

"Go right." Brian told him. "Then its three miles straight through downtown and when get past the city center it's a about a mile out. I'll tell you when to turn." Brian told him.

"We could have used GPS," Max told him gently.

"Probably. Don't know why we didn't think of that." Brian remarked, feeling like an idiot.

As they drove over a bridge, Max's eyes widened at the sight of what looked like a massive city that rivaled Dawson City. Its lights sparkled as towers rose and fell in size, with so many buildings that it seemed to on to the horizon. A train or rather several of them ran through the melee followed by riverfront accesses and cars and people buzzed all over it.

"Damn, that's Carsonville?" he asked, mildly surprised.

Brian followed where he was looking and he laughed gently. "No, that's Carson Chemical Plant, CCP. It's the big job provider around here. Makes all kinds of chemicals, medical plastics and high-tech polymers, which you should begin to smell right about.... now."

Without warning the most ungodly noxious odor wafted in through the truck's vents. It smelled like a demonic mix of sulfur, urine and for some reason nail polish remover, the scent of acetone nearly making their eyes water. Max gagged and Brian coughed as they crossed the bridge and got closer to the plant.

"Fucking Christ that is.... that is something..." Max said, tears in his eyes.

"You actually get used to it but it's pretty bad tonight..." Brian admitted and he turned on the air conditioner on high to circulate the air faster. In a few moments, the smell was gone and he was thankful. It was far more overpowering this time than any other time he had ever smelt it and he wondered if it was because his enhanced sense of smell and for a moment, he felt himself actually almost retch.

"You have a strong stomach if you lived here and didn't die from that." Max said glaring sideways as they left the chemical plant behind.

Brian nodded. "There were a few times where we didn't think we'd make it because the apartment we used to live in was closer than where my mom lives now. Hell, there was explosion at the plant one year and they never told us. We lived on the other side of the island too, not more than a mile from the damn thing."

"That is some bullshit." Max decided and Brian nodded.

"So, your mom doesn't live in that apartment anymore?"

Brian shook his head. "No. After dad was killed, the insurance policy from his death set her up for life especially after some friends at the force helped her invest it in the chemical plant. She could live bigger and better but she chooses not to. We moved out about a year after he died into a small house just outside the city, thankfully, far enough away so that the chemical plant isn't that big of a deal anymore."

Outside, neon signs flashed and fast food shops littered both sides of the four lane. The city around them was alive. A billboard advertised a law firm and further down, one advertised the Niswonger Children's Memorial Theatre.

As they drew closer to the outskirts of the city, Max looked at Brian again.

"Can I ask you something?"

"Sure." Brian replied, almost absently, looking out at his old home town as it flew by just outside the glass. For some reason he felt like he was in a mobile fish tank, seeing the world go by, helpless to be a part of it, only able to be taken for the ride.

"It's about the fight at the warehouse. I don't remember much after that fuck-face cold cocked me in the back of the head. I know I went down and then you were there. I remember flashes of you. You held your own pretty good but then you got grabbed and I sort of blacked out for a few. How did you get out of that? When I came to, there were bodies everywhere."

Brian turned and shifted in his seat, the leather creaking mildly. He thought about his next words carefully because that was a question that been floating around at the back of his mind since the fight as well.

"I remember I was stupid and dropped my guard. Three of them grabbed me hard and two of them pinned my arms back and the other one had me in neck lock. I remember the other guy, the big one with the rebar was standing over you."

As he talked, Max could hear Brian's voice shake a bit, with anger and something else.

Fear.

Brian went on, his eyes back at that warehouse. "He said he was going to kill you slowly, and then come for me. Something in me...I don't what it was.... Something woke up and I don't remember much after that. It was like I was asleep or drowsy, a passenger in my own head. I have flashes of blood...but not much else until I'm there beside you, checking on you and carrying you out of there."

"Was it an adrenaline surge?" Max asked as they slowed for a red light.

"Yes and no...it was something else. I don't how to explain it. It wasn't just the adrenaline...something actually changed. I felt like someone else took over and drove the car, if you get my meaning."

Absently Max rubbed his arm where Brian had bit him and when he realized he was doing it, he stopped immediately and hoped Brian didn't notice which of course, Brian didn't.

The light turned green and in a few moments, they had left the main city behind and were on more suburban two-lane roads and traffic had thinned out considerably. Trees and green lawns had replaced concrete parking lots and business offices. Fast food was replaced by mom and pop diners.

"Have you ever heard of anything like that in a werewolf?" Brian asked.

Max told him the truth, his eyebrows furrowing a bit. "I've been in lots of fights over the years and I can honestly say I haven't but whatever it was saved my life so I'm grateful for it."

Brian nodded and looked back out through the windshield and grateful to change the subject, gave Max new directions. "Take a right up ahead on Lamont and then go straight for two intersections and then a left onto Avalon Avenue. It's the third house up on the right, with the big tree and hedge row. Gravel driveway."

Following the directions, Max quickly spotted what he thought was the house.

"That one? The beige one with the front porch?"

Brian nodded. "Yup. Home sweet home."

As they drew closer to the house, Brian felt himself grow fidgety and he noticed as they pulled into the driveway, the gravel crunching beneath the truck's large tires, that he felt nauseous. His stomach suddenly started doing flips like a god-damn circus and his skin beneath his thick fur felt cold. He noticed, that some of his fur was actually standing on end and he felt his ears move back and couldn't help it any more than he could help it as his tail started to thrash.

Through the windshield, his mom's maroon Chevy Cavalier sat, dust upon its dark paint. The color was muted next to the tall green hedge that lined the drive-way, separating the houses. The house hasn't changed much, Brian thought. It was a simple structure, with two bedrooms, one and a half bathrooms, a kitchen, dining room and a living room. It was small and small was what they needed after their family unexpectedly shrank. His old bedroom was the one that was upstairs and he wondered if his mom had finally moved into that bedroom instead of the lower one downstairs. With its dark roof and beige siding with white trim, it was the picture of small-town Americana. Its wide front porch had a wooden swing and twin rock-ing chairs. It was lined with plants and there on the concrete steps leading up to the porch was a tiny fat green frog with bulging eyes and on the other side of the step, a black stone puppy with brown cartoon eyes.

The front yard was neatly mown and kept and it was surprisingly a good size. The chain link fence and gate, Brian thought, was new. The shed and garage were separate from the house and the same old street light poked up from behind it. The backyard was closed off by a tall wooden slat fence.

Max noticed that Brian was breathing hard, bordering on panic. He reached out a hand and let it rest on Brian's thigh and gave it a gentle but tough re-assuring squeeze.

"Hey, breathe. Don't pass out on me."

It took a moment for the words to register and Brian looked up at Max and realized he was nearly hyperventilating.

"Sorry. It's odd being back here after so long. I never expected to come back here like this. It's harder than I thought. I think I'd rather jump off a few more buildings."

Max smiled. "She's your mom. Trust her to make the right call. She will. "

Brian shook his head and as Max reached for the door handle and raised it with a click, Brian stopped him.

"Dude, I'm not sure I can do this."

Max nodded and reassured him. "Let me go first. I can be charming."

Brian raised an eyebrow disbelievingly. Max frowned and then his face softened.

"What? I can. I deal with customers and crooks to get intel. I know my way around how to bullshit. Let me go up and knock and then you can come up after. Sound like a plan?"

Sighing and understanding the longer he put it off the worse it was going to feel. He could sit here until the apocalypse came but nothing was going to change the fact that he had to get up and walk up that red brick walkway to his mom's front porch and look her in the face, fur be damned.

"Alright. Let's do it."

With a *thunk* of the truck doors, both of them stepped out into the late afternoon sunshine, their fur gleaming and lifting with the soft warm afternoon breeze. Brian lingered behind the truck and let Max take the lead, slowly moving out behind him. They stood before the chain link gate and Brian expected it to squeak or protest but it didn't. It glided smoothly open upon its thick steel hinges and in a moment, they were in the yard, the ground and grass soft beneath their feet. The gate closed behind them and there before them lay the strip of rectangular red brick that led up the porch.

The path stood out so starkly in Brian's eyes that it may as well have been a spot lighted fashion show runway in his mind with imagined millions on either side, all chanting for him to take that step and walk, walk, passion baby.

He shook the image as Max moved ahead up the path. His eyes saw motion behind the glass of the front windows and then that shadow moved and the front door handle jiggled. The sound was so loud it seemed. The time had come.

#####

Christine MacGregor was in her kitchen, making sure everything was properly set out and ready for dinner later. Her son was coming to visit and she was thrilled. She hadn't seen Brian in a year it seemed like. He was so busy with his job at the hospital that whenever he got free time he was exhausted and that she understood. Her day had been quiet, as they mostly were. She had been off the day before and free today. After her morning cup of coffee, Donna, her neighbor had dropped by for lunch and they had made crispy tuna salad sandwiches and yakked like a bunch of school girls and thoroughly had a good time and then, the phone had rung and when she had seen the caller ID, her heart had done a jump.

It had been Brian.

His voice had sounded different she thought. Not like he was someone else but heavy, like he was carrying a massive weight on his shoulders. They chatted for a few but it was when Brian had asked her if they could talk, she knew that something had greatly changed in her son's life and it had alarmed her. She had told him and his friend to come by and stay the night and that they could talk all he needed and she had meant it. She bustled around the kitchen, kicking herself for waiting too long to lay things out. She should have laid them out after she and Brian had gotten off the phone but the news on the television had caught her attention.

In the living room, the LCD television that was up on the wall was on MSNBC and on it the newscaster, a dark-haired man, was giving a situation report on a split screen with a white-haired older male in a dark suit.

The headline banners were running below the screen in red with white font.

BODIES FOUND IN DAWSON CITY DOCK WAREHOUSE. POLICE SUSPECT LINKS TO OTHERS FOUND IN THE CITY.

She glanced at the screen as the two men talked.

"...Mr. Mayor, with all due respect, the police reports are indicating that local law enforcement suspects you could in fact have a serial killer or a vigilante on your hands. Several bodies found in a local warehouse, all badly beaten with horrific injuries, a fourth found in an abandoned fishery and of course that's not even mentioning the three found the week before. All bodies showed signs of an animal like attack and brutal beatings, all of them gang members. If there is a vigilante running lose killing these gang members, why hasn't the city done anything about it? What do you do say to your opponents that say your office has gotten weak in the past two years to combat the rising crime rate?"

The older white-haired man, Jonas Tetch, the mayor of Dawson City, glared at the camera, put off by the insinuation, and not liking being put into a hard spot.

"Derek, listen, I don't know any more than you do, right now and I don't know how those police reports were leaked to you but I will say that we are doing everything in our power to find the individual responsible for this. We do not know at this time whether it's a vigilante or some other nutcase, and I'm not going to make wild accusations until we have evidence. As you know, with the political climate being what it is, I prefer the citizens of our city feel and understand that we have their safety and their rights at the foremost of our minds, even as we confront this sort of unchained violence. We cannot permit the law to be taken into the hands of ordinary citizens with a grudge, no matter how much good they think they are doing."

"That may be the case, but we also have sources saying that DCPD lack the man power to fully investigate, and there are new rumors circulating of police corruption and —"

Tetch shook his head. "I'm not even going to dignify that with a response—"

"What can you tell us about the reports coming out of the local hospital of a rising drug problem that could be tied to these deaths; some kind of new street drug?"

Christine flipped the set off and was grateful for the silence, sipping her tea from her cup. She wished Brian wouldn't have moved so far away, let alone to Dawson City. That place was a madhouse. Drugs, gangs, vigilantes. She worried about him living there but she also knew that she couldn't try to force him to do anything and that she needed to respect the fact that he was an adult. She took much the same approach when Brian had come out to her when he was sixteen. She didn't care that he was gay. She didn't need grandkids. Besides, he was her son.

That's all that mattered.

She only wanted him to be safe and happy and if he was both of those, then she could rest easy. His uncle hadn't been as accommodating and a rift had grown between them, primarily because her brother Donald was always trying to convert Brian to Christianity and Brian and he would get into heated arguments at family reunions that eventually evolved into shouting and with a sad thought, she admitted that was probably why most of the family didn't get together anymore. Just too many talking heads, each with an opinion louder and more important than anyone else's.

Everyone wanted to fight and no one cared. The family had faded away one by one over the years. Granted, she thought, she didn't really care for Donny either, to be fair.

The sound of crunching tires on gravel caused her to look up and she crossed into the living room to look out the window and to her surprise, she didn't see a bus or a taxi dropping Brian off but rather a large black four door truck parked behind her two door Chevy.

Her surprised expression became one of bewilderment as the driver of the truck got out and stepped out into full view.

He was massively built and tall at the same time. Six foot six maybe, easily, maybe taller. His body was well muscled and covered from head to toe in thick grey fur. A tiny bit of a silver blaze on his chest stuck up from under the neckline of his dark blue t-shirt. The loose shirt and the loose black cotton pants and shoes he had on did little to hide his powerful and imposing form. His head, she noticed was like a wolf: Long powerful muzzle, triangular ears, one a little more ragged than the other, and a thick neck with even thicker fur there.

A shifter.

His eyes were the brilliant ocean blue of a husky and he moved gracefully, walking up to the gate, opening it and stepping in to her front yard.

She didn't see the truck's passenger since her attention was purely focused on the large canine form on two legs walking up her path.

Moving from the living room window to the front door, Christine unlocked the door's deadbolt and slid back the chain, turning the door handle, opening the door cautiously.

As she watched, the taller bulkier shifter moved up the path and he didn't seem to meet her eyes yet but instead, he stepped aside just a bit to look behind him to make sure his companion was coming up behind him and that was when Christine saw the other passenger in truck. When she saw him, she felt the world slow down, sounds seemed to mute and the past came back to her so hard she felt her eyes sting.

He too was tall, but a bit shorter than the hulking grey wolf. His frame was muscular as well but again not quite as large as his companion. He wore a long-sleeved button-down brown shirt with the sleeves rolled up to his elbows, revealing his thick forearms, the shirt open to a clean white t-shirt beneath it. His jeans were neat and he wore ankle supporting hiking boots that looked new.

His fur was a smoky carbon black, so dark the sun just seemed to be absorbed. His face was noble, his muzzle clean and his ears pinned back along his head like a dog about to be punished. He was looking at the ground and then when he heard his companion stop to see if he was coming, the black furred shifter looked up and when he did, he saw Christine and Christine truly saw his face.

His strong wide head.

His long muzzle.

It was the eyes that did it. His eyes completed the image. They were such a vibrant and natural green that they looked like someone had taken an old-fashioned glass 7-UP bottle and held it up the bright midday sun.

When he looked her in the eyes, she felt the connection immediately and for her, it was like seeing a ghost.

The ghost of man that had been dead now for thirteen years, a man she had deeply loved, married and dearly missed and she knew in her rational mind that this wolf before her was not that man for that was impossible, but all the same, it was like her husband walked again and was coming up her driveway from a time before their son's birth. A bolt of white-hot grief shot through her heart, fresh as it was when she buried him years ago.

Jacob MacGregor was back and he was walking up her driveway after thirteen years. He was almost at the porch when he stopped and spoke and the voice broke the illusion. When he looked at her, she knew he saw her stunned face, and his ears fell back even further, his eyes large and his own chest going up and down, his tail tucked between his legs.

"Mom...?"

The tea cup in Christine's hand slipped down her fingers as her heart thumped and her chest heaved her blue eyes wide with shock. The cup hung on the edge of her index finger, the liquid in it spilling out and a moment later, the cup itself fell, smashing into the stone at the front entrance, exploding in shards of white porcelain.

"Brian..."

She heard her voice, felt her lips move and knew that she spoken, but not how she had formed words. She pushed open the screen door and stepped outside into the afternoon sun, her feet on the porch. The grey shifter looked between them and kept quiet and stood aside.

It seemed like it took everything Christine had to make her feet move out of the liquid cement of memory. She struggled hard and finally her feet did move faster as she finally moved down the short flight of steps and into the yard.

She stood before the tall black furred shifter, and quivering, shaking, she rose her small human hand up and laid it gently upon the side of face, just behind the back of his snout, where his jaws met. She held his face, looking into his eyes. His face and fur were warm.

She saw her husband's eyes again.

More importantly, as the ghost of Jacob faded, she saw her son, her beautiful son. It *was* him. The sun setting behind him was making the black tips of his fur blaze orange as if they were on fire as the sun passed through the individual hairs. She buried her fingers into the thick fur of his neck and threw her arms around him as best as she could.

"Brian....oh Brian..." she found words refusing to come out as the other ghosts of her past, this time the ghosts of decisions she and Jacob had made together to protect their son, their joy, came back with a vengeance and all she could do was look in his eyes and apologize.

"You look just like him.... I'm so sorry."

Brian took his mother in his arms and held her in an embrace.

"It's okay, mom. We can talk about it inside but for now...I'm glad you're okay with...me."

Christine pulled back and looked up into Brian's lupine features.

"What do you mean? Why wouldn't I be? You're my son. You're part of me. Nothing will ever change that."

Brian nodded as his mother stepped back and he put his hands in his pockets feeling sheepish as Max stood in the background, waiting patiently to be introduced, not wanting to intrude where he had no business.

Coughing, Brian tried to regain his composure.

"Um, Mom, this is my friend Max. Max Mullen. Max, this is my mom, Chris." Brian said, stepping back a bit. Max stepped forward and put on a warm smile, something Brain found was alien as of yet on his face in his experience with Max but he thought it made his face extremely handsome. Max stuck out a hand and Christine took it, her small hand vanishing into his meaty furry digits. He shook it gently and let go.

"Good to meet you." He said.

After a moment of staring at the two of them, Christine seemed to come to her senses.

"Oh god.... well, let's go inside, boys. We can talk there and I guess I can start dinner in little bit and Brian....you probably have a lot of questions for me."

Now that the hard part was over, Brian felt himself slowly, very slowly, begin to relax a little. His eyebrows raised.

"That would be an understatement."

Nodding, Christine motioned them to follow her into the house and bringing up the rear, Brian followed, his mother's words echoing in his mind as he turned over the one thing that she had said when she had seen him. It turned over and over in his mind as he tried to make sense of it from every angle he could but he couldn't, so he would have to wait for the answer inside. There was no need to get angry and scream and roar. It was a fact and facts cannot be changed but the fact was, his mother and father had obviously hidden something from him for some reason and the phrase she had used kept haunting him.

> *You look just like him....*

Given the context of the situation, Brian's sharp mind was making connections that made no sense but that he could not argue with. *Who was this "him?"*

The answer was obvious even as he moved up the steps and closed the doors behind the three of them, stepping back into the second of his two childhood homes.

Max leaned in and whispered to him.

"Boys?"

Brian shot him a look and elbowed him in the ribs. Max shrugged it off with a grin.

His father's face, his very human face, floated there next to the question and the connection between the two made his stomach turn a bit with anticipation.

> *You look just like him...*

#####

As he crossed the threshold, Brian's boots crunched on something sharp and the cracking sound brought him up short. He stopped, looked down and lifted up his right foot.

There in a puddle of clear brown liquid were several large shards of white porcelain.

A coffee cup or a tea cup, he thought, the one his mom had dropped when she saw him coming up the walkway and for a moment, he was fifteen again, seeing another tea cup crash to the floor and a sudden unexpectedly sharp pang of a memory squeezed his heart.

"Hey, mom, is the broom and dustpan still in the same place?" he said, looking up, his voice small in the foyer. Chris paused and turned and looked at her son and then saw his face and followed his eyes to the floor.

"Oh, fuck me. Christ, I don't know what I was thinking. Yeah, it's all in the same place. Let me grab it."

She came back past Max and made to go past Brian towards the broom closet but Brian reached up and stopped her gently with a hand on her shoulder, his massive hand seeming to swallow her shoulder in the process.

"Nah, let me get it this time." He said gently and from the look in his mother's eyes, the moisture that sprung from the corners of her eyes told him she knew what he meant and so, she simply nodded and stepped back.

"Thank you, Bri." She said, looking back towards him as he cleaned up the shards and the spilled tea. With a quick head shake she turned to Max and nodded.

"So, let's get you comfortable, Mr. Mullen." She said directing him to the open living room with its twin couches that faced each other with an old worn smooth coffee table between them. Max felt himself his face redden a bit under his fur.

"Ah...its um...you can call me Max. Mister makes me feel old."

"Nonsense, you don't look a day over 30 but point taken. It drives me batty when I get called ma'am. I'm certainly not a ma'am." Chris said as she cleared some magazines off of the sofa and with her direction, Max took a seat carefully, wrapping his tail around his right hip, letting it dangle off of the couch comfortably. The old cloth sofa hugged his large body snugly and within moments he found that he had settled in quite nicely which was rare given his large frame.

"Now. Drinks. Do you want soda, tea, water, I've got some Scotch too, if you need it? I know I do."

There was a sound of tinkling glass sliding off of a dustpan.

"Mom!" Brian said, coming back across the living room with a scandalized look his dark features.

Chris shrugged. "What? It feels like it's going to be that kind of a discussion so I just want to be prepared. Never go to a raid underfed or under drunk."

Max smiled. He was beginning to like this lady.

"Um, water's fine. Thanks." He said his eyes shooting between Brian and his mother. Brian moved to go into the kitchen and help her with the drinks but she shooed him back into the living room like someone was shooing away a cat from the porch. Max decided that the best strategy here was to wait and see and keep his mouth shut. Besides, this was golden, to see Brian squirm a bit. It was amusing, reminding him of himself when his mom would fawn over him any time he got a scrape or a cut or anything else for that matter. He never really had friends growing up and he imagined this was what it would have been like. It was, he thought, the very definition of bittersweet.

Brian was pacing when she returned to the living room, the soft glow of the lamps giving the wood paneled walls a gentle welcoming glaze. The central air unit cycled and somewhere a dog was barking.

"Brian, sit down honey. You're going to wear a hole in the floor."

Brian sat next to Max their arms touching and for a moment, his mom caught it and her eyes lingered but she said nothing. Brian and Max both adjusted themselves to give themselves a few inches as Chris sat down the glass of water for Max, a tumbler of Scotch on the rocks for herself and Brian smiled, seeing she still bought Mountain Dew, his favorite, even though she wasn't a fan of it herself, just on the rare chance that he could make the trip to see her for a while. That made Brian feel a twinge of guilt.

Not sitting yet, Chris looked at Brian.

"Before we get into this, I want to get something that will help. There are some things you need to see."

Brian nodded, watching her carefully as she vanished down the hallway past the stairs. He heard the hallway closet door open and heard her shuffling around as things were moved and replaced. He heard the tinkle of ceramics and the jumbling tumble of flotsam.

Brian felt a soft nudge in his ribs and looked down to see Max's elbow resting softly there. He looked up to find Max looking at him.

"You are so nervous I can smell it coming off of you. Are you ok?" Max asked quietly, leaning in.

Brian shrugged and whispered back. "I can feel my teeth tingling."

"Why?"

Shaking his head, Brian looked at Max and tried to explain, glancing down the hallway to see if his mom was coming back.

"I don't know, Max. I can't tell if I'm afraid or eager or angry. So much is going through my head. It's like she's about to tell me something I suddenly already know and that what I know is threatening to tear down something I've held so close, but what lies beyond...beyond that person...I don't know whether or not to be afraid of it and what it means for me."

Max's eyebrows raised. "You think you know what she's going to say?"

Nodding, Brian replied. "I've got a feeling ever since she said what she said in the driveway, and its sitting in my gut like bad oysters. I hate oysters."

Brian watched as Max squirmed a bit and reached into his pocket, pulling out his truck keys. Perplexed, Brian saw Max fiddle with them, pulling something off of the rings, the keys jingling. Max handed it to Brian and Brian looked at it, unsure of what to make of it.

It was a medium sized deep well socket, a 10mm socket to be specific, that had a hole drilled through it for a keyring to pass through. It was well worn, scratched and dented but it obviously held some sort of importance for Max to modify one of his tools like that and carry it around. The steel was warm from Max's body heat.

"What's this?"

Max grinned. "Lucky socket."

"What—"

Suddenly Chris was back and the two pulled apart with Max surreptitiously sliding his keys back into his pocket, leaving Brian confused holding the small socket in front of him. He quickly shoved it into a pocket as his mom sat down a medium sized box on the coffee table before them with a surprisingly heavy clunk, jarring the pictures of Brian and his mom from years past as well as the photos of a dark-haired bearded man with green eyes whom Max took to be Jacob MacGregor.

Brian looked at the box with a sense of growing trepidation. He felt his stomach flip around and he knew that once he looked into that box, much like Pandora, there would be no taking it back, no undoing, no unknowing of what he would learn.

Chris sat on the other couch and for a moment she suddenly found she couldn't speak so she took a few deep breaths. Brian let her take her time. The more time she took, then the more time she gave him more time to prepare himself for what he was going to learn and that was time well spent. He suspected that nothing he could ever do would keep his foundational world views of who he was and where he came from intact, and he knew that ultimately, he was emotionally delaying the inevitable.

"Brian, before we get into this, I just want to say a few things." Chris said at last, her eyes cast down.

"I want to say you are my son and I truly, deeply, love you. Your father did as well. You are our world, our sun. Our lives revolved around you and you are the best blessing a family could have ever asked for. Your father and I were and are so proud of you. I know he is because I am."

"I also wanted to say," she continued, and when she looked up, her eyes were wet with tears that threatened to fall. "That I'm sorry. I'm sorry that your father and I didn't tell you the truth and for the mistakes we made. All I can ask is that you look into your heart when you see what is in that box, that you can hopefully begin to try to forgive us for what we did. We did it because we loved you and now I know that what we did was wrong..."

With those words, Chris pushed the box towards Brian. Brian looked at the box and suddenly, he knew the answers were inches in front of him and all he had to do was lift off a cardboard top. Brian felt his jaw tremble and knew his ears were practically pasted to his skull. He felt the fur on the back of his neck raise and he knew that if he wasn't covered in thick fur, he'd have goose flesh.

He felt Max give him a pat on the shoulder and in that moment, he didn't care if his mom saw it or not as he reached out and took the box and pulled it to him, setting it down on the floor in front of him. His fur covered finger tips caressed it gently, tracing the edges of the lid, the course pads on the underside of his fingertips making the smallest raspy sound. He noticed the box was duct taped together and had been for a very long time. Knowing that putting it off any longer wasn't going to help anything, he poised his index finger over the tape, pushing his blunt short claw against it.

He sighed and took a deep breath and ripped the tape off, lifting the lid and when he saw what was inside, he felt his throat go dry.

"We wanted you to have this if something ever happened to both of us but...things being what they are...we never expected...I think now is as good a time as any." Chris said meekly.

At least two photo albums filled the box up with their bulk. Surrounding it were dozens of other photos and pieces, all framed or put away in envelopes. The photo albums were the big three ring binder types, filled to the brim with clear plastic sheets, with each sheet having multiple pockets for photos and mementos. Each album was a rich navy-blue book with gold trim and he recognized them immediately as belonging to the set his mom and dad had on the old bookshelf in the apartment before his dad died. There were always two albums missing of the numbered set and his parents had always told him that they didn't know what happened to them and theorized they were lost in the move to the apartment from the smaller run-down unit when he was a baby.

Staring at them now, he felt a cold shiver run up his spine as he raised his head and looked first at the bookshelf, now next to the TV, the same one he had eventually grown to overlook a thousand times and saw the set of blue albums there and saw there were the same missing two books, just like years ago. He glanced at his mom who didn't say a word, and he saw that she was suddenly struggling to maintain her composure and unable to find words himself, he lifted the albums out and set them on the table.

Below the albums and below the pictures was an old leather jacket, a black one with vertical red bars on the sleeves between vertical white lines and there, to the right, was a black box with gold hinges. Its small size told him what he would find in there as his shaking fingers picked it up.

With a click, it opened, springing up and there, resting on blue velvet inside was his father's police badge with a simple black band across it made of silk cloth. His jaw trembled again as he ran his fingers over the shining brass. He had not seen that in years. Ghosts threatened to overwhelm him.

Closing it, with a deep breath, he set it aside gently and went back to the albums. Picking up the first one, he pulled it into his lap and flipped open the cover. The image he had of his father in his mind with his light skin tanned from being outside so much, the rough skin of his knuckles, the wavy dark hair, his black beard with hints of gray and green eyes rose before him and they shattered into pieces so small they would never come together again.

The first few pictures in the album were of a werewolf, a shifter, who to his shock, looked just like him. Covered in head to toe in jet black fur with sharp green eyes and a wide happy smile as he embraced a young sandy-blonde haired human woman dressed in bellbottoms and a brown t-shirt; in the image, both of them were laughing hysterically in silent mirth, forever frozen in time. She was tiny next to him. It was his mother. Both of them were flipping peace signs and his mother had a crown of pink and white flowers on her head. His dad was rocking a fully grown out silver beard, the same shade as his own chest blaze.

They were outside somewhere, and behind them a red brick building rose up, and judging from the look of it, it was Carsonville Community College, only decades in the past if the cars were anything to judge by.

As Brian flipped the pages in stunned silence, trembling with each flip, his heart pounding, more moments from a past he never remembered came up to him, moments from the time before he was born, moments of the lives of his younger mother and yes, he had to admit it now, his father.

So many memories, so much time and all of it was at once alien and instantly familiar as three lives finally crashed together as one. There were photos of his parents graduating, with a surly shot of his uncle Donald looking angrily at the graduates, his dad not caring, raising his diploma to the sky, tossing his hat into the air, his triangular ears and tail gone wild. In one image, this one deeper into the books and obviously a few years later and judging by the radio on the kitchen sink, in the early eighties, his mom stood with a spatula in one hand, holding the hand of a black furred shifter who was just out of frame as she danced wildly, singing into the kitchen implement, her shirt covered in dough and flour.

The next image hit him harder than many others.

It was in a field, and the sun was high in the sky, and a bridal arch had been constructed by hand, white painted and curved, covered in curled ivy and pink and white flowers. There were at least a dozen people, including a few shifters in the crowd and he noticed by this point in the album, his grandfather on his mom's side had stopped showing up. Brian knew that he had died of a heart attack not long before his parents had gotten married and the thin drawn figure of a small woman with gray hair in a floral print dress that reached her ankles drew his eye. His grandmother, Grandma Annie.

There, under the arch, was his father, the only person it could be, he thought, swallowing hard. His father was built like Brian himself: powerful, tall and broad shouldered with jet black fur and stunning green eyes. He wore his police dress uniform, and the same badge that Brian had just seen in the box was in the photo, proudly pinned to his chest. He father stood in front of his mother who herself was dressed in a simple flowing dress made of white cotton with one shoulder exposed, her skin radiating in the afternoon sun. A crown of flowers sat upon her head and she held his father's hand, looking deeply into his eyes as a minister, dressed in traditional suit, gave them the rites of marriage. The minister, Brian noticed seemed familiar, almost like...

Father Raymond.

It had to be but couldn't be, His parents weren't religious but Raymond had been a good friend of theirs and had agreed to perform the ceremony. But this minister was a shifter in his canine form, looking like a dark gray furred Schnauzer. Raymond himself had died, they said, just after he turned seven. Natural causes, they had said. Doubt began to bloom knowing what he knew now about shifter biology.

In the wedding pictures he had seen on the mantle and on the tables around the house growing up, his father been human and so had the minister. Granted, those photos, he now thought, seemed zoomed in, cropped. The more he thought about it, the Schnauzer could only be Father Raymond. The eyes were identical.

What were these then? What were all these photos?

He moved onto the second book and in it, going through the pages, he knew he could no longer doubt.

The first images in the second book were of his birth. His mother lay on a hospital bed, dressed in a gown, a privacy screen shielding her knees and private areas as the doctors handed her a chubby squalling baby very human boy. Standing next to her at her shoulder was that same black furred shifter, his eyes wet with pride as he beheld the miracle of his son and the angelic beauty of his wife. The look on his face said it all really. He was father and proud of it. This was his family.

The image below that one, was the exact same but instead of the shifter standing there, Brian saw instead the familiar human man that he had known as Jacob MacGregor, his dad, all of his life.

A part of his brain nudged him and he pulled the pictures out and held them up side by side, and with trepidation, turned them over to see the dates and times.

His answer was now in front of him and it was sinking in very quickly as to why his mother had said what she did a few minutes ago.

The time stamp on the photo with the shifter next to his mother was marked MAY 1,1990 17:34:35. The second image, with the human next to his mother bore the same date, May 1, 1990, but the timestamp was nearly three minutes at 17:37:12.

He recognized military time and quickly converted it.

5:34 PM and 5:37 PM respectively. May 1st was his birthday. He knew he was born in the afternoon.

He knew what the two separate images meant and he knew it was not a result of photo manipulation but rather a set up. One photo to keep for real and one staged photo to put on display for...

Display for who?

Display for me, his mind finished.

All of the information that he had gotten from the photos told him everything he needed to know except one thing. The *why.*

His father had been a shifter and he and his mother, for some reason, had hid that from him his entire life, going so far as to hide real photos and then take second ones as to avoid suspicion or the curious mind of an intelligent child. The picture of a man he thought he knew as his father, the human man, was gone and in its place now was a figure, split between time, a man, and a wolf.

"Why?" he said when he was finally able to speak. "Why didn't you guys tell me? What was so wrong with it that you had to hide from me who my father was this entire time?"

Beside him, Max sat in stunned silence as well, and he made a cough and tried to excuse himself but found himself restrained by Brian's powerful grip on his waistband, yanking him back down to the couch and Max instantly interpreted that silent signal for what it meant without a word.

Don't go. I need you. Please stay.

And so, he did stay.

Chris's hands shook, the ice in the tumbler in clicking together like old bones.

"Brian....you have to understand that things back when you were born, even before, were much different. The world was a harsher place. Not as accepting. Your dad and I, once we got married and knew that you were on the way, we simply didn't want you to have to experience any of that pain, any of that rejection. We didn't know if you were going to be like him and gifted but you grew up and never showed any signs and so we relaxed a bit and just let you live and have a full happy life. Until your father passed away, I never thought twice about what he and I agreed to do...but now...I see it was wrong. There were things that we didn't want you get involved in so that you wouldn't have to experience any of the...any of the hell...that people... people like him went through as a child."

"What do you mean?" Brian asked quietly, his voice shaking. Chris set down her glass, untouched and reached forward and gently turned a few pages in the album in Brian's lap.

"Your father and I were both activists. We were involved in marches for shifter's rights. Sometimes, those marches got ugly. It's how we met in college. One thing led to another and we fell in love and he was so good to me, Brian. He loved me so much and I loved him. Love blinded us when you came along."

Brian looked down and these images he saw were much older, almost sepia toned, some of them were black and white. He remembered pictures of the Civil Rights marches with Dr. King and these were similar, with thousands of people marching on Washington, hundreds seemed to be shifters, others were human. Officers at the sides of the marches held back dogs with snarling open mouths and as he turned the pages, he saw images of cops spraying shifters with fire hoses, sending them sprawling as their human and shifter companions tried to shield them.

The next image was of his mother and father, hand in hand, staring down the gleaming rifle barrel of a military guard.

"We wanted a better world for you. A life where you didn't have to fight for the right just to survive. We made a promise to each other to hide the truth if you were born without the abilities your father had. When you didn't show any of the signs of being like your father, we were relieved because it meant you'd never have to feel what we did, getting kicked out of restaurants or having guns pointed at our faces."

Brian swallowed, looking at the pictures, his throat dry. His father and mother had been activists, like Draco and his eyes quickly scanned the images, looking for Draco's noble face but he didn't see it. His mom and dad had been fighting for change for people they didn't even know and had experienced firsthand the hatred that people can throw out. Brian had to admit, growing up had been mercifully easy and mostly free of bullies. Now, he knew why his father had made such an excellent cop and why he had specifically worked homicide and later drug enforcement. He literally had the nose for it. *Did his co-workers know?*

"One of my co-workers back when I was pregnant with you..." Chris said sniffling a bit. It took her a moment to collect herself. "One of them told me I should abort you or give you up for adoption and Brian that hurt me so badly. I wanted you more than anything. You were mine. My child. I could never do that."

Brian's eyes widened. He had never been told that story.

His parents had hidden an entire side of their lives and selves from him, all to protect him from the social and cultural storm sweeping the country and had raised him and kept him against all odds, and genuinely had no idea that he carried the gene. His father had given up an entire part of himself. Brian thought the technology to detect the gene back then didn't even exist and even if it did, the Lycanthropic Genome Project wouldn't have been even started at the time. They had taken a gamble and stuck by him because they loved him.

He wanted desperately to be mad, to scream and yell and throw something over being lied to but he couldn't bring himself to do it. Instead, what settled in that emotional storm's vacuum was a quiet acceptance of the truth. He had always watched the battle for shifter rights from the side lines, angry at the idiocy people had towards others, having no idea that his parents had actively fought it during its worst period. It was the secret legacy of his father, to be a fighter for peace and he died as a man of justice. His mother had stood by his father as well, just as much as a fighter for progress and change.

Max's family, Brian thought, had pulled Max out of school to protect him and spent years homeschooling him and making his world as safe as they could, too; *it seems, we have a lot more in common than we thought.*

Chris had stood up and stood before Brian, looking very small, her eyes red, her face wet, her head bowed.

"Brian, I'll understand if you're angry. I'll even understand if you don't want to talk to me for a while but please...don't leave me. You're my son. You are the light and love of my life and the only part of your dad I have left. You are my family. Your grandparents and most of the rest of the family didn't care for your dad. He started hiding it from them too after a while and everyone pretended it was normal. His side of the family didn't think it was wise to marry a human. We don't talk anymore."

Brian stood as well and standing before her, he threw his powerful arms around her and pulled her close.

Chris buried her face into the thick fur of his chest beneath the cloth of his shirt, and in that moment, the emotions Brian had been holding back broke and together, mother and son finally wept and perhaps, they saw each other for the first time as truly complete people.

Brian nuzzled the side of his mother's much smaller human head, breathing in the scent of her hair, the smell of fresh flowers and spring days.

"I'm not going anywhere, mom. Not ever. I'm not mad at you and I understand. I love you. Thank you...for letting me know who he was and who you were. I think," he said, thinking as he blinked away moisture in his eyes. "I think I know who I am now. Everything makes so much sense."

Pulling away, Chris took Brian's big head in her hands and held it there, looking up and deep in his green eyes.

"I'll tell you who you are. You are an amazing person. A strong person. A good person. Just like your father."

Brian closed his eyes at her touch and savored it. There was nothing on the planet that could heal any pain, any wound, any faster and as deep as a mother's loving touch.

A few moments more and Chris tossed a glance over at Max.

"And you have good taste in men." She said, a smile forming on her lips as she wiped her eyes clear.

Brian felt his face go red and instantly went to protest, his ears flattening even farther if that was possible. He stammered and Max started to protest gently as well, but Chris silenced them both.

"Please. You two should know by now that a mother can tell. A mother knows. It's just something we do and nothing makes me happier than to know that Brian has found someone to love and who cares about him in return. I can tell you do, Max. You keep him safe."

Unable to say anything and finding that stammering objections was useless, Max simply nodded, his face flushed so hot he thought if he touched his own skin that he would burn himself, fur included. Brian sank back down onto the sofa, the box at his feet, the albums on the coffee table. There was so much more in the box but he couldn't bring himself to go through it all, not just yet.

"Now then!" Chris said, coughing and cleaning her face as best as she could. "I am going to get dinner started and you two can sit there and don't even think about moving into kitchen, or so help me I'll swat you, Brian. You too, Max. I want to cook dinner for my son and his boyfriend. God, I've always wanted to say that." She said and headed toward the bathroom to properly restore herself to normal.

Brian watched her go and slumped against the couch, breathing slowly and smiling a bit. His mom was something else. *She always had been.*

"I guess the cat's out of the bag," Max said, sheepishly. Brian looked over at him and grinned a little, his eyes still moist.

"Yeah. I guess so. Is that a bad thing?" Brian asked hesitantly. Max shook his head and gave that typical Max macho reply.

"Nah. I don't really care. I don't give a shit what people think. You should know that by now. Besides your mom was right. I like her. She reminds me of my mom."

Brian nodded and looked down at the box between his ankles and the albums on the table. His mother, he thought seemed greatly relieved and to be honest, right now, he was numb but it wasn't in a bad way. He was just processing everything he had learned and all it meant. He was quiet long enough for Max to give his shoulder a gentle shake.

"You ok?"

Brian smiled and looked over at him. "You keep asking that." He smiled.

Max nodded sagely, his ears swiveling towards Brian.

"And I'll ask it every day and you'd better believe it."

With a tug, Max pulled Brian over to him and Brian didn't resist and laid there in Max's arms, lying up against his powerful warm body, letting his head fall gently onto Max's broad chest, and enjoyed the thumping beats of Max's heart. A moment later, Brian felt Max's arm fall across him and embrace him tightly, wordlessly.

Sometimes, Brian thought, you didn't need words and this was one of those times. Max silently placed his chin on the top of Brian's head and Brian could feel his thumb making tiny slow circles in the fur of his shoulder, a silent reassurance.

The fear, the panic and the anticipation that had been building in him for weeks, the same emotions that had worn a wound into his psyche seemed to hurt less lying here, propped up against Max. They seemed to finally start to fade and maybe, Brian thought, they would heal after all.

CHAPTER 6

Jackson sat behind his curving desk in the tech room of Forest Glen. The tech room was his domain, the place where he felt the most comfortable. Unlike the rest of the ancient manor, the tech room was fully modern and used to be the manor's ballroom. Draco had allowed him (and paid for him) to remodel it into the thriving beating electronic heart of the manor itself. Composed of walls of bulletproof transparent glass and supported and braced by beams of matte black steel, it was a haven for him. From this point, he could control every system in the manor; every door lock, every sprinkler, every security system (there were several) all while monitor the grounds and surrounding woods.

He had custom designed the entire system, including the operating system. Here, Jackson felt safe from the awkward social interactions that always followed suit when he was involved. It wasn't that he didn't like people, he thought, pushing his glasses up on his nose. It was that people tended to not like him, because he had an annoying habit of saying too much too fast and making it worse by trying to fix whatever harm he had unintentionally caused. Of course, all this would be made so such simpler if people would just say what they mean instead of speaking in metaphors and analogy.

A graduate with honors of MIT, Jackson had worked for Towson Consolidated, a super company whose headquarters was in the heart of Dawson City, a direct competitor to Madison Genetics. He was their head of I-T during his time with the company, he had created and built a vast fiber optic network, keeping the entire building running smoothly, as well as analyzing new technologies, both bio-organic and technological in origin. For him, taking apart a super computer was as easy as breathing and yet here he sat, casually dressed, his brown and white furred face and eyebrows knitted in frustration.

For the last week it seemed like, Jackson had been trying to undo the systems damage someone in Raven's lab had done, either by intention or accident, by brute force wiping data from the OS itself and its storage banks. The super computers downstairs were thankfully intact but the electronic mayhem that had been wrought was something that was fast, surgical, and he had to admit, rather good. The more he had worked on it, the more he had come to suspect that it was not in fact an accident but rather a deliberate act of sabotage.

He sat between the two curving desks of what he called his operations center, a raised reinforced glass and steel platform from which he could control everything. Banks of flat screen monitors lined the desks as well as flat keyboards and one large piece of computer hardware that Jackson had to admit was his favorite. It was a 27-inch flat screen computer that seemingly had a tiny body and was in fact, seemingly made up of all screen that sat on thick pivot joint angled up at the user. The Lenovo IdeaCentre A720. The perfect touch screen device for an active and heavy computer lifestyle, he thought proudly.

Jackson whirled in his wheeled leather chair and spun around as he slid back across to the other desk. His brown and white furred hands flew across the keys. Images on the screen flew by.

There, he thought, seeing the binary damage flash by once again. He isolated it, enlarged the window and executed a heuristic algorithm that would surely repair the damage.

A moment later the screen flashed with a red error message.

"Damn it," he cried in frustration. He took his glasses off his round head and slammed them on the desk, rubbing his dry eyes in irritation. He leaned back in his chair and tried to relax, to calm down. This wasn't going to help find out whatever that someone was trying to hide, he knew, and he took a few deep calming breaths.

He heard a knock and his big floppy ears swiveled towards the sound. Cracking open his fingers, he peeked over at the glass and steel door.

Molly.

Jackson jerked his head and a moment later, Molly entered the tech room, the door sliding open with a hiss and closing behind her. She was dressed as she always was: a dark pant suit and a white blouse with dark heeled shoes. To his surprise, her jacket was off, the most comfort she would allow herself to have. Her blue-green eyes and short red hair also looked a bit frayed, as if she too had been working harder than usual, which Jackson knew she had. He had told her and Draco about the erasure and damage to the systems and Molly had been probing her extensive former government sources from her time as an FBI agent to help find some way of cracking the problem and so far, she had had as little luck as he had.

Draco was concerned about the erasure and he had ruled out saying who he thought it may be, though obviously everyone involved had their suspect and it wasn't Raven; the question is why Rakinos would have done it. Molly and Jackson had both objected to him being present but Draco had overruled them, feeling confident in everyone present would behave themselves. Obviously, someone hadn't.

"Going for casual today?" he asked with a smirk. She gave him a small one back and moved straight to business.

"Any luck?" Molly asked, stepping up onto the platform, coming up beside Jackson, standing with her arms crossed, looking at the red flashing error screen.

For a former agent, she wasn't bad and he liked her.

"None. I've tried every algorithm I know for reconstruction but so far, it just throws up errors. I can't figure out why. I engineered entire networks. I can hack the Pentagon for Christ's sake but I can't fix this. It's driving me insane. Whatever it was, was a lot of data." Jackson sighed. He squirmed a bit when Molly raised an eyebrow at his mention of his prolific skills and he quickly back tracked.

"Not that I would ever do that. Not that I have done in a long, well, I would never commit a felony. I mean, prison food is nasty. So, I've heard."

"Right." Molly said and her hard expression melted a moment later and she put a reassuring hand on Jackson's shoulder, her gold cross around her neck winking in the fluorescent lights and LEDs.

"Call up the raw data block." She said thoughtfully and Jackson could hear an idea forming in her voice. She always got a certain sound in her voice when an idea was hatching and Draco trusted it and that meant Jackson did too. He entered a few commands, hands flying over the clacking keys. The windows on screen changed size, zoomed out and zoomed in, revealing a huge section of binary code that was missing entire chunks, the whole thing flashing red.

As she studied it, her sharp eyes flicking line by line, Jackson wondered what she saw that he did not.

"Have you tried heuristic algorithms? .NET code recovery? Reverse compilation?"

Jackson nodded. "All of the above."

Turning back to the screen, Molly frowned. "The security tapes from the lab, the only place anyone could have accessed a terminal. Did they show anything?"

Jackson nodded. "Just Raven and Rakinos testing Brian and Max's samples. The resolution isn't good enough to be zoomed in on screens and believe me, I've tried zooming, cleaning, restructuring. Nada."

"Doesn't every station have a work ID code so its actions can be traced?" Molly asked, standing up and back.

"They do and I'm pretty sure by this point it was the one that Rakinos was using so I'm pretty sure he's our guy but as to what he did or what he was hiding," Jackson growled in frustration. "No dice."

Something about the image looked familiar to Molly and she knew that she had seen it somewhere, but where.

The numbers ran up and down in rows, zero then one, then zero, zero, then one. Besides the layer of encryption, the manor used on its network, there was something...

"I know what this."

Jackson's ears perked up. "You do?"

"Yeah I do. Remember a few months ago when you helped the FBI crack that hack-and-slash attack on the Hoover Buildings computers? This same signature was left behind. It's a binary decay initiated by a processor overclock command. Simple, brutal and effective. Have any of your processors been overheating?" Molly asked looking at him as realization dawned on Jackson's beagle like face.

"Yeah. Yeah there has been a set overheating in tower three and I couldn't isolate it. I didn't connect the two."

"Which computers does tower three service?"

Groaning at his own oversight, Jackson turned back to the keyboard, his fingers racing. "The lab and medical bay scanners and simulators. I should have seen that. If this is binary decay from an over clock command, I can reverse and rebuild it with a Hols-Arnon equational algorithm!"

"How long will that take?"

"Not sure, shouldn't be more than 12 hours tops. That's a lot of data to recompile but when it's done we'll know what Rakinos tried to hide." Jackson said proudly, swiftly entering commands, feeling a renewed sense of purpose.

"Want me to call Raven and tell Draco?"

"Yeah."

Molly nodded and headed out of the tech room to leave Jackson to his work since he was already far and away long gone into his binary digital world.

#####

"You did WHAT?"

Harvey Madison stood in his lab coat, arms crossed, face wide in shock, the anger in his voice apparent, loud enough to hear in the halls only if the room itself wasn't soundproofed. He had spent all day at the office; days, in fact, trying to direct the board's attention away from the accounting errors that had been found by one nosy little shit of an accountant and so far all he had managed to do was get himself in deeper. They were moving forward with an official inquiry and he was effectively powerless to stop them. It was his goddamn company, he had thought savagely and here, come to find out, his partner had in fact went ahead with testing without telling him or having him present.

Rakinos sat at his desk, hands and fingers steepled under his powerful chin, his scarlet eyes tracking Madison as he paced the room. Rakinos could feel his blood pressure climbing with every instant he spent in Madison's presence.

"I told you. It worked. The effects of the bane were stabilized by the introduction of MacGregor's DNA. The triple helix withstood the ionizing effects of the radiation long enough to allow the bane to fully activate. It had a side effect as well. The bane seemed to trigger a third transformation in the shifter subject and it interacted with the DNA. We knew it was possible; we didn't know how useful it could be, only its potential. And now...it seems there is so much more than we imagined." he told Madison quietly.

Madison whirled on and got into Rakinos' face, pointing a scrawny finger at his nose.

"You wasted our entire supply of that DNA on what, a science project? A freak? We needed more time. More testing. We don't know if that thing you've made is stable. I can't take it to the board and sell it to them. That DNA was priceless!"

Rakinos held back a snarl. For now, but how long he was going to hold back, he thought, wasn't going to be long. He was tired, utterly, of Madison and his mewling. It had been mewling since day one, unending.

"I'm not proposing we take the dog soldiers to the board—"

"Dog soldiers? Is that what you're calling them? You think just because you finished what they couldn't in World War 2 that.... Jesus Christ, this is a disaster. You've made a Frankenstein instead of a viable controllable bio-weapon, you idiot."

Rakinos felt a switch flip somewhere deep inside and realized that Madison was never going to shut up. He was never going to stop mewling. He would never allow true progress because his mind was too feeble, to limited. His earlier desire for a human test subject had gone unused, out of patience, but now, that patience had run out.

He let his hands fall to his side as he stood up and walked around his desk, deliberately taking his time.

Coming up to Madison he sighed and stepped around him. Madison was still ranting.

"What are we going to do now? We don't have enough DNA to replicate. We can't just go and kidnap him and force him to give us what we need."

Rakinos stood before a locked metal cabinet and slowly, carefully, he unlocked it. With a click it slid out and he reached in and when his hand came out, it held a tiny vial with a blue-green glowing fluid inside of it. Not the bane, but something just as good.

He ran a finger up and down the glass casing.

Turning around, he looked at Madison.

"That's exactly what we are going to do, doctor. I don't see any reason why we can't."

"Are you fucking crazy? If we get caught trying, our whole operation will be exposed!" Madison snarled, throwing up his hands in frustration.

"Of course, the easiest solution is to make him come to us. Hanging around Max Mullen won't do him any favors. Sooner or later, he and Draco will put two and two together and do something stupid, and I'm going to force their hand."

"You've lost your mind, what little is left of it, Rakinos."

Rakinos held up the tiny hypodermic injector in his hand, the blue glow bleeding out over his blood red fur.

Madison glared at him and for the first time, he realized that he was in fact, alone in the room with Rakinos who had expertly worked Madison into a corner.

"What's that?"

Rakinos looked surprised at the thing he held and then he pretended to finally see it.

"Oh. This? Well, you see", he started, his deep voice sending shivers up and down Madison's spine and Madison realized why a moment later. It was the same death purr a cat would give a mouse it had cornered.

"This is what's left of the replicated triple helix DNA from MacGregor in its pure and undiluted form, just enough for study or for use on a specific subject. I held it back. It's really a great set of options when you think about it and doctor, by the way, your services will no longer be required."

Madison bolted but Rakinos was faster, arm barring the man roughly across the chest like a clothesline. With a cry, gravity yanked Madison done hard onto the stone floor, his head smacking wetly into the hard-unforgiving rock. A trickle of blood seeped out from his scalp as his vision blurred and he tried to stand but was too dazed.

Rakinos knelt down and with his free hand, yanked Madison to his feet and in the same smooth motion, slung him into wall hard enough to splinter it, driving the wind from the doctor, pinning him there, holding him a foot off the cement floor.

Rakinos leaned in close to Madison's face, baring his fangs and Madison too dazed to understand what was happening to him and he looked down that gaping maw of teeth uncomprehendingly, his vision swimming, his back burning, his legs strangely numb.

"I need your help one last time, doctor."

Madison saw Rakinos' other hand come up, his blurred vision and concussed brain seeing the glowing injector coming closer in slow motion. He tried to yell, to fight but all that came out was a strangled gurgle of snot and blood.

The injector's flat base was suddenly pressed on his neck and Rakinos paused, looking into Madison's eyes, his own eyes flaring scarlet.

"Thank you for your service."

With a click, he depressed the firing stud and Madison felt a lance of steel rocket into his neck and a moment later, liquid fire entered his veins. Rakinos watched every drop of the liquid be injected, the chamber draining slowly before he tossed it away and dropped Madison to the floor like a sack of rotten potatoes.

On the floor, Madison lay crumpled but not for long. His body began to rack with convulsions as every vein in his body began to glow blue, first faintly and then with more and more light. Madison himself felt like his insides were melting, cooking in their own juices. Somewhere in his pain overloaded brain, he could hear them frying and he tried to scream and instead what came out was a gargled strangled high-pitched shriek of agony as he bucked on the floor, his hands and fingers breaking themselves into new shapes.

Rakinos watched Madison's spine grow so hot it fluoresced through his lab coat which soon split at the shoulders. Madison spat up a wad of blood and he looked up at Rakinos, begging for death, begging for mercy, bleeding from his ears and eyes.

Rakinos simply stood back and calmly watched as Madison's mewling and moans soon turned to high pitched blood curdling screams of agony.

Madison should know better, Rakinos thought. *There is no mercy. Mercy is for the weak.*

Stepping up to the door that led to his office, Rakinos pushed the button and the door slid open with a hiss. For a moment, as he stepped out of his office, Madison's horrific screams echoed and rippled up and down the hallway before being silenced a moment later as the door sealed shut. Rakinos turned to head back down to the lab when suddenly a shifter scientist, a female with long dark hair came up to him and nervously stopped him.

"Sir?"

Rakinos turned and looked at her expectantly and she withered under his scarlet gaze.

"What?"

"The DNA analysis on sample two you asked for. We finished it." she said, her voice trembling as she held up a tablet and flicked the screen on. "There's a..."

"A what?" he asked calmly, his voice laced with death.

"There was an anomaly. We found a match to sample 2 inside our own archives."

Rakinos' ears perked up and his eyes widened. Sample two was Max Mullen's DNA sample.

"Who's?" he asked.

Shaking, she handed him the tablet and Rakinos unlocked the screen, the blue glow lighting up his face. He studied the readouts, the numbers and the genetic profile comparison. He had ordered a full work up on both Brian MacGregor and Max Mullen. Reading the outcome of the testing on sample two, that of Max Mullen, made a hot shiver run up his neck and he felt himself strangely feel something he hadn't felt in many years.

Cold realization and fear sinking in followed by white hot rage.

"Yours." she finished and quickly ducked away.

Rakinos let her go, too stunned by what he was seeing on the tablet. He didn't realize he was squeezing it until the Gorilla Glass that made up its screen splintered and finally shattered.

#######

Draco stood in his study on the second floor of the manor, looking out over the now moon kissed fields and forests behind the house. The mountains rose in the distance, cobalt blue sentinels older than man, and their peaks reaching towards heaven, forever falling short. The sun had set about two hours ago and if he strained, he could hear the crickets outside and the wind as it passed through the trees like a ghost. He looked at his reflection in the glass and contemplated.

For the first time in days, he had left the suit jacket behind and wore a light gray t-shirt that was loose on his enormous frame. It was plain, unadorned and that was how he preferred it. There was no tie, no buttoned-up shirt. While he insisted on decorum and presentation, there were times that it was ostentatious and became more of a burden. He had traded his business suit pants for cloth warm up pants and his feet were bare, the pads of his toes resting gently on the Persian rug that covered the floor in his office, the residual heat from the day seeping into his feet, feeling quite nice. His long silver-gray hair he still kept in his favored ponytail, and that was something he had kept since he first grown it in long almost fifty years ago now.

His ocean eyes and silver fur were both dark now in the soft dim light of the study. He always turned the lights down low when he was thinking as it helped remove distractions. Draco had many things on his considerable mind: the final impending vote on the Lycanthropic Registration Act, forced through the Senate by a landslide vote by the GOP and its fellow right-wing groups. The act was trash and it was sold on fear. Fear that shifters presented some kind of threat to the human population, that any mother or child could turn feral and go on a killing spree at random. Draco frowned as that thought came through his mind, because they were never so eager as to curb the epidemic of violence brought about by the psychotic worship of the assault rifle and its deadly siren call.

A ghostly gunshot echoed in his mind from the past.

Another thing on his mind was how extremist groups on both sides were not making the issue any easier to see through: Lupine Freedom, the werewolf extremist group that launched a devastating attack on the Library of Congress was making it harder on werewolves. Odin's Spear, their human equivalent fighting for human supremacy, was also muddying the waters, making it harder for werewolves to trust humans.

On that level, at least one of those groups he could understand their motivations. Odin's Spear was founded and led by a former KKK Grand Wizard, Elias Stone, and Stone wasted no time in stirring up panic and rage and fear among the KKK elite, building a group set about specifically to combat what they saw as the erosion of humanity itself.

The loss of identity, or the perception of such, was a powerful motivator, Draco thought.

The other group, Lupine Freedom, was much more mysterious, and despite all his probing, all his contacts, he had been unable to determine who their leader was and what they ultimately wanted, or thought that they gained, by pulling horrifically violent terrorist attacks against human targets or symbols of humancentric life. The rage over mistreatment and prejudice he could understand-- but the sheer violence, the brutality, the insanity of literally defeating the purpose of living peacefully side by side with their fellow man was what he couldn't understand. It made no sense unless of course, their leader had no intention of ever living peacefully.

Despite these thoughts, the ones that floated on the surface of his mind most of all were those concerning Brian MacGregor and Max Mullen.

Ever since Max and Raven had brought him to Draco to see if any answers could be given about how he was still alive and now a werewolf himself, Draco couldn't get Brian out of his mind. The boy himself seemed to be a good person, albeit somewhat impatient and in many ways naïve. In the week that Brian had spent at Forest Glen trying to master his shapeshifting abilities, Draco had noticed he was also fiercely determined but that he didn't take failure well. MacGregor also possessed a sharp mind and an even sharper wit, often with a self-depreciating edge to it. He and Max had formed a deep bond and that much was evident to anyone know who knew Max well enough to spot it. That was enough to make Draco more than intrigued with Brian, since Max didn't really bond with anyone.

Max himself was a special case and honestly, Draco admitted to himself, one of his harder ones to ever crack, simply because of the sheer amount of emotional and mental trauma Mullen had been through. Draco reflected on how he first met Max Mullen and smiling, he would never forget it.

It was the warm end of summer of 2012 when they had met, quite by chance. Back then, Draco had been more involved in marches and rallies instead of being cooped up in stuffy boardrooms and conference halls with the rich and powerful and in a way, he missed those purer times. The people he marched with were real.

The people in the boardrooms were cardboard cutouts.

It was the third rally he had had in Dawson City and it had been raining hard that day, quite unusual given the heat. The sky had been blue grey, the wind had been fierce and everyone had been soaked but they marched on, standing in front of city hall, peacefully carrying their signs. Draco and Barbara (he felt a pang of regret hit him, thinking of his sister) had been leading the crowd, making sure everyone stayed calm. Odin's Spear hadn't yet risen up to become the ballsy group there were now under the current administration, but they were a threat simmering in the background that year.

The governor had refused to come out and speak to the crowd, nor would he address the grievances brought to him by Draco. Out of the corner of his eye, Draco had seen a figure, leaning against the brick wall of the building next to city hall, dressed in a tattered worn ugly grey hoodie, torn jeans and even with the hood up, Draco could tell it was a shifter and it was a face he had seen lurking around before.

The figure stood stock still, watching everything, not joining the protest but simply drinking it in, his blue eyes thoughtful and lost in the shadows of his hood. There was something about him, the way he was dressed, the dirty ripped clothes and the smell of blood on him, the smell of pain, that made Draco pause and he had asked Barbara to continue the speeches while he stepped aside for a moment.

Moving quickly, he had crossed the open space, working his way past the crowds and the moment the gray figure had seen Draco coming towards him, he had turned and moved, bolting into the shadows.

Draco had increased his speed, moving much faster than his size would belie and as he turned into the trash filled alleyway, he saw the dark figure already more than half way down to the other side and he knew that unless he took drastic action, the grey wraith would be gone. Something about the person in the grey hood was compelling and for reasons he couldn't explain, Draco had found he was compelled to pursue the young shifter; taking off, he chased him sprinting and leaping, dropping down in front of the young man, bringing him to a complete and rather sudden stop.

"I'm not going to hurt you but I've seen you at my rallies before. You never take part but you've been there. Who are you?" he asked, catching his breath as he stood up to his full imposing height. The grey hooded shifter refused to meet his eyes and instead seemed to be considering running the opposite direction but gave up and instead stood his ground, dropping into a fighting stance.

"Leave me alone." He snarled, his eyes flaring yellow in the dark of his hood.

Draco held up an open palm. "I'm not your enemy. I just want to know who you are."

"Why? I don't matter. It's none of your business."

Draco had frowned and carefully scented the young man before him. He smelled like water and wet fur, like he hadn't bathed in days. Draco smelled blood on him and his clothes seen up close were thin and ragged. His frame was thin and his voice shaky but the power in his emaciated frame was evident regardless.

Flashes of information came with the scents: Soggy cardboard boxes, the spaces underneath buildings, squealing rats biting and nipping. Yelps of pain, fist fights in bars, beatings so severe that they had left residual trauma for days. The clatter of train wheels and long stretches of open lonely roads and deep below it all, blinding white fresh snow, ice. And strangely, fire and the chemical scent of propane and burned hair. Bloody seared hands bandaged and tears of pain.

This young man had been through hell and was still trapped in it. He was broken, utterly so, so much that Draco realized he didn't even believe himself worthy of a name anymore.

Draco sighed and lowered his hand, and the figure seemed to relax lightly, not much but some, and most importantly, he didn't run.

"My name is Draco Riley. I'm an activist and I also help people like you. I help them get back on their feet. You know I can smell your pain, your suffering. Let me help you. It's your choice but I'm here now, extending a hand. It's your choice if you want it."

The figure in the ratty grey hoodie seemed to be taken back. No one had ever put it so bluntly before to him and no one had ever left the choice up to him. They had most likely taken pity on him and just assumed he had wanted help but Draco knew that this one wasn't like that.

Draco held out a hand again, this time lower, open, fingers extended.

The figure moved forward, slowly, cautiously, hesitated and then extended his own, carefully, gingerly taking Draco's and giving it a wary shake before pulling back.

"Now, what's your name, or do I call you Hoodie?" Draco asked, a roguish grin tugging at the corner of his muzzle.

"My name..." the figure in the hoodie said carefully, as if he hadn't said his own name in many years. "My name...is Max Mullen."

That night, Max had come home with Draco and Barbara and over a period of weeks had begun to put on weight and his fur began to grow back in. It had taken them a short time to learn that Max couldn't shift into human form. Max himself slowly tried to put his past together for them though it was a difficult and painful journey of memory reconstruction from dreams and nightmares and memory and sometimes, all three blurred together. Using his name, Draco had been able to find out that Max was the son of a couple in Nome, Alaska, though whether or not that was their original home was undetermined. His mother had been a teacher and his father had been an oil pipeline worker.

A few months after Max came into the picture, Draco met Molly and had established a deep connection with her as well. Molly was a former FBI agent who had grown sick of the corruption she saw the top and wanted to be able to make a difference and so she had sought out Draco and his crusade, offering to be his personal assistant and bodyguard. Draco had taken her on and she had used her contacts to try and find out more about Max's family but to no avail. There were records that went back to Max's earliest school days, showing a history of him getting into fights with bullies and eventually the family pulled him out of school altogether.

Then there came that horrible night when Max was seventeen, Draco thought, his heart hurting for Max then and now, while flashes of Barbara echoed in the room like a ghost. From the police statement the young boy had given, terrible people had come for his family and they had taken everything the boy had ever known from him. There had been an explosion and Max was left with severe burns on his hands and arms, as well as memory loss from the concussion he had gotten from being thrown clear. Max had told Draco that he remembered waking up in a hospital later with no memory of how he got there, with his hands and arms wrapped in bandages and the doctors not understanding that he would heal on his own.

He told them he had no memory of how he had gotten there and lied about who he was. To them, he was just another shifter that looked the same as any other and one night, during shift change, facing the prospect of being placed in a group home, Max had snuck out of the hospital. He had lived on the streets, migrating south, ever since, never settling, never having a goal in mind, just wanting to get away from the memories that haunted him every night he went to sleep; the guilt, the rage, the fever of revenge that burned in him.

Molly did find one interesting record relating to Max and his family, a set of papers about the termination of parental rights but the papers were fragmentary and as far as they could tell, Max's family had no other children and there were no other records of them ever having done so. The records themselves were sealed and were only on paper which meant they couldn't be hacked or accessed remotely, meaning the only way to get them would be to get a court order and that meant more pain for Max, so all them, Max included, had dropped it, and their summation was that at one point, Max's family may have been considering giving Max up for

Anthony Milhorn

adoption to give him a better life, but that was only speculation. Max seemed deeply bothered by the thought and so no one had ever brought it up again.

The next year Max had attended his first rally at Draco's side and again it was in summer but this time Rakinos had showed up and so had Odin's Spear.

A ghostly gunshot echoed and Barbara's ghost faded away. Over time, Max had distanced himself from the rallies, blaming Rakinos and his incitement for Barbara's death, and Draco had moved away from them as well. Time went on and times changed, got more vicious, more violent. Draco had seen Max's aptitude for mechanics and creativity and had helped him set up his own shop and helped fund its restoration and for the first year, the upkeep until Max was self-sustaining. That same year was when Ash, Draco's younger brother, stopped coming around and things changed so much.

And now, Rakinos has returned...

Draco shook his head and tried to get back on his original train of thought.

The bond between Brian and Max.

Max was like a son to Draco. Over time, the two of them had grown closer and to see Max finally starting to come out of his shell a bit was encouraging. He suspected that perhaps Max found Brian more interesting than he let on and that in fact, he also suspected that there may be more than friendship between them, despite their differences and tense relationship at first when Draco had first met Brian.

If so, that was great. It meant Max might finally be stabilizing.

Brian himself, Draco mused, was a relatively unknown factor. When Molly had done his background check, there was nothing to stand out. He was an average student in high school and college, though he never finished college itself. He had no prior criminal history; social media presence was sparing and seemed to indicate a moderate left leaning political view. The only dark spot on his record was the death of his father, Jacob Alan MacGregor.

Jacob had been a police officer with the Carsonville City Police Department and had been on track to make detective due to his excellent track record. He had worked drug enforcement, homicide and interestingly, hate crimes. All the public records of Jacob that Molly could find showed him as a human male with dark hair and green eyes with a friendly face and a strong jawline. The official police records about his death were also sealed and not even Jackson had been able to crack into them, as if they had been deleted instead of locked and that made Draco wonder why.

The public cause of death for Jacob was a drug investigation gone wrong. What was there to hide about that? Tragic, yes, hellish on a young boy and mother who

168

suddenly found their family torn apart but it made no sense as to why anyone would hide those records. He wondered if perhaps, Brian's mother had requested them sealed or perhaps his father had a directive of consent. It was impossible to know.

Still, Draco had felt sorry for Brian, and he had felt bad about not being able to give the young man the more concrete answers that he sought. Draco truly had never heard of a human surviving a shifter bite let alone becoming a shifter afterwards. It was a phenomenon that caused him much consternation to the point that he had reached out to Rakinos for help. Rakinos, despite their differences and their turbulent past, was a lycanthropic genetics expert in his own right, who had delved into far deeper and more shadowy aspects of the subject than Draco would permit himself to study.

Rakinos, in his own way, was far more knowledgeable than Draco himself, and even Raven's considerable genius, even with all three of them combining their efforts, they still hadn't been able to provide any answers. And so, Draco felt responsible for letting Brian down and now with the knowledge that his I-T expert and his best friend both suspected Rakinos knew more than he was letting on and had actively set out to hide that data was eating at him. Draco had been hesitant after his discrete contacts in Washington had put Rakinos' contact information in his hands but he had decided with no other choice, that perhaps time had softened the once hot-headed man, had given him perspective, so Draco had welcomed him into his home, however briefly, hoping they could let old bygones be bygones.

And now, Jackson had told him that someone in the lab had tampered with their computers and Draco knew it wasn't Max or Raven.

How foolish I was.

There was a knock on the door that broke him out of his thoughts.

He could hear through the wood and knew who it was. He smiled warmly.

"Come in, Molly."

A second later, the door opened with as soft click and he heard her soft purposeful foot falls cross first over the hardwood and then become quiet as she walked onto the thick carpet of the rug. She appeared next to him a moment later and stood by his side, as she always did. He sighed and looked down at her, turning away from the window.

"Something on your mind?" he asked gently.

Molly sighed. "We think we have a way to reconstruct what Rakinos tried to destroy. Jackson found a way to rebuild it but it's going to be about 12 hours before we can see it. He's already started the process."

Draco nodded. "What do you think it is? Why would Rakinos do that? Do you think I made the right choice in contacting him again after all these years? I thought time would have...." he trailed off.

Molly shook her head, the moon light falling upon her pale skin and red hair.

"I can't try to understand the mind of a psychopath, Draco and if I did, I'm afraid that to do so, we'd have to follow him into madness. Whatever he did, whatever he found in that lab, he thinks it will serve his own ends, whatever they may be. He will always be self-serving. We can never compromise ourselves like that."

"I agree. How's the security system itself?"

"Uncompromised to our knowledge."

"Max and Brian?"

"Raven has been trying to call them all day but neither one is answering their phones. I had Jackson ping their phones just in case and it looks like they've been in Carsonville most of the day and are still there. I had him cross reference the address and its Brian's mother's house so they aren't in any danger."

Draco nodded. "Raven?"

"Angry at Max for not answering. Irrationally so. I think the two of them are up to something but it's only a hunch. Did they say anything to you?" Molly replied.

"No but I've also suspected it. Something about the way they were talking when everyone was here last week. I just hope they know what they are doing."

Draco turned back and looked outside into the night, his thoughts turning a dark shade of midnight black as worry began to eat at him and he bore its teeth in silence.

#####

Dinner had gone amazingly well and Brian sat feeling as stuffed as he ever had been, feeling like no time had passed at all since he had last been home. Everything felt so normal, so safe and sane that the outside world and all its demons seemed to be trapped far away and it was almost so good, that it felt like his dad was going to walk through that door; only this time, in his mind, Brian saw not the human face but the werewolf that his father really had been.

For some reason, this didn't bother him as much as it should and in fact, made him smile to himself a bit.

Before him, the steaming bowl of orzo pasta draped in steaming meat sauce, seared peppers and onions and melted parmesan was begging for more attention and so he gave it more, savoring the explosion of flavor. Next to him Max sat and he seemed to be enjoying him a bit more than usual, though still never quite breaking through the ice. His mother was more than thrilled and had seemingly had a 180 degree turn from where she had been hours ago. Now, they all sat around the dining room table, laced with food and bread and drink as his mom told stories to Max from Brian's childhood, eliciting great embarrassment from Brian and gentle almost laughs from Max himself.

"Do you remember when you cut off your hair in third grade and insisted that I leave it the way it was? Your dad nearly busted a gut from laughing and I was mortified. But you went anyway." His mom, taking a steaming spoonful of the thick pasta. Max raised an eyebrow and looked over at Brian.

"Well, it was a phase. I thought it was getting too long and it was a hot summer!"

"Honey, half your head was bald." Chris said laughing through a mouthful.

"Wouldn't be much of a problem now." Brian ran a hand through the thick fluffy fur on his head. "If I did that now, I'd probably look like a dog with mange."

Chris giggled. "Or with fleas."

Brian's eyes widened and he looked at Max. "Dude, are fleas a thing?"

Max shrugged. "Wouldn't know. Never had em. Though there was this guy at the bar I always suspected having them. Real rangy type."

Swallowing, Brian filed that away for future reference. *Fleas.*

"So," Brian said, quickly changing the subject. "Dad's jacket in that box. What was that from? I never saw him wear it."

At that Chris's tone changed a bit but not in a sad way but drifted more into the realm of fond memory.

"That," she said, swallowing and smiling, "was another one of the reasons I fell in love with him. I didn't actually meet him directly on campus per se. See your dad had a thing for motorcycles and he was actually a motocross driver for the Carsonville Dirt Devils. One of their best riders. That jacket was part of his uniform that he would wear. There was something about watching him on that bike, flying through the air, bouncing over the dirt, taking those daredevil turns that just...well...you know."

"Wow. I never knew dad used to race dirt bikes. That's actually pretty cool."

Chris pondered. "That jacket should just about fit you now. You are about the same size he was then. You should try it on sometime. He would have wanted you to have it if we hadn't tried to hide so much. God I feel like such a bitch..."

"You aren't, mom. Relax. It's fine. I'm glad you told me. I feel like I've gotten to know you both a bit better. You both sound like you were pretty bad ass back in the day." Brian told her honestly.

"We just did what we thought was right."

After a few moments of silence in which they wrapped up their dinner, Chris sat her spoon down with a clink and sighed, very full, and looked at Max.

"So...Max... tell me about you."

Brian shot a look at Max who for a second, visibly stiffened but quickly hid it. He sat down his spoon and took a drink from the glass next to his bowl and cleared his throat.

"Well, there isn't much to tell. I'm a bit of a country boy I guess. Was born in Alaska, moved to Nome when I was a kid. Dad worked for Exxon laying pipes and my mom was a teacher."

"That's fantastic! I've always wanted to go to Denali Park."

"It's beautiful up there. No matter what time of the year it is." Max told her, memories drifting behind his eyes.

"What did your parents think about you moving so far south? I would have panicked if Brian pulled that."

Brian scowled at her gently, knowing she was taking a gentle dig at him living in Dawson City. Chris shot the look back.

Max shifted in his seat a bit and Brian saw his tail slap down hard, brushing the floor and noticed his ears tried to flatten but Max stopped them both.

"My parents passed away when I was seventeen, so I was on my own for a while. I moved down to the lower forty-eight and honestly, I was in a bad space for a few years. Then I met Draco—"

"I'm so sorry...." Chris said quietly. Then Max's words seemed to sink in.

"Wait. You mean Draco Riley, the activist? The billionaire?" Chris said, perking up as his words sunk in.

"Yeah. You know him?" Max asked warily but glad for a subject change.

"Not directly. Jake and I attended a few of his rallies before he stopped doing them more or less. This was years ago before Brian was born. I don't think we ever met him directly but he was inspiring to watch. He seemed like a good-hearted man." Chris told him.

"Yeah. He is. He found me and took me in. Helped me get back on my feet and now I run my own mechanic's shop on the lower east side in Dawson City. Make a decent living and its simple, just how I like it." Max finished. "Then this knuckle head showed up and turned it all upside down." Max jerked his head good naturedly toward Brian who felt his face flush warm.

"How'd you two meet and how did all this come around?" Chris asked, sipping her tea.

"I'll let you tell this one." Max said, carefully side stepping that minefield.

Brian shot him a dirty look but dove in as best as he could.

"Well, mom, you know that I work for the hospital. One night about two weeks ago we had a really fucked up druggie come in and he was out of his mind. He hurt some of the nurses pretty bad and me and Elijah were called in to take him out before he hurt anyone else. The doctors couldn't figure out what he was on but it was bad. We managed to get him out and the cops took him."

As Brian told the story for the first time to his mother, he felt the sharp pricks of regret and anger rise again but he wouldn't let them. His mom deserved to know. He knew that an exchange of truth wasn't complete unless both parties engaged and it wasn't fair for her to tell him everything and him to hold back the truth from her.

"That morning after our shift was over, I was walking home and I was jumped by the druggie's gang members. I think the cop that took him in was on the take. They weren't happy I'd helped taken down one of their own."

"Jesus Christ Brian...what...you could have died..." Chris said, her eyes going wide.

Everything he said now, he could feel was in a monotone, the monotone of memory.

"They hurt me pretty bad.... I would have died if it wasn't for Max. He happened to hear the fight and he came and... well...he fought them off and saved my life. He did what he had to do to save me. They went after Elijah too...at his house. He...He didn't make it, mom."

Chris took that news in dumb founded silence, unable to form words. "I didn't know...oh my god. What do you mean Max saved you? How is Ellie doing? Honey...I'm sorry...my God...Elijah...Are you okay?" Chris eyes grew moist.

"Max bit me. Mom, I was dying. There was no way he couldn't have gotten help fast enough and he did the only thing he thought of. He didn't know if it would kill me or save me but at that point, there was nothing else to be done. It worked and I started healing. He carried me away from the fight scene and let me rest up and heal at his place. As far as Ellie goes, I guess she's okay. She's not talking to me much right now. I think she needs her space. I went and saw him at the cemetery. I'm.... I'm taking it day by day."

Chris face turned deathly pale. "Oh my god...."

Brian took a deep breath and let it out.

"But I'm fine I promise. A few days went by and Max asked a doctor friend of his to come look at me because we knew that something wasn't right. I was seeing things, hearing things and smelling things. The doctor, Raven, was one of my co-workers at work and I didn't know it going to be her that Max knew. She tried her best to figure out why I wasn't dead and what the changes going on in me were but she couldn't and then one night, I got restless and went out on my own and something happened....it all came together....and this happened." Brian said, indicating his fur and ears and tail.

"I didn't know what I was doing and I think I almost hurt Raven and I did hurt Max."

Chris looked from Brian to Max.

Max shrugged next to him. "I've had worse. Your son, coincidentally, should have played football. He has one hell of a mean tackle."

Brian felt a sheepish grin sprout on his face and it helped to diminish the sudden dour mood at the table. He went on.

"But Raven and Max took me to Draco's for a week, and between the three of them, they tried to help me adjust and so far, I've done really well. I just can't seem to master changing back and forth. It doesn't bother me as much now as it did at first, especially with what I know now about dad. It makes sense. They said that if I didn't have a dormant shifter gene, I would have died so in a way, dad saved my life."

Chris was up from the table in a heartbeat and she flung her arms around Brian's thickly furred neck, squashing his ears flat to his head in a tight embrace.

"Brian you could have died. If I had told you, maybe you could have been prepared but it doesn't matter. You're alive... I can't believe Elijah's gone.... he..."

Brian felt even his airway be choked off, even as he hugged his mother back.

"Mom...can't...breathe...."

Chris let go immediately. "Sorry..." She looked over at Max and went over to him, and even sitting down, he dwarfed her. She stood next to him and her eyes were moist.

"You saved my son, Max. You brought him back to me, my only family I have that left that hasn't turned on me for loving his father."

She moved in to hug him as well but Max pulled back a bit.

"I'm not much of a hugger," he said sheepishly.

"I don't care. You are a miracle and I want you to know that. You're getting a hug so deal with it."

Before Max could protest, Chris moved in and threw her arms around his powerful neck as well, giving him all she had. Max resisted lightly for about half a second before stopping and giving in, and in that giving in, he felt something inside him click that hadn't clicked in a very long time. He put his arms around Chris as well, careful not to hurt her.

She spoke into his ear.

"Max you are a hero and as far as I am concerned, you are a member of my family. Family isn't always who you are born to or who gets taken from you but sometimes the people you chose to let in and those who love you if you let them. You'll always have a family here."

Max felt a strange feeling go through him, a warmth that spread from the back of his head down to his navel and for some reason, in those moments, the scars of the past didn't hurt so much and the pain diminished just by the absolute smallest amount. Flashes of his mother's embrace shot through his mind and he found suddenly that he didn't want to let her go just yet.

"Thank you..." he said quietly as Chris pulled away and stood up, giving his shoulder a tight squeeze.

As she stood there composing herself, Chris sighed loudly and tried her best to go back to normal.

"So, you boys can have Brian's old room upstairs. I haven't changed much in there, just kept it clean. I did have some neighbors move my old bed into there. A king size just seemed just too big for me by myself anymore and I took your old queen, Bri. Should be plenty of room for you both. I'm not making you guys sleep apart like some puritanical old cunt."

She sniffed and began to move around the kitchen, gathering bowls and plates and when Brian stood up to help her she shook her head. "No sir. You and Max take some time. I'm going to get my head on straight and cleaning helps me do that. I'll handle this."

Brian went to protest. "But—"

"No buts. Scat."

Brian looked at Max apologetically. "No use arguing with her."

"Damn straight." Chris yelled back at them good naturedly.

CHAPTER 7

It was well past eleven o'clock when Chris decided that she needed to crash and Brian and Max had followed not long after. After making sure the doors were locked, Chris kissed them both good night and even gave Brian a good scratch behind the ears which for some reason made his right foot want to jump around. She had laughed heartily at that and told them good night. Upstairs, Brian and Max were finally alone. As they entered the bedroom, Brian went in first and turned on the light.

He felt the strangest feeling of déjà vu looking around his old room.

The room itself was the larger of the two bedrooms, and like the rest of the house, had rich wood paneling with white wallpaper and solid hardwood floors. It had a walk-in closet and room enough for a good-sized dresser, two-night stands and of course the king size bed that his mom had given up in exchange for Brian's old queen. At the end of the room facing the street and the front of the house was a large window. Crossing over to it, Brian closed the white blinds and drew the deep blue curtains closed. He switched off the main overhead light after twisting on the two bedside lamps, casting a warm gentle glow over the room.

The bed itself Brian had seen many times in his mom's room. For years she had kept it after his father died. It had been their marriage bed and to see it, knowing his father had been there and now that he was going to be there as well, was odd, and he couldn't pin down why. Max came in behind him and gently closed the door. His tall frame thankfully had plenty of room because the roof was peaked over this part of the house, otherwise his ears may have been touching the ceiling.

"Good god what a day..." Brian said, sitting down on the left side of the bed facing the door, putting his head in his hands.

Max nodded. "Yeah that much I can agree with. On the other hand, I do like your mom. She's pretty cool." Max put a reassuring hand on Brian's shoulder.

Brian looked up and smiled at him as Max crossed the room, idly looking over the odds and ends he found.

He picked up a stack of old comic books. Brian recognized them. Those things were thirty years old by this point and he had spent many hours during rainy days deeply absorbed in them.

"Guessing you never really got a chance to get into comics." Brian said leaning back, placing his hands on the bed as he stretched out his legs as he lay on his back, his tail twitching.

Max shook his head as he turned some of the pages. "Not really. I did like the X-Men though. Read a few of those."

"Huh. Which one was your favorite? Character I mean?" Brian asked, surprised a bit.

Max chuckled low in his throat as he came back to the bed.

"Beast."

Brian smirked sardonically. "I thought you were going to say Wolverine."

"You'll find I'm full of surprises." Max chided him gently.

Brian sat up and kicked off his boots as he pulled off the brown over shirt and sat there for a moment before tossing them both in a pile next to the headboard. He was too tired to really care about being neat. Out of the corner of his eye, he saw Max lift up his shirt and pull it off and found himself staring at Max's broad thick back and loving the way his muscled arms bunched as he moved.

He followed suit, standing up as he did, tossing his shirt into the pile and un-buckled the belt and soon his pants followed, leaving him standing only in his black trunks.

Max simply shucked off his warm up pants and stood there in his Under-Armor compression trunks.

"I don't think I'll ever get tired of seeing that," Brian said gently.

Max's eyebrows went up. For a moment he looked confused and then he under-stood when he followed Brian's eye line to his crotch and his behind.

"You're delusional." He said playfully. "But I have to admit, I know what you mean." He returned Brian's stare and Brian felt his face flush.

Throwing back the blankets, Brian hopped into the bed and slid under the clean white cotton sheets. Max approached the bed warily and gave Brian a look.

"What's wrong?"

"This bed.... will it hold us?" Max asked, standing there.

Brian shrugged. "It should. It's not a traditional slat bed. It's a two-part frame with interlocking steel support. Should be good for a lot. Hop in. I need some fur."

Max grinned and slid in next to Brian pulling the blankets up to his belly button. For a moment, Max lay on his back, hands behind his head, staring at the ceiling. Brian did the same, just letting the day work its way out, his mind turning circles within circles with all the information that was running through his head.

Brian felt a tap on his shoulder and looked over at Max. With a grin, Max motioned him over and Brian moved, sliding across the sheets, laying his head on Max's chest and a moment later, Max's arm fell behind him, holding him close.

"We need to shower." Brian said, sniffing.

Max almost laughed at that. "Yeah we probably do. Is it bad?"

Brian sniffed again, this time burying his face into the light silver fur near Max's under arm, eliciting a small bit of a squirm out of him and a chuckle. He inhaled Max's musky scent and felt a part of himself stir.

"Actually, not really. It's kind of enticing at this level. I think we'll live."

"Good."

For a while and Brian wasn't sure how long, the two of them lay there, in the dark, the thrumming of the central air unit cycling and the sounds of the house as it settled in for the night: The gentle hum of the refrigerator; the sound of water moving through pipes. The creaking as the wood expanded in the heat of the night. It was so familiar it was going to lull him to sleep if he kept listening.

Max was gently massaging Brian's upper shoulder with his thick fingers and it felt wonderful, the deep pressure working the tension out of the muscle there.

Sighing he nestled deeper into Max's silver chest fur, feeling his hot skin there.

"That feels great. You'll have to let me do that for you some time..." Brian said sleepily.

Max grunted. "I'll take you up on that. Did you find out what you came here to?"

Yawning, Brian took a moment to think. Had he found out what he needed to know?

"I think I did. I thought I knew my mom and dad so well but really, I didn't know them at all it seems like. There's just so much more to them. I guess growing up they were just THERE, you know? I guess I never saw them as fully human as me and you."

He felt Max nod and felt his muzzle tickle the edge of his ear as tilted his head to reply.

"I don't think of us really see our parents for who they really are. We see them as God, but really, they're just like us. Hopes, fears and dreams. We just never get to see it because I think they give all that up for us."

A look of realization lit up on Brian's face and he pushed himself up onto his elbow and looked down at Max, meeting his blue eyes with a look of wonder.

"You know, you are far more philosophical than you let on."

Max smirked. "Tell anyone and I'll have to kill you."

Brian poked him in the ribs with a thumb. "I'll take my chances."

Max reached up with his thick neck, boosting himself up a bit on his elbow, pressing his thick furred body against Brian's and met Brian's lips with a gentle deep kiss that lasted far longer than either of them measured. He laid back and smiled contentedly.

"I've needed that all day," he said. Brian nodded.

"Me too."

Brian settled back into his spot at Max's side and thought for a while.

"You know, this explains a lot of strange things growing up." he said, looking up at Max.

"Oh?" Max asked, his hand working the muscles in Brian's back, rubbing out the hardness there. Brian winched as he hit a sore spot just above the small of his back where his tail was.

"Yeah. Family reunions were always tense and I never really knew why. My cousins never were allowed to play with me much. I guess it makes sense now in retrospect, they were afraid of me. I didn't care for the reunions anyway and was glad when they stopped and why a lot of dad's relatives never showed up and the ones that did always looked like they'd rather be anywhere else."

He felt Max shift his legs a bit and then Max nipped his ear gently before letting go.

"So, you never really got close with your aunts or uncles?" he asked as Brian ran a hand over Max's stomach, swirling his fingers absently around Max's navel as he played with the silver fur.

Brian shrugged. "Not really. Circumstances being what they were, I guess, now that I know about them, though some of them get under my skin. My mom's brother Donnie is an idiot. Religious nut cake. He and I used to get into screaming matches after I was old enough to understand what he was peddling. Didn't have any aunts, at least on my mom's side. Never really knew about dad's much."

He felt Max's grunt of reply through Max's chest.

"I didn't really get to know much of my family either. I guess we have more in common than we thought."

Brian nodded. "I guess it comes down to quality over quantity in the end."

Max's hand had slipped lower, his hand sliding under Brian's waistband to just below his tail at the top of his butt cheeks. As Max rubbed the thick muscle there, Brian felt his legs quiver.

"Damn, I didn't know I was that sore." He said, arching his back a bit.

"We sat most of the day. I'm surprised you're not hurting worse than you are," Max replied as he switched cheeks.

"Fair point."

Brian felt himself begin to drift off until Max worked his hands up under his tail and then he felt something else altogether, a very pleasant shudder running down his spine causing him to groan a bit deeper than he realized.

"Hey now..." he said. He heard Max chuckle in his ear.

"What, I'm not doing anything."

Brian pushed his hips forward a bit into Max's oak banister of a thigh and Max felt the rock-hard pressure there and realized just what he was doing. He almost laughed again as he slowly stopped.

"Tease." Brian told him, nipping him gently with the corner of a fang.

Max jumped reflexively and gave Brian a good squeeze.

"It's only teasing if I don't ever intend to finish."

Brian acknowledged that was a fair point. "Well hey you...let's finish that when we get back to your place when we aren't so tired."

"We're gonna have to." Max said and with a grin, he pulled Brian's hand over and pushed it below the blankets.

Brian cupped his hands around Max and found that he was sporting a rock-hard erection through the sheer fabric of his compression shorts.

Brian gave him a hard squeeze and pulled his hand back. "It's a deal. Let's get some sleep because we should head back in the morning."

Max scooted over and gave Brian a bit of room as they snuggled down into the blankets settling into their sleep positions.

"I agree." Max said with a yawn, revealing his massive fangs.

"Night, Max." Brian said as he felt Max settle down beside him. He could definitely get used to sleeping like this and genuinely hoped there was more of it to come.

"Night, pup."

#####

The dream had changed.

The snow fell in slow motion, drifting down towards a thick blanket of ice and powder that had turned into sharp dust. The pine trees stood dark and thick against a midnight sky as pin pricks of stars extended as far as he could see. He was standing in the thicket clearing just before he got to his house but this time, he was totally naked. He had no gear on. No clothes, nothing to shield himself from the cold. The cold knew it, and drove at him even harder, digging deep into his thick fur, screeching in pained silence raking his skin beneath it, making his teeth chatter. Tears from the pain of it that were welling up at the corners of his eyes froze as they fell into tiny gems.

Max threw his arms around his chest to try to shield himself and stay warm, his ears and tail fluttering in the winter storm. He looked at his hands as he moved and he knew that those were not his hands, at least not his hands now. These were the hands of his seventeen-year-old self. Lifting his head, his blue eyes not glowing with their typical night vision yellow, he looked out of the clearing.

Through the storms ravages, he saw his home, a beautiful two-story log home his father and mother had designed and built together with him over a year. Not that he could do much back then, at least, not more than carry stuff to his dad and the few people that came to help them build it. The big windows were ablaze with the warm glow of the lights and lamps inside and smoke drifted up from the chimney. It was home.

There were no men in black robes, no shouting and frowning, knowing even in his dreams he was remembering and hated it, Max forced himself to step forward, the frozen ground nipping and biting at his bare feet, the crystals stabbing painfully into his foot and toe pads with every crunching step.

Around him, no matter how hard the wind blew, the trees did not bend and sway and the stars began to revolve in the night sky faster than they should have throwing crazy lights to dance upon the ground. Shivering from the excruciating cold, he stepped out of the clearing and into his front yard. There were no other houses for a few miles and it was alone here in the open fields with a single gravel driveway buried under the snow that led out to the main road.

The little solar powered lights that lined the driveway shone under the snow like the lights of a sinking ship already condemned to the depths of the sea.

Eric Mullen was outside and he was standing facing someone. A huge some-one, someone that dwarfed even his father's tall broad frame. His father's dark grey fur and silver blaze, so much like his own, was encrusted with ice and snowflakes. His eyes were livid, burning yellow in the dark, and his fangs were bared, hands thrown up as if in defense.

The other figure loomed above him and was made of twisting burning shadow with streaks of shimmering red. Its body was massive; its arms screamed with power and its raised open hand, fingers spread, claws splayed, hung in the air, ready to fall at a moment's notice. Its face was lupine, Max thought, but far too large, ears too pointed, neck too thick. He couldn't make out its true features and they swirled there, just out of sight in the smoky crimson flame that made up its form.

There was something strange about the figures of his father and the crimson beast. It took him a second to see that they were both frozen in time. As Max came closer, stopping mere feet away, he saw that they weren't really frozen but were rather moving so slowly as to be almost imperceptible. He stood, watching this scene play out. It had become something different this time, rather than the same imagery he had seen a thousand times before. Always before there were men in dark robes, faceless and meaningless with hate led by a single large shadow. Now, there was simply this lone monster, alone, with no men. Just it and his father.

He knew his father's fate but had never seen him before it befell him. If he could move fast enough, if he could shove him out of the way, if he could change things, then this time, this time, maybe, things would be different. His heart thudding in his ears, not caring about the cold, Max moved. He feet dragged like they were in cement. The moment he made to move to intervene, he found himself snared by whatever force was holding the two figures before him in suspended time. He was half way between his father and the menacing demon when he felt himself stop entirely. In that moment he heard voices, or rather a voice that echoed, forever stuck in a loop.

Eric's terrified and defensive yell.

"DIANE, GET OUT OF HERE!!"

Max looked up, only his eyes moving, tracking up the side of the house to the second story and there he saw frozen in time like they were below, his mother with her dark hair and saw that her blue eyes were wide in fear and surprise....and something more? Recognition? They were the same eyes that had brought him comfort and solace in the darkest days of his young life and now they were seeing the destruction of their entire family and in those eyes, Max saw just how helpless she was. How afraid.

He knew her fate as well but not if he could change it in this strange new moment.

Looking back down to his father he saw movement at last.

Eric's eyes slid slowly towards him and from his mouth came one word. Never before had his father been alive at this point in his memories or nightmares and Max

183

heard the word as clear as day, as if his father were reaching from beyond the grave to acknowledge his son.

"Run."

Max saw movement and then he finally saw the face of the shadowy crimson monster. It turned its fang lined muzzle towards him and there in its burning scarlet eyes, he saw its true face.

The things face was his own, covered in blood so red that it turned his fur scarlet.

Max felt his eyes go wide as the raised clawed hand finally fell like a sledgehammer and it caught him directly in the face.

Stars and suns exploded like in his head and he felt every bit of the pain as it threatened to split his skull. He heard himself yelp in agony, felt a hot spray of blood as his muzzle was split open four ways, the blow jarring his head so hard he thought it was flying off but no, it wasn't his head that was sent flying but rather his entire body. The snow rushed up to strike him in the face and a momentary blackness overtook him as searing hot pain dulled into a numbness. He opened his eyes, blinking away tears and blood, his ears bleeding, as he watched the figure fall upon his father.

The struggle was brief but explosively violent. His father never stood a chance and never did in any of the dreams.

In seconds, the looming smoky crimson version of himself with its red eyes held his father's body above the pristine snow, painting it red. His father was still alive, barely, his immune system trying to repair the damage that had been done and it would have succeeded had it not been for the figure placing its free clawed hand upon Eric's chest and digging in with its fingers. Max heard his father struggle and then finally heard the ear-piercing yelping scream of agony that lost all semblance of humanity before his father's body jumped once, twice and then went limp as the smoky red monstrosity pulled its hand back.

Something was in its hand, something oblong and round, something wet and damp with scarlet. Yanking Eric's limp body close, the monster seemed to whisper something to him and then tossed him aside, dumping his body in the snow like a rag doll.

It crushed whatever was in its hand and tossed the remains on the ground with their owner who landed with a heavy sickening thud that was far too loud.

The smoky red figure now burned as flames began to lick off of its shoulders. It looked back and saw Max laying on the ground. Max couldn't stand.

His legs weren't responding. Everything seemed so far away now as gravity seemed to chain him to the ground.

He wanted to scream, to cry to do anything but his dazed brain wouldn't *comply, couldn't comply.*

All it would allow Max to do was watch as the figure raised a smoking flaming hand and laid it against the side of the house with a searing sizzle.

The wood there charred, turning black, and a moment later, with a snarling whoosh, flames erupted. The fire crawled quickly, engulfing the entire bottom floor. The house screamed as wood protested the increase in heat and glass exploded. The figure reared back one of its massive legs and kicked down the front door with a spray of sparks and flame, shattering the door frame into splinters, ducking through to the inside of the house that was now a raging inferno.

Max knew where he was going. There was only one place for him to go.

"N-n-no...." he grunted through clenched teeth, forcing the words out, spitting out blood. He tried to get to his feet and failed, collapsing back to the icy ground. Nearby, his father's dead body leaked crimson, staining the snow a cherry red.

Growling in frustration, Max pushed harder and still he couldn't get up.

He heard his mother's voice, heard her speak words he couldn't make out because his ears were still ringing, his face still burning.

Finally, he heard her scream.

Summoning everything he had, Max put his hands up under himself and shoved, ordered, screamed at his body to move.

It moved an inch.

A sound was building in him, one that he would never make again in his entire life. It was a sound of desperate consuming rage, a primal snarl, a growl of defiance as he stood at last, the snow tumbling off his body and when he stood, he was his thirty-nine-year-old self, no longer the child that he was.

He bolted for the collapsed front door of the house as time resumed its flow. The flames had begun to lick at the upper floors. The house was going to be a total loss he knew but his mother....

He could not sit here. Could not simply watch.

The door was blocked by burning wood and debris. That thing that wore his face had done extreme damage but the fire itself was moving unnaturally fast. The house was falling apart. There was no way through.

Max growled in desperation, knowing the back door was covered in snow up to the roofline. The windows were pockets of searing hot flame.

The doorway beyond the fallen debris was clear. He could see the stairs leading up to the second floor.

Without thinking, he reached out and grabbed the debris, shoving it, pushing it, pulling it.

185

The sound of his own flesh searing and cooking as it made contact was lost to him as a tiny wet hiss. He smelled burning fur. He didn't care. The debris didn't move. The pain got worse and he heard himself screaming but he kept pushing.

Snarling in rage and frustration, he rammed the mess with his shoulder.

All he got for his trouble was sheer agony as the flames bit into the thick meat there, grilling away his fur there in a great black patch of burnt hair.

Finally, he gave in to his rising adrenaline and slammed the debris again and this time, it exploded inward, clearing the way to the stairwell in a spray of blazing embers. He nearly fell as he crashed through the ruined doorframe, barely catching himself.

He moved, feeling his feet cook on the red-hot wood like a hamburger at a cookout. He didn't care. Max could feel the pain radiating up to his knees, could smell it, taste it even, but nothing mattered. The living room floor had collapsed and through the hole, he see down through to the basement. He could see all of their family's history, sitting under a pile of flaming cross beams and burning memories. His first-grade pictures. His mother's paintings. His father's tool set that he had taught Max to use. All of it was lost to the inferno. Max could hear a whistle like a tea kettle coming from outside but had forgotten its importance as he bounded up the stairs, his body screaming for mercy, his hearing dampened. He knew had a concussion. Maybe worse. Everything seemed so quiet and so loud at the same time with an odd ring to it. His vision was blurry, his eyes watering from the smoke.

There, at the top of the stairs, he saw his parent's room at the end of the hall, the door was open, the flames having not reached this part of the house but every second the floor grew hotter, the air thicker, harder to breathe. Smoke was beginning to turn everything black.

The figure stood over her limp body and looked up at Max.

It still wore his face, its eyes burning scarlet; the thing's smoky flaming fur had turned a deep blood red maroon.

The creature looked at him like he was nothing and without a word, it turned and leaped, crashing through the window and vanishing into the night. It had smiled, he thought.

Max ran into the room, skidding on his knees to his mother's side.

Diane Mullen lay in her favorite pair of jeans and her loose around the house sweater. Her shirt was stained red from the torrent that had poured from her throat and chest. Max grabbed her and held her to him, whimpering like a child, his cries useless he knew but unable to help himself regardless. He used his hands to try to stem the flow from the ugly red gashes. She was alive but barely, and her breathing was already slowing down.

"Mom...mom...no... not this time..." Max heard his voice say as if he was far *away listening to himself from another room.*

Diane's eyes fluttered open and she seemed to see him and tried to raise her hand to his face. Max took it and held it as her eyes grew distant, seeing some farther shore. She spoke to him, her voice terribly shaky, her words quiet, smothered by her own life being drained out of her. All but the last were unclear but the final ones, buried themselves into his heart like a javelin:

"...Love....you...Max..."

Her eyes glazed and the light went out of them, winking out as if they were a sun that had burned off all its fuel and finally had gone dark in the cold depths of space. The life that was in her body fled and her arm went limp in Max's grasp.

Max felt himself pull her hand to his face, just to feel her touch one last time, felt his eyes stinging as tears fell and he wept, whimpering as he did, his chest heaving and falling.

The whistling sound grew louder and more insistent.

Max lifted his eyes to the hallway, looking out towards the living room, and suddenly remembered that the propane tanks outside had a safety valve on them to vent in case of increased pressure or heat to avert an explosion.

That was the last conscious thought Max had.

With an enormous roar, the world went white, the red then orange. He felt his mother's touch be ripped away from him as he was picked up and thrown through the wall of the house, smashing out through thick timbers, insulation and burning studs. Glass rained down and the night lit up for miles as the fireball finally consumed the house, the propane tanks finally unable to stand the pressure any longer as they gave in to the hellish fury inside them, rupturing into searing titanic clouds of fire.

The ground itself shook violently and the trees closest to the blaze were seared free of their branches; others were leveled by the shock wave.

Max felt a dozen tiny fires all over his body, eating at him as he flew and finally he smashed down hard in the snow, a good hundred feet from the house itself, the icy fluff cascading around him like a mini avalanche.

He heard something crack and lights exploded in front of his eyes as, at the precise moment, his head crashed into the thick rock buried under the snow and the world went black...

Gasping for breath, Max woke, sitting straight up in the bed.

He was drenched in sweat, panting, his eyes blazing yellow, pupils wide and afraid.

For a moment, he was disoriented and looked around wildly to get his bearings.

Wood floors, white wallpaper, an old dresser lined with knick-knacks and a stack of old comic books.

Slowly, he caught his breath as he remembered where he was.

It was 2018, not 1996, and he was in Carsonville, not Nome. He was in Chris MacGregor's house with Brian not lying unconscious in a snow field as his childhood home burned behind him.

Collapsing against the headboard, Max put his head in his hands. He felt moisture around his eyes and angrily wiped it away. Letting his hands fall, he stared into the darkness, the dream hanging with him like the smell from the chemical plant when they'd first arrived. It penetrated him, poisoned him and sickened him. It was different. For as many years, it had been the same nightmare, the same dream-scape over and over and now, it was different.

The dream had changed.

"Brian...?" he asked quietly in the dark, reached out and looked down at his left and frowned.

The space Brian had been occupying was gone. There were simply rumpled sheets and a pillow with a shape indented on it that was vaguely like that of Brian's head.

Swallowing, Max swung his legs over the edge of the bed and in the dark, found his pants and pulled them on hastily. Moving as quietly as his large frame would allow, Max opened the bedroom door, hoping it wouldn't squeak and stepped into the hallway. The lights were out in the house and he could hear Chris in her bedroom below, snoring lightly, like a sleeping cat. The security system hadn't been tripped and nothing else looked askew.

Sniffing a few times, Max tried to find Brian by scent and there it was, that earthy scent like warm sunlight. Feeling relieved, he followed it down the stairs and then down the hallway, the floor creaking gently beneath his weight.

Catching a glimpse of himself in the hallway mirror, Max shook his head. His fur was rumpled and he had dark circles around his eyes, even though the fur on his face.

Like a ghost.

The scent led him past the hallway and turned right to lead to another door, one that led to the backyard. The main door there was open and the white metal screen door was closed. Through it, Max saw the backyard itself for the first time.

It was a wide-open space, generous given the size of the house and was completely enclosed in a tall wooden privacy fence. A single large tree grew up in the corner of the yard, throwing shade over a picnic table and grill. There were a few solar powered garden lamps and a bird bath set aside to the left. There, sitting on the table under the tree, was Brian.

Opening the screen door, Max stepped barefoot out onto the cement patio, closing the screen door gently behind himself. As he stepped out onto the grass of the yard, the blades tickling his feet, Brian didn't look up and he was apparently lost, deep in thoughts only he could know. Max approached carefully, not wanting to startle him, the warm gentle night breeze picking up his fur on his bare chest and belly like the fingers of an invisible and gentle lover.

In the dark, Brian's fur was so black that if it hadn't been for the moonlight, Max could have easily missed him, even with his night vision. It looked like just a white shirt floating in the dark. Brian's eyes stood out brightly in the ebony blue night as twin gleaming green circles, his pupils large in the shadows. Those eyes slid towards him and Brian sighed, his tail unconsciously wagging just the slightest before settling down, his ears pricking towards Max.

"Hey, Max."

Max nodded gently. "Hey. Mind if I sit with you?"

Brian shrugged. "Plenty of table."

Max came up and got up next to Brian, sitting comfortably on the aged wood as it creaked a bit under their combined weight.

For a while, both of them sat there, in silence. Brian himself was only partially dressed in his white t-shirt and black trunks. It was obvious he had been awake a while, Max thought.

Brian turned to him and looked him up and down.

What he saw alarmed him. Max's fur was rumpled and his eyes were wild, as if he had seen a ghost, and more, there was pain in his eyes, like a fresh wound. The fur around the corners of Max's eyes was wet and it was obvious that he had been crying.

Brian reached out immediately and put an arm around Max's broad shoulders.

"Hey...what's wrong? You look awful..."

Max shrugged, pushing the fur back up and out of his eyes. "Tell me about it."

Brian half grinned. He gave Max's shoulder a soft squeeze. "Dreams?"

Max nodded. "Yeah. Same one but...this time was different."

Brian frowned and let Max's shoulder go as they sat together in the dark under the tree.

"How?"

Max sighed and tried to explain. The more he spoke the more his voice shook.

"I don't know...it was so clear this time. There weren't any people in robes...no metal claws...I was alone...and it was me that killed my parents and burned my house down. I can remember seeing my dad up close this time...he was alive until...until I or something like me...killed him. Then it went after my mom and Brian I can remember her hand.... The thing that killed them...it was wearing my face...my face..."

Brian could feel the shakes slowly start to go through Max's big body. Max hung his head. He sniffled once and tried to hide it.

"When your mom hugged me earlier...it was like my mom was alive again...for the briefest moment.... I didn't' want to let her go."

In the dark, Brian, for the first time since he had known Max, saw something he never thought he would see.

Max was the tough guy, the fighter, the beer drinking mechanic who took no shit from anyone.

Max, he saw, was trying to hold back his emotions and despite it all, the corners of his eyes had turned silver with moisture.

Tears. Max was crying and trying desperately not to.

Reaching up, Brian wiped away the tears that had formed there and he took Max by the chin and gently brought Max's head up to face him, eye to eye.

"Max... look at me.... please..."

After a moment, Max did and for a change his eyes weren't blazing yellow in the night but had turned back to their ocean blue. Brian didn't know why and he didn't care.

"It's okay to feel. It's okay to grieve. It's okay to fight...let it out. You've fought these monsters so long it's no wonder your dreams finally changed...you've been blaming yourself for so long it's tearing you apart. I'm here and I can't take it away but I'm going to have your back...or your face. Whichever I can reach first."

Brian said, choking up a bit himself as he tried to smile. Seeing Max like this was hard, far harder than anything Brian had felt in a long time.

Max smiled a bit or tried to anyway.

"Thank you."

Brian tugged and Max came forward and laid his head onto Brian's shoulder and for a while, there in Brian's arms, in the shadow of an old oak tree surrounded by sprigs of purple pink heather, Max did cry and Brian held him, neither speaking and neither needing to, and instead, was simply there.

Time passed and finally Max's quiet tears faded and he sat up, looking Brian in the eyes, deeply searching for something that he had at long last found.

Coming together, the two of him embraced followed by a long passionate kiss that wasn't sexually charged but rather charged with the warmth and radiance of passion born of standing together. They pulled apart slowly.

"Why do you put up with me? Why do you want me? I'm a wreck..." Max asked after, shuffling his feet on the picnic table seat.

Brian shrugged and put a hand on Max's. "Because I care and you've been there for me. You saved my life. It's the least I can do is to save yours. I care about you a lot."

Max sniffed. "So... what are you doing out here?"

"Just thinking mostly, about my dad...who he was...and who I am. I feel like I know a story now that I only half knew before, like it was whispered to me and I only caught the faintest edge of its dream, but the story isn't told yet. There's still so many pages..." Brian told him, as Max leaned up against him, his big head resting on Brian's shoulder.

"Yup, you're a writer." Max said with a chuckle.

"You know you can laugh, sometime, right?" Brian told him gently. Max snorted.

"Maybe some time, I will, when I feel like I don't have so much weighing me down..."

Brian nodded with a tiny chuckle of his own. "Then it's my personal mission to help you lift that weight one day at a time because I want to hear what it sounds like. I like your voice. I can just imagine what you sound like guffawing like a lunatic."

"A lunatic is right."

More time passed between them, each one just enjoying the others company, each one's individual pain becoming lessened around the other. Eventually, each breath from the other fell into sync together and Brian could hear their heartbeats in tandem.

"I came out here," Brian said to Max quietly, "to find myself. Ever since the change, I've felt like something was wrong with me in my head. What I saw in my head wasn't what I saw the in mirror. I mean, don't get me wrong, its turned out to be a blessing and I'm starting to like it but...there was always something off seeing myself as not myself...if that makes sense."

He felt Max nod his head. When he spoke, Max's gruff but now gentle voice was in his ear. "I imagine it was confusing as hell...like your identity had been taken away.

Not to mention that black out you had."

Brian nodded.

"Yeah, that was scary. I hope that doesn't happen again. I was starting to feel like I didn't know who I was anymore, and then I found out about my dad today...and everything changed. Now I know all this is part of me as much as that old image I had in my head of who I was and what I was. I feel like the pieces in the puzzle are almost together again. I can almost see myself, Max. I'm so close..."

He felt Max's head come off his shoulder and he turned to meet his now glowing yellow gaze again. Brian wondered if emotions could impact their abilities as shifters and he thought it made sense.

Max looked thoughtful.

"I wonder...if now that you can see the pieces... if you could try shifting again. See if it helps." Max suggested.

Brian thought about that. The idea was intriguing but at the same time he had tried so hard for days at Draco's and failed. He had gotten so frustrated, so annoyed and Brian was well aware that failure was one thing he didn't take well.

What I really am, is afraid, he thought. *Afraid to fail again. Afraid to go through so much pain again.*

"I don't know, Max..."

Max sat up and put a hand on Brian's back. "I think you could do it. You've got all the pieces now...just gotta put them together and take a picture."

He pulled Brian into a quick hug. "I believe in you, like you do in me."

Brian sighed. *What the hell...*

"Alright. I'll give it a shot."

Boosting himself off of the table, Brian dusted his hands off on his hips and walked about three feet out from the table. He stood, just outside the shade of the tree, under the silver light of the waning moon and stars. Closing his eyes, Brian thought back to the days at Draco's when Draco and Raven had both tried to teach him how to shift his form:

"Relax. See in your mind your human face, the one you know, the familiar aspects of it. Release all the tension in your muscles, starting from your toes up. Let go. Breathe." Draco had told him, watching him carefully and nodded, gently, teacher to student as they stood on the warm sunlight grass of Forest Glen.

Somewhere, Brian could hear Roy's lawn mower going, the blades turning, *whum whum whum* in their metal shield. He had closed his eyes and pushed past that sound, reaching inside himself for something he didn't know, a picture that was scrambled.

He remembered hearing the beeps of Jackson's phone as he tapped it on the patio. Raven sat next to them, offering guidance as well. They had been at this for hours.

Brian had breathed in deeply and let it out, trying to find his face in the darkness, flexing his toes and fingers, working out the tension there. The only face he saw in the dark was that of his wolf self and try as he might, nothing seemed to be happening.

"Damn it...nothing..." he had spat, frustrated, throwing up his hands. Raven stepped up to him.

"You're trying too hard. Remember it should be gentle, like flowing water. There's nothing in your genetic profile I've seen so far that says you can't. You've just got to visualize."

"How am I supposed to visualize when the face I see now isn't mine? I've not seen my old face in over a week and it feels like it's slipping away." He had replied dejectedly, kicking a clod of dirt out of the ground angrily.

"We are never truly lost, but sometimes we can get misplaced." Draco added and encouraged him to try again.

"Ok one more time..." Brian had grumbled and closed his eyes again. He tried desperately to bring up his face, his human face and saw only jumbled pieces, like someone had taken a picture and smashed it into billions of bits that can never again make sense. He concentrated harder and the picture began to come together, bits fitting with bits, an eye forming, brown hair, the pinkish tinge of his skin.

There was a slight tingle at the back of his neck, like a nascent tickle waiting to be born and for a moment, it began to had spread like warm heat down his shoulders and he felt his heart begin to pound.

This was it!

It was happening!

Then the picture fell apart into shards and the feeling vanished with it, leaving him standing there, in the grass, feeling stupid, lost and utterly confused.

Brian snarled as he had opened his eyes. "Goddamn....I just can't get this, guys. Maybe I can't change. I need some space...."

That had been over a week ago now. Ages.

He remembered the look on Raven's face, the look of confusion while the look on Draco's older features was one of regret.

Now, standing in the shadow of the oak tree, alone, with Max, Brian once again closed his eyes.

He didn't know if that was something that was needed or not but it felt like something that was right to do and he tried to clear his mind of all the little needling thoughts, the nagging doubts and whispers of his already set in stone failures.

In his head, Draco's voice came again.

"Relax. See in your mind your human face, the one you know, the familiar aspects of it. Release all the tension in your muscles, starting from your toes up. Let go. Breathe."

In his mind, Brian pulled up an image of himself, his true self and in the dark space of his mind, an image began to form. Slowly at first, its features defined only by shadow and lines and there it was, his wolf face, his muzzle, his snout, his eyes and ears.

He shook his head; that wasn't the right image.

Trying again, he pushed deeper in his mind, past the broken memories, past the death of his father, past his own fear and a new face began to form and when it did he felt his breath catch.

His father's human face.

So much like his own.

Brian wanted to hear his voice again so badly after so long. And, just like the ghost that he was, his father too faded away, leaving him in the deepest part of his mind, where no memories lived, only thought, feeling and color.

He sat there for a while, in his mind, feeling the darkness and invisible colors he knew were there. They tickled his fingers like fish in a pond, begging to be used, to be lit up and shown. Twisting his hands on the mental plane, he took the colors by the tail and moved with them, directing them. Somewhere in the dark, he felt something move with him as invisible eyes watched curiously. He ignored it.

Externally, Max watched as nothing seemed to happen but something clearly was going on in Brian's head as his eyes were tightly closed in concentration but moving behind his eyelids, his ears pinned against his head, his tail twitching, the muscles in his legs quivering.

In the mental mind space, for all of Brian's efforts, nothing seemed to happen, even with all his energy and he sighed, about to surrender, to give in when suddenly he saw something he hadn't seen before. It had been hidden behind his anxiety, his apprehension, his pain and his fear but it was there nonetheless, finally revealed from his acceptance of his father's true nature, understanding that the wolf was as much a part of him as his human face and with Max there, Brian felt a surge of confidence he didn't have before. As this washed over him, the thing slid out from behind those feelings as he sat alone in his mental space and he finally saw it.

It was a face.

A face that was familiar with its thick but trimmed auburn beard, amber eyes and short but messy brown hair.

He stood and approached it as it hung before him, an inverted mirror image to his own wolf features but human, nonetheless. Raising a hand up to it, he felt it pull to him, call to him and he touched his own identity at last. Brian felt that warmth bloom at the back of his head and spread to his shoulders and this time, it did not fade away. This time, there was no pain.

As Max watched Brian, something indeed was happening. The fur on his body slowly began to ripple. Something about his face changed. His snout got smaller. His ears began to recede. A smile lit up Max's face as the process took over and Brian's entire body began to shift, changing, flowing like black water as the fur drew back into his arms and his form shrunk. His tail drew up and was gone.

His muzzle faded back into his skull and at last, Brian MacGregor, the scruffy looking bearded human that Max had first met weeks ago, stood before him again, dressed in a baggy white t-shirt and trunks that finally properly fit again. His fur-less skin shone in the moonlight, the tips of his hair and beard flared orange as the moon light passed through them. Max stood up and went over to him and when Max stood before the now very human Brian, Brian's eyes finally opened.

For a split second, his eyes were bright glowing green, and faded to white and then faded back in to the amber-brown that Max hadn't seen in a very long time.

With a sigh, Brian looked down at himself and felt his jaw drop open in shock.

"Oh my god..." he said touching his chest, his hips, his arms, holding up his hands in front of his face and there, past them, he saw Max, standing with a proud look on his scruffy muzzled grey-furred face.

"You did it." Max said smiling, his yellow eyes twinkling.

Brian laughed. He looked from himself to Max. He laughed again.

"Hell yes!" he cried happily.

Max crossed his arms and stood in the moon with Brian. "Never doubted you."

His voice seemed to break the reverie as Brian stopped and looked up at Max. Confusion seemed to cross his now human features and then a swift shadow of sadness and panic.

"What's wrong?" Max asked, his arms falling a bit.

"Nothing it's just...I'm different now. I don't know if I'm still what you wanted anymore. I can stay the other way but...I..."

Max shook his head and gently placed a hand on Brian's now smaller shoulder and in that moment, he looked into Brian's eyes and dropped his walls, his barriers and protections.

"Brian...I don't care what you look like. I didn't fall for one or the other. You're still you, either way....and I...."

Brian flinched, terrified of what Max was going to say.

"I... I think I love you." Max finished.

Brian felt his eyes go wide and the world swayed as he looked up at Max. He stepped forward and put his arms around Max, for the first-time feeling Max's thick fur on his bare skin instead of fur to fur, enjoying the heat radiating out from Max's body, even the slight musky scent of him. His body solid, warm and gently fuzzy.

"I think I love you too."

Closing his eyes, Brian concentrated and this time, it was easier, simpler, the face came faster; his eyes blazed green, and his body flowed, changing in Max's arms, growing without pain, as fur sprouted from his skin and in seconds, he stood, eye to eye with Max again in his wolf form, and took Max' head in his hands and together, their lips met under the starlight and the shade of an old oak tree.

Afterward, the two of them stood, side by side, under the stars, each of them with an arm around the other's waist as they looked skyward and Max laid his head onto Brian's shoulder and Brian leaned into Max, their ears touching gently.

Neither of them heard the tiny footsteps come from the house and neither of them saw Chris MacGregor, standing quietly behind the screen door, watching them together, seeing them standing by side by side. For a moment, she felt the slightest pain, but it was the pain of a mother watching her child grow up in a way that was beyond her control but at the same time, it filled her with pride. A mother's pride, and to see her son happy for the first time in many years brought a gentle smile to her face as she turned and went back to bed, giving the two of them their space.

Overhead, the skies turned and the stars cycled and for both of them, time, at last, seemed to stand still, just for a little while.

".... And I'll use you as a warning sign
That if you talk enough sense then you'll lose your mind

...And I'll use you as a focal point
So I don't lose sight of what I want
And I've moved further than I thought I could...

...And I'll use you as a warning sign
That if you talk enough sense then you'll lose your mind

...I'll use you as a makeshift gauge

Of how much to give and how much to take
Oh I'll use you as a warning sign

That if you talk enough sense then you'll lose your mind

Oh and I found love where it wasn't supposed to be
Right in front of me."

- Amber Run, "I Found." (2014).

Anthony Milhorn

Made in the USA
Middletown, DE
02 April 2025

73713350R00109